The Colors
of
Denver Andrews

AN ELIZA GRAY NOVEL

J. Willis Sanders

BUGGS ISLAND BOOKS

Cover art by MiblArt

Also By J. Willis Sanders

The Eliza Gray Series
The Colors of Eliza Gray
The Colors of Denver Andrews
Coming soon: *The Colors of Tess Gray*

The Outer Banks of North Carolina Series
The Diary of Carlo Cipriani
If the Sunrise Forgets Tomorrow
Love, Jake

Writing as J.D. James: the Reid Stone Series
Reid Stone: Hard as Stone

<u>***Content Advisory for this Novel:***</u>
Explores themes of grief, loss, and family tragedy.

loss

Denver had never known loss like this.

He had known loss when his parents had died. He had known loss when Eliza had left for Ohio, to be with her family after he had finally admitted to falling in love with her. It had amazed him how her family had moved here to be with her, even leaving the Amish to do so. Love brought them to her: a father's love and a mother's love, a sister's love and a brother's love.

Sitting on the wooden bench on the dock, Denver opened his eyes. June. Hot. The lake. Boat motors humming. No, he wasn't ready to see normal things. Better to relive the time that gnawed at his heart, or he might not know it was beating at all. He closed his eyes again.

His desire to be a father had stemmed from Absalom's love for Eliza, so on a cold December night a year and a half ago, when his and Eliza's daughter was born, the thrill of hearing the doctor announce, "Well, well, we have a girl," had sent an overwhelming wave of joy through him.

Until she didn't cry.

Denver let go of Eliza's hand to look over the sheet covering her raised legs. Black eyebrows. Black eyelashes. Headful of black hair. The image of her mother. The image of a father's love for his daughter. The image of a mother's love for them both.

They hadn't chosen a name, preferring to wait and see what love would bring them.

The doctor suctioned her tiny nostrils and popped the pale bottom. No sound. Nothing. He popped her bottom again. Still no sound. Still nothing. He rushed her to a nurse who took her to a table where they worked frantically. Denver held Eliza's hand until the doctor came over to say how sorry he was, that he didn't understand, that the heart monitor read a strong rhythm until their daughter was born. Eliza began crying. She didn't stop until she fell asleep hours later, exhausted.

Denver refused any further examination as to a cause of death. Just the thought of a cold scalpel touching his daughter's pale skin broke his heart even worse.

After the funeral, when the black-clothed mourners trickled away, sad-faced and shocked at the sudden loss of one so innocent, Eliza stood beside the tiny mound of red dirt beneath the blue funeral home tent, the beginning of a winter storm whipping her black hair around her face.

All of her loved ones tried to get her to go home. She said nothing, simply stood there, stiff and unmoving, jerking her hand away when one of them touched it.

Denver told Absalom where to find his old tent and a sleeping bag and a propane camp heater. When Absalom brought it, Eliza stepped aside. "Cut a place in the bottom. A place where I can hold her and keep her warm."

Denver did so with a pocket knife from his pickup, set the tent up over the grave, and held the sleeping bag open for her to crawl into. He zipped the sleeping bag. She unzipped it to open the slit in the tent's bottom and hold the tiny mound of red dirt. "Mamma's here, sweetheart. They all have left you. I never will."

God kept the storm away. Absalom left and came back with another sleeping bag for Denver. When Denver put it inside, Eliza wordlessly shoved it from the tent.

Almost two weeks passed. Eliza refused her follow-up appointment with her doctor. Absalom and his family brought food. The minister of the church let everyone use the restroom. Without a word, Eliza would nibble and sip and zip herself back into the sleeping bag, as if it were a cocoon to keep anything and everything from touching her, except death and misery

Denver called a psychiatrist. She gave him something to put into her food to make her sleep and had him bring her for a stay at a mental facility. Leaving Eliza there for a month had been unbearable. Eating alone had been unbearable. Sleeping alone had been unbearable.

When the psychiatrist said Eliza was well, Denver brought her home.

His mother-in-law, Oneita, had knitted a pink and blue baby blanket. His father-in-law, Absalom, had made a rocking chair. Until spring came, Eliza sat in it, the blanket held to her cheek. When summer came, she sometimes sat on the wooden bench on the dock the same way. When winter came again, she returned to the rocking chair.

She ate what Denver took to the table, slept in his sister's old room, and she either returned to the rocking chair or dock each morning if the weather allowed.

What it would take to bring her back to him, he didn't know, but it seemed as if their marriage had died with their daughter, to be buried with her beneath that tiny mound of red dirt.

Denver opened his eyes. He considered turning from the lake to look into the living room window. He started to but didn't, because the scene of Eliza sitting there was imprinted into his memory as clearly as if someone had carved it into his brain.

A sudden breeze rippled the lake's surface, creating a V beside the dock. As a boy, he had thought these Vs were ghosts running their fingers through the water's surface.

Could this V be made by their daughter come to visit? Come to see how they were doing without her? Come to see if they were dealing with her death like most people dealt with death, by understanding how life must go on instead of living it as ghosts themselves?

When he had lost Eliza that first time, he had paddled his canoe out on the lake with plans to drown himself. Now they were both drowning in a lake of pure anguish—too hurt to touch, too hurt to talk, too hurt to even sleep in the same bed.

Denver raised his eyes to the darkening sky. Behind him, to the west, the sun was setting, while in front of him, to the east, the distant clouds hanging over the trees across the lake burned crimson.

If only his and Eliza's hearts could burn like that again, with a love that had drawn them together as profoundly as anything he had ever felt, known, or experienced.

He faced the living room window of the home his parents had left him and Willow. He couldn't ask for a better sister. Not only had she given him the house when their parents had died, she had stayed with him and Eliza for a few weeks after Eliza came home from the mental health facility, to help out around the house and to help Eliza get back on her feet mentally.

If only that had happened.

Although Eliza's psychiatrist had said she was well enough to come home, and on subsequent visits had said that her sitting for hours and hours, either in the rocking chair in the living room or on the dock, was part of her personal healing process, as time passed, and the sitting continued, Denver didn't know if she was healing or giving up, on life as well as him.

Behind the living room window, Eliza's black hair reflected the light from the lamp beside her. Sometimes she turned it on as it grew dark. Sometimes she didn't. When she did, she would sit there until Denver persuaded her to go to bed.

Although he couldn't see the pink and blue baby blanket she held to her cheek, he knew it was there. At least she didn't cry anymore, wetting the blanket with her tears like she had wet the red dirt at the cemetery.

A fish splashed in the lake. In the woods to the right, a bobwhite quail called: *bob-bob-white, bob-bob-white.*

What a lonely sound, either from a male or female searching for her or his covey, or maybe for an old love gone missing.

Denver leaned over to place his elbows on his knees and stare at the dock. Tears dropped to the worn and scratched wood, gray with age.

Ever since he and Eliza were married, hope for their future had been their constant companion.

He wiped his runny nose.

No. Hope had died with their daughter, and for the life of him he didn't know how to bring hope back into their lives. Still, his worst fear was losing their love—a love they had fought so hard to attain, and which was now fading like fog over the lake on a summer morning.

The crimson clouds across the lake turned to ochre and then to gray. Over them, stars winked into view.

Rising to his feet, Denver gave them one last look and started up the gravel path to the second story deck and its sliding glass doors.

Inside, he went to the kitchen to warm leftover soup from last night and take it to the table, along with spoons and water. When he motioned Eliza to the chair across from him, she came and sat without a single word or sign, even when he took the blanket from her and lay it across the rocking chair back.

Night fell, darkening the yard and the lake. A boat engine whined, followed by its red and white running lights blinking on, visible through the sliding glass doors. Where might that person be heading? Denver could barely make out a single head at the console. Maybe the person was going home to someone who loved him or her, someone who would ask if they had enjoyed their day, someone who would say they would join them next time on the lake.

The only time Eliza wore her hearing aids now was during a psychiatrist appointment, although they hadn't been in months. Since that was the case, they sipped and drank quietly, without signs, glances, or smiles. Denver hated these meals. They were strangers joined by grief, their love foundering on the rocks of heartache.

The bobwhite quail called once again and no more. The boat motor's whine faded into the night. The air conditioning system came on, sending out a cool flow of air from a ceiling vent. It dried the sweat on his brow, sweat he hadn't even realized was there.

He risked a glance at his wife. A week after she came home from the mental health facility, she cut her waist-length hair to the back of her neck and left it in the bathroom. Afraid he would keep it in his room as a reminder of them not sleeping together—not that he needed a reminder—Denver donated her hair to one of those places that made wigs for people undergoing cancer treatments. Her hair now reached to her shoulder blades. She brushed it before rising in the morning and at night before bed. She brushed and flossed her teeth too. She even showered regularly. Such things might seem insignificant to some people, but Denver was grateful because he didn't need to remind her to care for herself, which meant that maybe some tiny piece of her still cared—not only for herself but for him.

The meal done, he washed dishes while she returned to her chair. Watching her, he dried them and put them away.

More than anything he wanted to know if she still loved him. Yes, he understood her grief, but she should understand his too, should understand how they could bear it better together than apart.

He took a beer from the refrigerator and twisted the top off the bottle, threw it in the trash and downed half of it in one long pull. Three more followed as he sat at the bar watching Eliza. A slight numb feeling swallowed him. Two more beers followed. Eliza never moved. The numb feeling extended into his body.

She once would chastise him about drinking after only one beer, saying and signing, both while grinning, that he loved alcohol more than her. Now he wasn't sure, or was the beer making him question his feelings for her?

He threw the last bottle away. It broke with the other five, creating a pile of gleaming brown teeth in the bottom of the trash container. If only he could crawl into those teeth and have them devour him. Then maybe he wouldn't hurt anymore when the alcohol numbness wore off.

He dumped the trash container into the larger one on the deck, brought the smaller one back inside to stuff a plastic liner into it.

Eliza never moved, never blinked, never offered him the slightest acknowledgement that he even existed.

At the bar again, he drank six more beers, dumped those bottles into the large trash container outside, and went to turn the lamp off beside Eliza so she would go to bed, which she did.

Bedroom door closed, he stumbled to the bathroom to brush his teeth, decided against it, and went to the kitchen for another six-pack of beer. Almost out. Better get more tomorrow. Better buy a fridge for nothing but beer if this kept up.

On the dock bench again. Two more beers downed.

The lamp in Eliza's room came on. The curtains parted. Her slender figure appeared.

Yes, they both were ghosts, thin from eating so little that their bodies appeared angular and sharp in their jeans and T-shirts, which was all they had worn since their daughter had been born.

He fell from the bench to the dock, rolled over to finish the beers. Dark brown bottles and metal caps caught starlight and flung it back at him. Eliza's curtains closed. The room darkened.

Denver crawled to the dock's edge and vomited into the lake. Wiping his mouth, he rolled over to stare at the stars. A sudden burst of rare agony—rare because he thought the mechanism for it was too depleted to function—tracked warm tears from his eyes and down his temples, until they pooled in his ears.

One way or another, he and Eliza needed to find their way back to each other. If not, death would take them—him from alcohol poisoning, her from a heart as cold as ice.

ice

After one last look at Denver on the dock, Eliza turned the lamp off and went to bed.

Her husband had become a drunk, and she didn't know what to do about it. Yes, their daughter's death had devastated him like it had devastated her, but at least she hadn't turned to beer for comfort.

The most difficult part of their shared tragedy was whether or not she still loved him, a question she never, not in her wildest dreams, would've imagined when they fell in love.

Still, she couldn't give up on him—they had fought too hard to be together—but she had no idea how to return them both to the time before their daughter had died.

Another difficult part of their tragedy was how she didn't know if she wanted to risk having more children, only to have them snatched away from her by death.

And still another part was how blame was etching itself into her heart, not only blame against herself for falling in love with Denver and leaving the Amish, but blame against Denver for coming to Ohio in the first place. If they had never met, she might still be miserable, but at least they wouldn't have lost their daughter.

No, although the stillborn baby was *their* daughter, it seemed she was more Eliza's daughter than Denver's. Eliza couldn't make sense of that feeling—it just *was*. Yes, to think that was wrong, but no matter how hard she tried to rid herself of it, the feeling clung to her like cockleburs embedded in her black Amish dress after picking corn in the field back home.

She rolled over to face the window. Through an opening in the curtain, stars glittered in the blackened sky. She once kept her hearing aids in to catch the sounds of the night: the chirping of crickets, the wind in the trees, an owl's *who-whoooo*, the rhythm of Denver's breath as he slept beside her. Long gone times it seemed, but only a few short years ago.

One certain star glittered brilliantly. How would it feel to be a star in the cold of space, where vacuum insulated a star's warmth from all those other stars around it?

She rolled over to face away from the window and the reminder of her own star-like self, insulated against anything and everything that might cause her to break down in the middle of the long, lonely nights.

Moments later, the minute vibration of stumbling footfalls signaled Denver coming up the steps to the deck. She could picture him fumbling with the latch on the sliding glass doors, could picture him finally getting it open and coming in, could picture him shuffling across the living room floor to the room that once was their room instead of his room.

Some mornings his sour breath hinted at unbrushed teeth, possibly from vomiting and passing out. She sometimes glanced in his room while he was outside. He hadn't changed his sheets in weeks, only washed his clothes when he needed more, only showered once a week and often smelled of faded deodorant and sweat. Oil glistened in his hair the day before he showered. Stubble grew on his cheeks, chin, and neck.

Yes, grief likely had removed his idea of caring for himself. It wasn't as if he showed her any affection anymore, so maybe, even though he had sworn differently when she had asked him during one particular counseling session, he blamed her for losing their daughter.

A heavy vibration traveled through the floor and to her door. It opened and she closed her eyes.

Could she smell vomit? Could she smell fear? Could she smell hate?

No, not really, but although imagination often lied, honesty might hide within the recesses of her disbelief.

More footfalls, soft, slow, and with the tread of a shuffling man, drunken and despairing, came to the bed.

She strained to hear him, strained to sense him, strained to catch the tiniest hint of his love for her.

The footfalls shuffled toward the door. The light from the living room dimmed as it closed.

How long could they go on like this?

She waited until the sliver of light beneath the door turned black and went to the rocking chair for the baby blanket. In bed again, she held the pink and blue weave to her cheek.

How she longed to feel Denver in her arms again, if only for comfort instead of making love. He needed comfort too, or he wouldn't drink so much. Why had he come to her bed like he did? Did he do it to curse her under his breath, to wish he had never married her, to wish he had never met her, to wish he had never learned sign language, which was yet another thing that had brought them together?

Her mind offered silence instead of answers.

She rose from the bed, fitted the hearing aids into her ears, and padded to Denver's door. No light shone beneath it. She eased it open.

The night had engulfed their home. Starlight dimly illuminated his face and chest. Eyes closed. Soft snores. Shirtless chest rising and falling. She padded to him on bare feet, the floor cold from the air conditioning.

In the sign language school in Ohio, when she had spent the night with him and the other teacher, Akina, while Papa was at home, Eliza had moved her sleeping mat beside Denver. How she loved him then, more than she ever thought possible.

Sometime in the night, when lightning woke her, she opened her eyes to find him looking at her. Through the windows, lightning brightened the room again, followed by thunder strong enough to vibrate within her chest. She had taken Denver's hand to place between her breasts and had told him she felt it in her heart. They had discussed that moment in those autumn days in Occoneechee State Park, where they had spent their honeymoon. Although he had admitted to loving her on the night of the storm, he hadn't known how she had loved him so completely back then.

That week at the park couldn't have been more magical. They hiked the woods and trails, fished from the bank below the rental cabin, made love endlessly, once even on the deck as red and gold leaves from a nearby oak fell down around them.

Without considering the consequences, she started to pull his hand to her chest but stopped when her fingertips touched his wrist.

He stirred, rolled one way and then the other, then turned away from her, revealing the muscular wall of his back.

No, it was more thin than muscular. Not only did they eat very little now, they didn't take the canoe out on the lake and paddle for hours like they used to.

She returned to her bed.

One way or another, something must change. If not, if they kept existing instead of living—and loving—something would happen they both might regret.

That huge star, brilliant and cold within the sky, glittered as if laughing at the joke her and Denver's marriage had become.

She understood how it might feel to be a star, for her heart to grow cold in the long and lonely night, with nothing but grief to keep her company instead of the comfort of the man she once loved.

Placing her hand between her breasts, she nodded. Yes, no doubts, no hesitation. Her heart mirrored that star, nothing but a ball of ice insulated from every joy she had ever known.

Including her love for Denver.

family

In his workshop shortly after sunrise, Absalom Gray took two chair runners from the steamer box, where they had formed to the perfect shape for rocking. He killed the power on the steamer, left the runners on a workbench, and went outside, mug of coffee in hand.

To his left, walking the stone path from the house to his workshop, Oneita carried a mug of steaming tea, her favorite morning drink. She stopped beside him and sipped. Being a foot shorter than his six-five height, she looked up into his eyes. "I miss the time when mornings like this, with the sun rising over the trees, could take away every little worry I had."

Absalom said nothing. She was a born worrier, strict for their children's sake, yet he knew what she meant: her worries—and his—weren't little because they were about Eliza and Denver.

She sipped again. "Should we see how Eliza and Denver are doing?"

Absalom didn't care to mention the obvious, but he should. "We can, but Denver would've told us if anything had changed. Even when we do visit, it doesn't seem to affect her mood."

"I don't need to remind you how we left the Amish and moved here to be near her. We even learned sign language well enough to speak with her about simple things when she doesn't wear her hearing aids. Now she won't even—" Oneita lowered her head. "I was going to say she won't even speak to us, but that's not important."

Absalom sipped his cooling coffee. Both he and Oneita had shared Eliza and Denver's pain when they had lost their child, as if the stillborn infant had been the daughter they had lost to an E-coli infection so long ago. To even begin to get over that loss, Oneita had demanded they move from Kansas to Ohio, so they both understood how grief could tear at the heart and soul. Thank goodness their grief had eased to the point of having four more children, the bright spots of happiness in their lives.

Absalom faced Oneita. Without warning, the memory of their daughter, all black curls and pinks cheeks, hit him as if it were a sledge hammer between his eyes. How he loved her smiles and laughter. Yes, although he hated leaving her in Kansas, being in Ohio had eased his pain from losing her too. He started to drink coffee, but it was too cool to enjoy. He emptied the dregs into the grass beside the walkway. "Do you ever think about going back to Kansas for a visit? It's been what, over twenty years now?"

"More like twenty-five." Oneita paused, possibly considering the reason for the question. "You're thinking about how we lost our daughter. I would like to visit Kansas sometime. I might cry over that tiny grave, but nothing like before."

Absalom kissed her cheek. "I would cry too, I'm sure. I'm surprised I haven't thought about it, but we would've been better off to recall the good times with her instead of the bad. Besides, she wouldn't want us to go on grieving for her forever. She would want us to be happy like she was happy while she was with us."

The crow's feet at the corners of Oneita's green eyes deepened from a slight smile. "Think we can bottle your idea of how to get over grief and give it to Eliza?"

"I'm sure that was covered during her therapy."

Absalom caught a glimpse of Tess in the kitchen window. At sixteen, she was taking driver-ed in high school and had been asking him and Oneita for a car, saying she preferred a smaller used sedan for saving money and gas. Unfortunately, she got a steady stream of phone calls from several boys at school. She called them "friends." Right. Her auburn hair like his and green eyes like Oneita's meant those boys weren't thinking about being friends.

"I see you looking at Tess," Oneita said. "When do we find her a car?"

"Have you heard from Ethan and Timothy lately?"

Oneita shoved Absalom's arm. "Don't change the subject. You know you can't stop her from driving."

"It's not the driving I'm worried about. Tess has a good head on her shoulders, but some of the boys who call her might not." Absalom cut his eyes at Oneita. "Before she dates any of them, I'll make sure they come here to pick her up. If I'm out here with my shirt off and splitting wood with my double-bladed ax, they might think twice about doing something they shouldn't."

"Better not do that." Oneita stood on tiptoe to kiss him. "It might make me drag you inside to the bedroom, you handsome man."

Absalom laughed. "It didn't take you long to forget our strict Amish ways."

"I came out to tell you Ethan called. He and Timothy have more sign language students than normal because more family members are coming. It's nice they want to learn so they can talk with their children."

"Huh," Absalom said, scratching his chin. "If Eliza went there to teach a while, I wonder if it could help her get over her grief?"

"I haven't thought of that," Oneita said. "It could help get her mind off of it, I suppose. Denver could go too. They have more than enough money invested from his parent's life insurance and her painting income to keep them from working."

Tess came outside. Absalom didn't mind how Oneita's blue jeans fit her, but Tess's were entirely too tight. She came up the stone walkway to meet them. "What are you two talking about this morning?"

Absalom winked at Oneita. "We're thinking about buying you a new car instead of a used one. My rocking chair business is doing pretty good for its third year."

"Really? That good?"

"Sure is, but it'll take me until after you graduate from college to buy it."

"Don't tease her like that," Oneita said. She faced Tess. "We'll find you a used car, but you've got to promise to behave when you start dating."

"That's not a problem, Mama. I know to wait until I fall in love."

Clearing his throat, Absalom narrowed his eyes. "Young lady, you *better* know to wait until you're married. Any man who loves and respects you will want to wait too."

"Yes, Papa. I don't want to end up a mama before I'm ready to fly out from under yours and mama's wings."

"Good," Oneita said. "That means we taught you well."

Tess raised her eyes upward, toward the sun clearing the trees. "I wonder if Eliza is sitting on the dock this morning?"

"We were talking about visiting her and Denver," Oneita said. "Is Ivy still asleep?"

As if on cue, Ivy appeared at the screened kitchen door in her nightgown, rubbing her eyes. "Mama!" she yelled, "I'm hungry!"

"For strawberry oatmeal, of course," Tess said. She faced Absalom and Oneita. "Did I wake up ready to eat when I was her age?"

"Pretty much," Absalom said. He waved at Ivy, almost four, with a headful of tangled auburn curls. "Go on in and fix her some oatmeal, Tess. I need to run to the golf course for a while."

"I thought you stopped working there to have more time to make rocking chairs?"

"I know how to fix one of the older mowers when the new greenskeeper doesn't. It's Saturday. The course will be busy. I like to run by now and then to make sure things are running well."

"And to hit a few balls," Oneita said.

Absalom raised his arm and touched his huge bicep, toned from his life of working on their farm in Ohio, and now, from splitting wood for the fireplace. "Gotta keep in shape, Oneita."

"Oh, hush, you big bear of a man. Finish whatever you have left with your rocking chairs so we can visit Eliza and Denver."

visit

After scrambled eggs, toast, and coffee, and while Eliza was showering, Denver went to the dock with a trash bag to clean up his empty beer bottles and caps. He really needed to get control of his drinking before it got *out* of control.

Bag filled, he dumped it into the larger container and took that bag to his pickup to take out later. Starting to the front door, he turned to the sound of a vehicle engine coming down the road. The vehicle cleared the trees bordering the lot. Absalom waved as he pulled into the driveway, Oneita beside him and Tess and Ivy in the back. They all climbed out. Tess ran to him and gave him a quick hug. "Hey, Denver. Is Eliza on the dock?"

"She's taking a shower."

Oneita took Ivy from her car seat and set her on her feet. She ran to Denver, who picked her up and whirled her around. "Hey, Ivy, you're getting to be a big girl." He put her down. She looked up at him and poked his stomach.

"Where's your tummy?"

Denver patted his stomach. "It's still there." Absalom and Oneita walked up. Absalom patted his shoulder. "How're things going, Denver?"

"About the same, Absalom."

Oneita rubbed his arm. "Does Eliza still sit all day with that blanket?"

"I'm afraid so. I guess she needs time to get over ... well, you know."

"How about you?" Absalom said. "You *do* look like you're losing weight."

"Not much of an appetite lately." Denver had used this excuse before, but it usually stopped the questions about his weight. He faced Absalom. "How's the rocking chair business going? Tess probably wants a car soon."

"I sure do," she said.

"We were just talking about it while ago," Oneita said. "She palmed his cheek. "You haven't shaved lately. Growing your beard out?"

Ivy went to Oneita. "I need to go potty, Mama."

"Go ahead," Denver said.

"Me too," Tess said. "Maybe Eliza's out of the shower now."

"Come along then," Oneita said, taking Ivy's hand. "I'd like to see her."

The front door closed. Except for a breeze rustling in the oaks at the edges of the lot, silence fell. Denver waited. Absalom likely had more to say. Either he or Oneita usually called before driving or walking over from their house two roads down in the lake subdivision. Since they hadn't, something was on their minds.

Absalom walked to the side of the front porch and pointed toward the dock. "It'd be a fine day for you and Eliza to take your canoe out."

Denver couldn't deny that, but the few times he had asked Eliza, she had turned him down flat.

The breeze turned into a hard gust rippling the lake. Yes, he would love to be out on the lake in his canoe. The problem was whether he would want Eliza with him or not. He despised feeling like that, despised everything and anything that had brought them to such a sad situation.

"Denver, are you all right?"

Denver faced Absalom. "What?"

"I said are you all right?"

"I get by. You're right about going out on the lake. I—" Lingering behind his eyes ever since their daughter had been born dead, the urge to cry struck Denver like twin ice picks into his optic nerves. How he wanted to be on the lake, like the times he and Eliza had paddled his canoe there. How he wanted to take their child there. How he wanted to teach her how to fish and camp. How he wanted to see Eliza teaching her how to paint her amazing pictures of nature. All gone now. All gone.

Absalom's hand fell on his shoulder. "Since you know how Oneita and I lost a daughter, you know we feel exactly what you feel. I'm sure this is placing a strain on you and Eliza, but it'll get better with time."

Slowly, gradually, the ice picks withdrew from the back of Denver's eyes. He missed Mom and Dad, missed how they could talk, missed how when serious subjects arose, they could sit and work them out. To have them here now might help. At least they would hold him while he cried his grief into their shoulders.

The breeze gusted again, sending a cool flow into his face, fresh and clean.

Absalom and Oneita were great in-laws, but they weren't Mom and Dad. Time to suck it up and be a man about this mess between him and Eliza.

"You're right, Absalom. Time will take care of it." The unspoken part echoed in Denver's skull: *one way or another*. He rubbed his bristly chin. "I guess I do look kind of scruffy." Another unspoken part echoed in his skull: *but why do that when Eliza might never touch my face or kiss me again?*

Absalom's crow's feet formed deeply etched chevrons as he smiled. "That's the spirit. Let's go see what our girls are up to."

Inside, Oneita, Tess, and Ivy sat at the bar between the kitchen and the living room. Eliza, hair damp and shining, no hearing aids in, wearing jeans and a white T-shirt, took milk from the refrigerator and filled a glass for Ivy, who was munching a chocolate chip cookie. Denver could see the expiration date on the bag on the counter. Still in date—barely.

Eliza raised her hands toward Oneita. "Coffee, Mama?"

Oneita sign, "No," and Eliza asked Absalom, who signed, "No" also.

Tess raised her hands toward Eliza. "It's a beautiful morning. We could all go for a walk."

"Or go out on the pontoon boat fishing," Oneita said.

"How about it?" Absalom said. "We can run home and make something for lunch and take it with us."

"I'd rather not," Eliza signed.

"Can you use your hearing aids?" Tess said. "I haven't talked with you in forever, and I miss it."

Eliza's chest rose and fell. She went to her room and came back with the hearing aids in. Her expression stayed the same: flat and emotionless.

Absalom and Oneita glanced at each other, concern in their tightened lips.

"I'd like to go fishing," Denver said.

"You go, Eliza said. "I'll stay here."

When Eliza first got her hearing aids, she went to a speech therapist and practiced so much that Denver used to tease her about it. Since she had hardly spoken ten words since the funeral, her words ran together as if she were speaking while eating.

Denver bit his lower lip. Press the issue or not? Yes, because something needed to break this wall of silence between them, and spending time with him and her family on the lake might help.

"I'd rather you go with us, Eliza. You don't have to fish. Just being out in the sun and fresh air on the lake will do us good. Remember how you used to love it?"

* * *

Once, twice, three times, Eliza blinked. With Denver in front of her and Mama and Papa behind her, she felt surrounded and worse—pressured. "You go. I'm not." She went to the rocking chair and sat.

Papa's thudding footsteps came from behind her. He took the arms of the rocking chair in his huge hands and turned her to face the living room instead of the lake. Sitting on the sofa, he waved everyone else over. Mama and Denver sat. When Tess and Ivy came over, Papa pointed toward the window. "Why don't you two go to the dock? We'll be out in a minute." Tess took Ivy by the hand and left. Papa faced Eliza. "I'm sure you think we're pressuring you into going fishing, but it's time you got out and did something besides sitting. You and Denver are turning into hermits, stuck here in this house."

"Denver goes out for groceries."

"That's not what I mean and you know it, young lady."

Heat rose in Eliza's cheeks. "I'm a married woman, Papa. I'm old enough to know what I mean and I'm old enough to know what you mean. Go fishing if you want, I'm not going."

Oneita slid forward on the sofa. "Do you plan to stay here until you dry up and wither away? You're only twenty-three, Eliza. You and Denver have long lives to live yet, and you need to enjoy them."

Eliza lowered her head. None of them understood how she felt, understood how she ached inside from having her daughter born dead from her womb, without a single cry, without a single whimper. She had even worn her hearing aids to hear that, and when she never did, her entire world had collapsed in on her. At the moment, beyond all the other moments of her life, even when she had considered killing herself because she thought she had lost Denver, even when Amish children had mocked her deafness, she had wanted to kill herself to join her daughter.

Denver rose from the sofa and went to the sliding glass doors. What did he see when he stood there? What did he see when he sat on the dock, but only when she sat inside? Maybe he saw another life, a happier life, a life with a woman who could love him and give him a child, one who would cry at birth.

But what did she see when she watched the lake all day? Nothing, nothing at all. It was if that icy star or grief gripped her heart and insulated it from anything and everything she once loved, including Denver.

She started to get up but didn't. Better to wait until the middle of the night to pack, and to leave Denver a note telling him not to look for her. She had more than enough money from selling her paintings to go wherever she wanted. If something happened to change her mind about starting over with him, she would return, but not until then.

Denver turned to look at her. His eyes said nothing, so his heart felt nothing. What did he want from her, if anything? Did love still live between them? Was there a spark still there of what they once had? If so, she couldn't see it in his blue eyes that she once loved to gaze into.

"What you two need," Papa said, "is to get away for a while."

"I agree," Mama said. "What do you think about going back to our old home and teaching sign language? Ethan says more parents are coming, so they could use the help."

"Jon added onto the house too," Papa said. "Plenty of room for you both to stay there."

Denver returned to the sofa. "What do you think, Eliza? I'd like to visit Ohio and see Jon again."

Eliza considered the offer. To see Jon and his wife, Becca, plus their children, Ellie, who should be about nine by now, and Samuel, who should be about three or four, might get her mind on something besides sadness.

"I'll think about it."

"Glad to hear it," Papa said. "He looked at Mama. "Your Mama and I are thinking about taking a trip too."

"We just thought about it today," Mama said. "We'd like to go back to Kansas, where we lived before we moved to Ohio. I should be able to visit your sister's grave now without being overcome."

"How about Tess and Ivy?" Denver said.

"We'll take Ivy with us. Tess starts waitressing at that bed and breakfast in town next weekend, so she'll stay home."

"How will she get there? She doesn't have her license yet, right?"

"And no car either," Absalom said. "Any chance you could give her a ride? It's just Friday and Saturday night."

"Sure, no problem." Denver patted his stomach. "Maybe she can get me a discount on that crab dip they make."

Eliza noticed Denver's familiar grin, the one he hadn't shared with her in so long. How could he do that with her feeling so terrible?

She stood and went to the window. Tess and Ivy were sitting at the end of the dock. The sun highlighted her sister's long auburn hair, down past her shoulder blades. Since she was no longer Amish, would she behave when she started dating? The boys would flock to her, admiring her fuller figure than Eliza's and green eyes like Mama's.

Denver came to her side. "Tess sure is gorgeous. I hope no one bothers her at the restaurant. Your Papa will kill them if they do."

Eliza returned to the rocking chair. When had Denver last told her *she* looked gorgeous? Then again, when had she last cared if he did?

Papa stood. "Denver, do you still want to go fishing if my daughter doesn't?"

Denver's chest rose and fell, his familiar sign of frustration. "Maybe another time. When will you go to Kansas?"

"We'll have to talk about it," Oneita said. "We'll let you know so you can give Tess a ride."

Eliza faced the lake. High in the blue sky, an osprey soared on wide wings, white and then darkening toward its body. If only she could fly like that, fly away from all her hurt and all her pain, fly away from her parents pressuring her, which included Denver, the man she had no idea if she loved or not.

Maybe time away from him would tell the story.

She lowered her head.

Or end it.

hope

For Denver, the day passed agonizingly slow. He wanted to bring up the subject of him and Eliza going to Ohio to teach sign language—just the thing to bring them together again.

Lunch passed with more soup, this time with a grilled cheese, which Eliza didn't touch. After washing their few dishes, he went downstairs to the easel where she used to paint almost every day. The shirt he had given her to protect her clothes—an old flannel thing she had once loved—was draped over the easel, covered in dust. He took it upstairs and added it to the clothes hamper, showered and shaved, washed and dried the clothes, and put clean cargo shorts and a T-shirt on, his summer attire when things were normal between them. He took the warm flannel shirt, smelling sweet and fresh from the drier sheet, and lay it across Eliza's bed. Maybe the memory of how she once loved it—and him—would come back with its aroma.

Around four he went to the grocery for a porterhouse steak, two huge baking potatoes, and the makings for tossed salads. Although he walked by the beer cooler, he refused to give it a glance. For some inexplicable reason, things were looking up, possibly to the point of returning back to the time before their daughter's death had ripped them apart. No, no sirree. No alcohol in any form for him tonight. Still, the red wine caught his eye, but no bottle wormed its way into his shopping cart.

Home again, grill heating, potatoes in the oven, salads made, he went to the living room window. Eliza sat on the end of the dock today. At least she had a bottle of sunscreen beside her and her feet in the water. Maybe she felt the hope in the air between them too.

Steaks grilled to perfection, potatoes cut and buttered, salads made, he took a chance on calling Eliza in from the dock. To his surprise, she turned toward him and waved. Since she had her hearing aids in, maybe they'd have a nice supper with some normal conversation instead of absolute quiet.

Eliza came in, cheeks somewhat pink from the sun despite the sunscreen. She looked more herself than she had in months. Denver held the chair for her and then sat himself. She took the hearing aids out, disappointing him. He raised his hands to sign, "Can't you put them back in? It's hard to sign and eat at the same time."

Her dark eyes focused on his face. Slowly, as if it pained her to raise her hands, she did. "What do we have to talk about?"

Denver rubbed his clean-shaven chin. If she had noticed how he had showered and shaved and put on clean shorts, including making this great supper, she didn't intend to acknowledge it, or his efforts. The night was *not* starting off well.

He sliced the tender side of the porterhouse and put them on her plate. "It's been a while since we had a supper like this, don't you think?"

No signs, not a one. She ate without looking at him, dark eyes staring at her plate, fork rising and falling in slow motion, a person eating only to delay death.

When her plate was half-empty, she started to rise with it. Denver grabbed her arm and let go to sign, "Sit for a minute and put your hearing aids in. I want to talk about going to Ohio to teach sign language." He paused. "I miss your voice too. Can't you talk to me?"

Eliza dropped to the chair and shoved the hearing aids into her ears. "I sound like a child learning to talk."

"That's because you haven't talked in so long." Denver placed his hand on hers. She looked at them on the table, then slowly pulled hers away, another sign that the night wasn't starting well.

Outside the window, the sky and the lake grew dark. Lightning bugs flickered in the oaks.

Denver brought his hand back to his lap. "Would you like to go to Ohio? I would."

Eliza took their plates to the kitchen and came back with a beer from the refrigerator. She sat it in front of Denver. "Don't forget one of these to get your night going."

Denver shoved the beer aside. Yep, she had noticed his drinking, or rather, his excessive drinking. Good thing he hadn't bought any more at the grocery. "I would've had one with supper if I wanted one. What about Ohio?"

"I might like that."

"Why *might*?"

"If I go alone."

"You don't want me with you?"

"We've been together every single day for a year and a half. I think we need some time apart."

The ice picks pierced Denver's optic nerves. Sure, he and Eliza had grown apart. Sure, she likely questioned her love for him like he questioned his for her. Considering everything they had gone through, with losing their daughter and the resulting grief, those questions might be natural. Still, the only way to find their way back to each other was to be together, not apart.

She rose from the table and went to the sliding glass doors. The jeans hung on her slender frame as if on the legs of a scarecrow, baggy and loose. She turned to face him.

"If you care about me at all, you'll let me go by myself."

The icepicks withdrew, replaced by anger. To want to go by herself meant he wasn't welcome anywhere near here. Then why didn't she just pack and go? Denver downed the bitter beer in one long pull. Talking to her was a waste of time. Never, ever, had he thought their relationship would sink this low.

As Eliza stood by the sliding glass doors, star began winking into view over the trees across the lake, similar to when they had taken the pontoon boat out to watch Clarksville's Lakefest fireworks show the first time, back before they admitted to loving each other.

That night couldn't have been more magical.

During their honeymoon at the cabin in Occoneechee State Park, she had admitted to turning the gas valve off on the outboard so they could spend the night on the lake.

What a night that had been, especially since it included her first art show before the fireworks, where collectors bought every painting she had created since childhood. Most also requested oil reproductions, setting off a whirlwind of work, more art shows in states throughout the east, and a schedule that barely left enough time for themselves.

Two years later, overworked and exhausted, Eliza had suggested another week at the cabin in the park. Two months later, she ran from the bathroom to jump on Denver in bed and to show him a positive pregnancy test. "I know it happened at the cabin," she had signed and said. "We just needed to get away to ourselves and relax." Smiling so huge that his cheeks had ached, Denver followed her announcement by giving her a massage and making love to her.

Those days were gone now, reduced to pain and anguish and grief. What would it take to get back there again?

Eliza returned to the table. "I'm not sure if I want to go at all. I need to think about it."

Denver covered her slender hand with his. "Will you think about me going too?"

They're hands stayed together instead of parting, the warmth of days and nights past, possibly to never return. Still, he took it as a positive, no matter how insignificant.

"I'll ... I will."

The hesitation in her voice hurt Denver. He took his hand from beneath hers. At least the ice picks hadn't plunged into his optic nerves.

Eliza went to the rocking chair. He washed their dishes, dried and put them away. Opening the refrigerator, he momentarily regretted not buying more beer. No, he didn't need it yet, but if kept drinking like he had last night, he would give it up completely. The last thing his and Eliza's marriage needed was for him to become an alcoholic.

With that thought still in his mind, he took the last two beers from the refrigerator and walked in the dark to the dock, where he sat with his bare feet in the summer-warmed water.

As he twisted the top from the first bottle, footsteps crunched in the gravel path behind him. "Hey, brother-in-law. Could you use some company?" Tess sat beside him. "Mind if I have your other beer?"

Denver didn't see the harm in one beer. "Go ahead. Just don't tell anyone I said it was okay."

Tess opened the bottle and took a swallow. "Kind of bitter but I like it."

Denver took a cold swallow. "That's your first beer? I thought you might've had some with your friends."

"One tried to get me to drink at her house when her parents were away. I didn't think I should."

"But you think it's okay with me?"

"Just to keep you company." Tess looked over her shoulder. "I see Eliza in the rocking chair." Denver said nothing. Tess leaned her head onto his shoulder. I hate how she's treating you. She acts like it's your fault and it isn't."

Denver started to tell Tess to not lean against him, but when he turned to speak, the floral aroma of her hair stopped him cold. He missed everything about being married, including making love to Eliza, and the warmth of Tess against him reminded him of just how much he enjoyed sex. He eased away from Tess. "I appreciate your concern, but—"

Tess sat up straight. "But you're married, and I'm Eliza's sister and I'm just sixteen, right?"

"Pretty much."

"What if you weren't married and I were eighteen? You know I'm almost seventeen."

"I'd still be kind of old for you."

"You'd be twenty-seven. What's nine years difference?"

"I meant you're under age now." Denver couldn't believe this conversation. Not only was Tess attracted to him, she was actually flirting with him. Even though that was the case, the worst part was how he was attracted to her too, and at sixteen of all things. He bumped her shoulder with his. "You know your papa would kill me if he heard us talking like this. I wouldn't blame him either."

The night darkened further. Scattered clouds dimmed the stars, leaving the lake to resemble a vast sheet of black road.

Tess swallowed beer. She looked over her shoulder. "Eliza turned the light out and it's dark inside." She raised her hand to Denver's chin and turned his face toward her. "I really do think it's terrible how she's treating you."

The clouds moved. The night brightened. Starlight glittered in Tess's green eyes. She leaned toward Denver, breath warm against his lips. Gorgeous? No doubt about it, but alluring too. She licked her full lips, which caught the starlight like her eyes. The urge to kiss her or pull away fought each other. Which would win?

Tess leaned closer, a hair's breadth between their lips. Denver pulled away. "Tess, this can't happen."

Her smile shone bright in the starlight. "I'm just teasing you. I've seen you and Eliza tease each other often enough." She gave him the beer. "It's okay, maybe I'll like wine better. The restaurant has wine. Maybe we'll share a bottle one night after you pick me up."

"A whole bottle might get us in trouble."

"Half a bottle then, and a moonlight swim." Tess kissed his cheek and stood. "I've always wanted to swim naked in the lake."

The vision of her naked body in the moonlight popped into Denver's mind. Trouble with a capital T. "I hope you're teasing again."

"Sure I am, unless you and Eliza ever divorce."

"You talk like you want that to happen."

"Not at all. I love my sister and I love you. Like I said, I hate how she's treating you. You deserve a wife who'll love you instead of grieving her life away. I understand how she feels, but life goes on."

Denver stood. "You haven't lost a daughter, Tess. There's no way you understand."

"I get that." Tess waved her hand toward the lake. "See all that beauty?"

"What about it?"

"Not just the lake, but the sky and the stars and me too. I don't think I'm ugly, do you?"

"No, but—"

"Hush, it's like I've been saying—life's too short to live it sad. Don't you want to try for more kids?"

"I do."

"Do you think Eliza does?"

"I won't pressure her about it. It takes time to get over what we've been through."

Tess faced the lake. "You don't know her like I know her. Except for Papa, deafness made her turn away from our family. Every chance she got, she went to the woods and the river. It wouldn't surprise me if she left you one day."

Denver didn't care for the turn in this conversation. "If you mean she'd leave and not let me know where she was, she wouldn't do that."

Tess faced him. "Like I said, you don't know her like I know her." She slipped her fingers into his. "Yes, I've been teasing you, but know this—you're a great guy and you deserve a great life. I haven't decided what'll I'll do after high school, but I could do a lot worse than making you happy."

She stood. "There I go, teasing you again. Let me finish my walk." She started away and stopped. "Oh, Mama and Papa are going on their trip to Kansas next Saturday. I'll call you for my ride to the restaurant around four." Her tan shorts and green blouse faded into the night. Beneath her sandals, gravel crunched along the walkway from the dock and went silent as she disappeared.

Denver sat again, emptied both bottles, and lay back on the dock to stare at the stars. Never would he have dreamed the shy Amish girl Tess had been would tease him like she had—if that was what it was. Regardless, it better be teasing. As much as he missed making love to Eliza, if Tess caught him alone after he had too many beers, she might have her way with him.

More beer. He needed more beer. He got up, started to his pickup, and detoured inside before he got there.

Idiot, the last thing he needed with his gorgeous sixteen-year-old sister-in-law stalking him was more beer.

outing

The following Friday, Eliza rose early to make breakfast. During Denver's two trips to the grocery this week, he hadn't bought any beer, so she felt a begrudging notion to do something decent for him.

When his bedroom door opened, he wore cargo shorts and a T-shirt. Like every day since her family had visited this past Saturday, he had shaved every morning, and this day was no different. He had stopped by the barber too, and his trimmed brown hair ended neatly above his ears instead of curling over them.

She took scrambled eggs and sausage to the table and returned with coffee and slices of cantaloupe, which Denver had bought from a farm stand in town.

Glancing at her curiously, Denver brought silverware. "What's the occasion?" he signed and said.

Eliza sat. "No occasion."

As they ate, Denver continued to glance at her after every other bite or so. "You look ..." He blinked several times. "You look great. What did you do?"

"Nothing."

"Well, you still look great." He blinked again, wiped the corner of one eye with a napkin.

She drank coffee. "Want to go out on the lake later? We can take the canoe and lunch and hike in the park."

"I— Be right back."

Denver left for his room. She gave him a moment and followed. The bathroom door was closed. She listened beside it but couldn't make the noise out. She turned one hearing aid up and listened again. Soft sobs and sniffling. The rattle of the toilet paper roll turning. Him blowing his nose. She returned to the table to wait for her weeping husband. Maybe he still cared and he felt relieved to think she cared too.

Eliza took scrambled eggs, swallowed, and followed it with more coffee. But did *she* care? Part of her wanted to spend the day with him, to give them a chance, to see where it would lead. Still, part of her wanted to pack a bag and fly to some remote corner of the world to see if being without him would hurt worse than being with him. With all the traveling they did during her art shows, she could travel either with or without him, and had for a few shows. Not only that, she kept her own bank and credit card accounts and paid them by smart phone. Yes, if she wanted, she could leave him without a trace of evidence as to where he could even begin to look for her. She ate a bite a sausage. Maybe it wouldn't come to that. After all, fairness—and her wedding vows—demanded she give them a chance.

Still sniffling, Denver returned to the table. "Must be my summer allergies acting up."

Eliza said nothing. He had never shown any allergy symptoms, let alone summer allergies.

Breakfast ended. Eliza washed their few dishes while Denver dried and put them away. Such a simple task—one they had once enjoyed by talking, teasing, and laughing—now dull and lifeless.

Denver put the last cup away. "I'll drag the canoe from under the deck and spray it out with the garden hose. It probably has enough cobwebs in it to start a silk factory."

Smiling enough to let him know she thought his joke was funny, Eliza glanced his way. "I'll make sandwiches and fill a container with water."

"Wanna pack a quilt to eat on?" Denver's blue eyes, crinkling at the corners, suggested how he wanted to use the quilt for anything but eating.

"If you'd like. I see you drank all your beer. Do you need to get some?"

"What kind of sandwiches are you making? If they're from that turkey I bought, I could run and get a bottle of white wine. You used to love wine, once you got used to it."

"Sounds good. Get some before you wash the canoe."

"Cool." Denver started toward the door but stopped. "Mind if get more than one bottle?"

The unasked question hovered on Eliza's lips. *Why, so you can drink yourself to a stupor and vomit in the lake again?*

Denver waved. "You okay? You look like you're thinking about something."

"Get whatever you want. I'll vacuum while you're gone. I might even look at my art supplies to see what I need to paint again."

"Really? I didn't know you were thinking about painting again." He came to her, placed his hands on her shoulders and looked her in the eye. "You make me happy, you know that?"

Eliza fingered a stray lock of hair behind her ear. "Go get your wine. See you when you get back."

Eliza got out the vacuum and gave the wood floors a quick cleaning. In the basement, she wiped a fingertip across the cases of oil paints and fingered the brushes. Everything was as dusty as her urge to paint, which faded as she eyed her dirty fingers.

She opened the blinds over the sliding glass doors. Back when she had come here to give her first art show in Raleigh, where Jan, Denver's past girlfriend worked, he had bought her many of these supplies. His thoughtfulness had touched her heart, but that star of ice burned within her chest, as cold as her feelings toward him. Still, she needed to see what the day might bring.

The upstairs door creaked open. Denver came down the steps. "How's it goin'? Any creative ideas?"

"Maybe. Go ahead and wash the canoe. I still need to make our lunch." Eliza passed Denver on the stairs. The sliding glass doors thumped shut behind him.

In the kitchen, she checked the refrigerator. No beer, but four bottles of wine, two white and two red. Her husband, the alcoholic.

Lunch made, she put everything in a cooler, added ice from the maker, and went to her bathroom to shave her legs and underarms. Denver hadn't said anything, but both were bristly. If the night miraculously advanced to them sleeping together, she should be as smooth as his face.

Done with that task, she dabbed perfume on her wrists and beneath her ears, where he once lived to kiss and where she once loved him to kiss. How she missed those kisses, but what it would take to love them again, she had no idea.

She took a quilt from the chest at the foot of the bed in his room and left it in the kitchen. On the upstairs deck, she waved to Denver. "I'm going to walk to Mama and Papa's."

Denver looked up. "This thing is filthy, it might take a while. Tell them I said hey."

Five minutes later, Eliza had left their road and had turned onto a walking path in the subdivision where she and Denver and her parents lived. Oaks, maples, and hickory trees lined the road. Two gray squirrels crossed in front of her and scampered up a tree, chattering away. Not fifty steps away, a doe and her spotted fawn left the woods, saw Eliza, and raised their whitetails while running back into the woods.

The mid-morning air carried the hint of leaf mold and fresh cut grass. Sweat trickled from her underarms and left a cool trail down her sides. She turned at the next right and walked another five minutes until she arrived at her parent's interior lot.

In the open double doors of Papa's rocking chair shop, he waved and trotted to her for a hug. "Look at you, out and about." He took a step back. "You look as fresh as a flower."

Eliza raised on arm. "After sweating, I doubt that, Papa."

"What's the occasion? Getting the blood flowing on this beautiful morning?"

"I just felt like walking. Denver and I are going out on the canoe for lunch later."

"Really?" In the workshop, leaning over a bench with a sanding block, Tess stood up. "Mind if I come along. It's hot and I'd like to swim."

"Maybe another time, little sister."

Tess came over to stand beside Eliza. "Papa, do I look like a 'little sister' anymore?"

"Not really. As much as I hate to admit it, you're practically a woman."

"See?" Tess said to Eliza. "I'm just a little younger than you when you met Denver."

Eliza recognized her sister's 'gotcha' tone. "Two years isn't just a little younger. You'll find out when you start dating how relationships are hard."

"How did Denver get you to go out on the canoe for lunch? He bribe you?"

Absalom cleared his throat. "Tess, that's rude and you know it."

"I don't mean anything by it, Papa. I'm glad for Denver. He doesn't do any of the things he likes to do anymore."

"Aren't you glad for me?" Eliza said.

"You know I am."

Papa went to a table for a glass of ice water and drank. "Tess walked over last night. She told Denver how Oneita and I are leaving for Kansas tomorrow."

"Driving or flying?"

"Driving. We've always wanted to see Mt. Rushmore, so we might drive up to South Dakota for that. We talked about making a big circle and seeing some of the Great Lakes too."

"Cool," Tess said, facing Eliza. "Denver will have to give me a ride to work for who knows how long."

Papa lowered the glass. "No more than two weeks. We might drive up to Ohio later this summer and visit some of our friends."

Tess faced Papa. "I thought we were shunned for leaving the Amish."

"We'll see how it goes. If nothing else, we'll buy baskets and visit our old friend's farm stands. We'd like to see Ethan too."

"I better get home," Eliza said. "You and Mama have a safe trip." She waggled a finger toward Tess. "Denver and I will tend to this child while you're gone."

Tess's cheeks reddened. "Good luck with that."

Eliza left for the road. It hadn't taken long for her sister to lose her Amish ways. Hopefully she wouldn't shame the family by doing something she shouldn't with any boys she might date. As Denver had said, she certainly was gorgeous. Well, voluptuous was more like it. Back before their lives had gone so awry, they used to stroll the streets of Clarksville on Saturday mornings, stopping at the indoor mall, the thrift shop, and a place that had great hot dogs and ice cream, on main street around the corner from the thrift shop. Eliza couldn't number the young men who had stared at Tess as she walked by.

Home again, she washed her sour underarms and applied deodorant. Coming from her bedroom, she found Denver walking toward his. "I need a shower. I smell like a wet dog."

"Everything's ready. Want to go when you get out?"

"Sure. See you in a few."

* * *

In the shower, Denver couldn't help whistling. His and Eliza's marriage looked to be on track again. If the day went well, she might even join him in bed tonight, even if only to sleep. Gotta start somewhere, and just holding her in his arms would be an amazing way to do just that.

Dressed in fresh shorts, a T-shirt, and sandals, he met Eliza in the living room, where she was watching TV. She turned at his footfalls. "I'm watching the weather for tonight and tomorrow. Looks like a nice day."

"You got something else planned for us?"

"Not really. I just like knowing the weather in case I do something."

Denver tilted his head to one side. "Like what?"

Eliza thumbed the remote; the TV went blank. "Like packing up and leaving you, how about that?"

Denver kissed her cheek. "You and your teasing. I sure have missed it. Let's hit the lake."

Denver drug the canoe and two paddles to the dock. He steadied it while Eliza climbed in the front with the cooler.

Paddles dug into the water. The bow left a feathering wake. The sun gleamed down on them. Sweat beaded at the nape of Eliza's neck, bare from her hair in a ponytail.

Denver steered the canoe toward Goat Island. "Mind if we have lunch before we go hiking in the park?"

"Goat Island does have a nice beach." Eliza switched sides with the paddle, and the bow of the canoe took a definite turn toward the wooded island, about a half a mile down the lake.

A pontoon boat went by. The couple sitting behind the console waved. Denver returned the wave. A bass boat roared toward them from the mouth of Grassy Creek, leaving a wake that jostled the canoe. In the sky to the south, a pair of Bald Eagles circled, heads tilting in their search for a fish.

Sweat trickled between Denver's shoulder blades and settled into the hollow of his back. Luckily, the ozone aroma of the lake interested him more than the smell of his sour self.

They paddled until the canoe's aluminum bow skidded into the sandy beach. Eliza hopped out and pulled it up farther. Denver climbed out and took the cooler to the edge of the woods, where Eliza was spreading the quilt on the sand.

They once came here often, remarking each time how the beach formed a C where they could hide from curious boaters while they kissed and got entirely too excited.

Eliza sat cross-legged on the quilt, and Denver did likewise. "I'm really glad you suggested this." He offered her a sandwich from the cooler.

"Me too." She took the water container out; ice tinkled inside the stainless-steel bottle. Sandwiches done and washed down with icy swallows of water, Denver lay on the quilt. Eliza stood. "I'm going to walk the beach a while."

Denver patted the quilt. "Might as well join me for a nap when you get done. It's nice here in the shade of those oaks behind us."

"We'll see."

As Eliza left, Denver sat back up. Whatever she had in mind with this canoe trip, kissing wasn't part of it. No need to pressure her. After all, just suggesting this trip was a step in the right direction. He lay down again and closed his eyes.

Waves washed against the sand with a soothing back-and-forth swishing sound. From toward Clarksville, a bass boat's engine roared as if it were a giant mosquito.

Tess.

A vision of her on the dock at home popped into Denver's head. She sometimes swam there on hot afternoons, wearing a one-piece swimsuit. Yeah, she must've been teasing him about swimming naked. Like she had said, his and Eliza's teasing had rubbed off on her.

More memories of the dock streamed into his mind, of him, Willow, Mom, and Dad swimming and fishing there, of his and Eliza's first kiss there, on the night he brought her home so she could attend her first art show at the gallery in Raleigh where Jan worked.

What was Jan up to these days? She had dated a steady stream of guys but had never married. Although their relationship ended badly when Jan realized he was in love with Eliza, they had mended their friendship.

Then there was Akina, the ex-marine who taught sign language with him at the school in Ohio that Jon had built. What a mess she was back then, but a mess who had comforted Denver during one of his more poignant memories of Mom and Dad, which had resulted in him and Akina having sex for more than a month.

The last Denver had heard from her, she and Dan, the teacher who had taken Denver's place, were still seeing each other. As far as teasing, Akina gave as good as she got. Talk about fun.

Carrying that ozone aroma of the lake, a warm breeze kissed Denver's face. Might as well take a nap for real until Eliza came back.

* * *

On the way back to the quilt, Eliza sat on a piece of driftwood at the lake's edge. Denver's chest rose and fell with the rhythm of sleep. Was he dreaming? If so, about what? If she were him, she would dream of a wife who cared for him like she used to, one who wanted children, one who loved him completely instead wondering about it. Still, the day was young, and she had to see what the night brought before giving up on their marriage.

She leaned over for a rock and threw it into the lake.

No, no matter what she did, she wouldn't give up on their marriage until she was sure it wouldn't work. What that would take, she didn't know, but she hoped it would be clear when it happened. No marriage deserved to be tossed aside like a piece of trash, not even theirs.

She went to the quilt and lay beside Denver. For two years she had loved watching him sleep, loved touching his face to wake him after a night filled with love. Try that now to see how it made her feel? Maybe, but not enough to wake him. If that happened, he might think she wanted sex, and she didn't want that here on this beach, where a boater could come by and see them. Then again, did she want sex at all? If so, tonight might tell the story.

Raising a tentative fingertip, she touched the tip of his nose, the cleft in his clean-shaven chin. Leaning close, she took in the aroma of after shave lotion, mild yet sweet. She sniffed his hair, loving the aroma of fresh air and sunshine, and a sexual tingle burst within her. What a welcome feeling, one she hadn't expected. She brushed his lips with her fingertips, resulting in another tingle, but warmer and more intense.

Denver's eyes fluttered open. "Hey."

"Hey yourself." Eliza waved a hand in front of her face. "The flies are out today."

Denver rubbed his mouth. "That must've been what woke me up." He took in a deep breath. "A perfect day, fresh air, and you here with me—it doesn't get better than that."

His words touched Eliza's heart. Maybe he still loved her after all. "You ready to go home?"

"What about hiking in the park?" Denver said, sitting up.

"I thought I might run to the grocery for something special for dinner."

"Like what?"

"Can't it be a surprise?"

"Sure, but—"

"No buts. You can walk over to Mama and Papa's while I cook. Take your phone, I'll call when it's ready."

prophesy

At home again, Denver walked to Absalom and Oneita's house. When he got within sight of the single-story structure with white siding, they were sitting in the shade of several oaks in the back yard. Nearby, in an inflatable swimming pool, Tess was pouring water over Ivy's head. She sputtered and coughed. "You made me spangle, Tess!"

"It's strangle, you monkey." Tess waved at Denver. "Want to come in and cool off?"

Although Tess wore a one-piece swimsuit, her curves drew Denver's attention until he managed to lower his eyes. Gorgeous for sure, as gorgeous as any woman he'd ever seen in the movies or on TV.

Absalom pointed to a lawn chair. "Have a seat, Denver."

"What's Eliza up to?" Oneita asked.

Denver sat, glad to share the good news. "We took the canoe out to Goat Island and ate lunch."

"Whose idea was that?" Tess asked.

"Hers. Then she asked me to visit y'all while she went to the grocery for something special for supper."

Tess got out of the pool, took a towel from another chair, and sat to wipe her face. "Is supper a secret?"

"She wants it to be a surprise."

"Praise the Lord," Oneita said. "She's finally seeing some sunshine at the end of the storm."

"Glad to hear it," Absalom said.

Tess lay the towel over her legs. "Me too. If she had kept sitting around, someone was going to have to do something desperate before it cost you two your marriage."

Oneita cut her eyes at Tess. "Denver and Eliza are in love. What makes you say such a thing?"

"I know that, Mama, but love sometimes get buried beneath all the stuff that comes along with life. When that happens, someone might need to shovel it out so it'll grow again."

"How'd you get so smart?" Absalom said. "You love someone we don't know about?"

Grinning, Tess popped his knee. "Oh sure, Papa. Only about half the boys in my class."

Ivy climbed from the pool, fell in the grass, and let out a wail. "Mama, I'm dirty."

Denver took the towel from Tess's legs and scooped Ivy into his lap to wipe the grass from her knees. "There you go, doodlebug." He wiped water from her face and kissed her cheek. "That better?"

Ivy hugged his neck and returned the kiss. "Love you, Den."

Tess took the towel and covered her face, muffling soft sobs. Denver gave Ivy to Absalom and knelt by Tess. "Hey, what's wrong?"

"I know what's wrong," Oneita said. "She knows you and Eliza would make wonderful parents and wishes you could have more children."

The revelation that Tess cared about him and Eliza to the point of tears shook Denver. Still, he understood how she felt. When he had held Ivy and kissed her, along with her saying she loved him, the first thing that came to mind was how his and Eliza's child would say the same thing. That is, if they ever had a child.

Tess's sobs quieted. He gently took the towel from her. "How about it, you big doodlebug, don't I get a hug too?"

Sobbing again, this time much worse, Tess ran into the house.

"Wow," Denver said, facing Absalom and Oneita, "I didn't know she was so tenderhearted."

Absalom gave Ivy to Oneita. "She cares about you and Eliza. Remember when she saw you both smiling at each other in Ohio that day you came to pick up Eliza's paintings for her first art show with Jan?"

"Ethan saw them too," Oneita said. "That's what made us think they loved each other, after we had time to think about it."

Absalom left for the house. Minutes later he returned with Tess, who wore shorts and a blouse. "Ignore me," she said. She took Denver by the hand. "Come on, brother-in-law. Let me show you mine and Papa's next woodworking project." She led him into the workshop, which smelled of sawdust.

Absalom came in behind them. "My middle daughter's going into business with me, Denver. What do you think of that?"

"Your rocking chairs are selling that well?"

"We're expanding to foot stools to go with the chairs. If they sell well, we might try other types of furniture."

"Phooey, Papa," Tess said. "That's dull stuff." She took a thick book from a work bench and showed Denver the cover. "I love acoustic guitar music. I want to learn how to play, but I want to build my own guitar."

Denver took the book. "I've always wanted to learn to play myself."

"If you and Eliza work things out," Absalom said, "you can learn with Tess when you have time."

"You can learn how to build guitars too," Tess said.

"We'll see." Denver patted his father-in-law's shoulder. "If, like you say, things work out, I'd like to be a daddy eventually."

Absalom's crow's feet deepened. "Not to tell you what to do, Denver, but you know she might need time before that happens."

Denver took the suggestion to heart. He and Eliza needed to find their way back to each other with a lot more than a canoe trip, a beach picnic, and a surprise supper would accomplish.

"I hear you, Absalom." He faced Tess. "Okay, doodlebug, show me how you plan to build guitars."

* * *

Leaning over the workbench to read a line about the difference in sound between a guitar built with mahogany back and sides versus rosewood back and sides, Denver straightened. "Wonder what time it is?" he asked Tess. "I forgot my watch and phone."

Tess pointed at a clock on the far wall of the workshop. "Five-thirty. You better get home so Eliza can surprise you with whatever she's cooking." She glanced toward the house and faced Denver again. "I'm glad Papa went inside. I like being with you alone."

"More teasing?" Denver asked.

"Yes and no. Seeing you and Eliza happy is my goal."

"That's sweet of you to say, Tess."

Tess's green eyes crinkled as she smiled. "You just found out I'm sweet?"

"Well, I'll just say you're a lot different than that little Amish girl in Ohio I met a few years ago, how about that?"

"In a good way, right? I saw you looking at me in my swimsuit."

Denver swallowed. This gorgeous sister-in-law of his sure had his number. And yes, she *was* sweet. He tapped her nose. "Hey, I'm just a guy. Sue me for noticing you."

"No suing needed, Denver. More than anything I want you and Eliza happy. She better not mess up and do anything stupid like leaving you like I told you about. I'll wait until I'm eighteen and not a day longer. After that, your sweet self is mine."

Denver took a single step back. Teasing or not? Didn't sound like it. "Look, Tess, we've talked about this. It can't happen."

She glanced toward the house "If Eliza messes up, you do realize I could make you forget all about her. If she messes up bad enough, like divorcing you, we'll be married less than six months after I'm eighteen and build guitars together, wanna bet?"

"Your Mama and Papa would kill us both."

"Nope. Their Amish ways are still in them. They value family. If Eliza doesn't want you, I doubt they'll mind if I want you."

Denver rubbed his chin. Yes, the Amish *did* value family. Not that Eliza would ever leave him, but if she did, and if he and Tess fell in love after she turned eighteen, and if Absalom and Oneita approved the match, he could do a lot worse than marrying their middle-daughter. He took his hand from his chin. If he were alone, he would've slapped it instead of rubbing it. What an idiot, thinking stuff like that.

Tess licked her lips. "Thinking about it?"

"I'm thinking I better get home to my wife."

Denver left the workshop for the road. Behind him, Tess yelled, "I'm just teasing! And don't forget my ride to the restaurant tomorrow!"

At home again, the savory aroma of supper met Denver as he closed the front door. In the kitchen, Eliza waved him toward his bedroom. "Your shirt is wet with sweat. Shower. Now."

Denver saluted. "Yes, ma'am. Right away ma'am. You know I love a take-control woman like you, ma'am."

Done with the shower, Denver stood in the open bedroom door naked. "How do you like my supper attire?"

Leaning over to look into the oven, Eliza said nothing. Denver's upbeat mood dropped a notch. He had hoped his teasing her would lighten their mood even more, like Tess's teasing—*if* she were teasing—had lightened his mood.

Dressed in fresh shorts and a button-up shirt, he padded to the kitchen on bare feet. "Whatever you're cooking smells great."

Between two covered bowls on the counter lay Eliza's hearing aids. That explained her lack of commentary about his naked self. At the stove, she was stirring something in a pot. Denver kissed the nape of her neck, still bare from a ponytail. Wide-eyed, she whirled around and pushed him away. "Don't do that! I could've burned myself!"

Denver raised his hands. "Hey, you don't have to yell. I'm right here." He didn't care for her tone, as harsh as if she were disciplining the child they never had.

She snatched the hearing aids from the counter and worked them into her ears. "What did you say?"

Still that same tone. Denver's upbeat mood dropped another notch. "I said I'm sorry, okay?" He sounded like a child being disciplined too, and he didn't like it one bit. If she kept treating him like this, it would brew one of their rare fights.

"I didn't mean to scare you. Let's just eat and forget it."

Eliza shot her hands toward him. "Oh, it's all about you eating, is it?" she signed, hands slashing the air.

Denver shot his hands toward her. "Where do you get that? You're the one who wanted to make a surprise supper."

"Don't use that tone with me, I'm not a child."

"I didn't say anything, I'm signing."

"I don't like your hands flying around like that."

"*My* hands? What about *your* hands? You look like you're trying to take off and fly over the lake."

Eliza sucked her lower lip into her mouth. Her eyes narrowed. Her nostrils flared. She turned away.

Denver started toward her, but stopped when she turned around, a huge smile on her lovely face. She giggled, laughed, and laughed harder, holding her stomach. All he could do was watch. Here was the woman he had fallen in love with, the woman he would never stop loving no matter what, the woman he wanted to hold and kiss and make love to, and eventually have a family with.

Eliza wiped her eyes. "It's been a long time since I laughed like that. I guess I did look like I was trying to fly."

Denver gave her a paper towel. "Me too."

She wiped her eyes. "Not that we've made love in a while, but it felt almost as good as that."

"That's been one of the things I've always loved about us, Eliza—our teasing and joking."

She threw the paper towel in the trash. "Let me get supper on the table."

Denver got silverware and dishes. Eliza brought the covered bowls. "You sit. The biggest surprise is on the way." She went back to the kitchen, where the sound of an electric knife whirred. Holding a platter of sliced meat with a bowl of gravy on the side, she returned to set it on the table. "Turkey and gravy for our late Thanksgiving and Christmas."

Denver said nothing. The thought meant a lot. Then again, they hadn't celebrated any holidays because of dealing with losing their daughter.

She took the foil off the two bowls, revealing mashed potatoes and green beans. Denver's mouth watered, not only from all the food but from the aromas filling the table. "Wow, Eliza, this is great."

She left for the kitchen and came back with spoons for the bowls and a bowl of cranberry sauce. "There, now we can eat."

Denver took her hand in his. "One more thing." He bowed his head. "Dear Lord, thank you for this day and thank you for Eliza. I know we don't understand everything that's happened in our lives, but I understand how You love us and won't give us any challenge that we can't overcome without your help. Amen."

Eliza took her hand from his. All during the blessing, he had tried to entwine his fingers within hers, but she wouldn't let him. It was if they were a wall of flesh and bone between them.

She added food to her plate, a single spoon of each item and one slice of turkey. Mouth still watering, he filled his.

Except for their blowup about him kissing her neck—no, even that had ended great—the day had gone better than Denver had ever hoped. If the rest of it went as well, maybe they'd spend the night in their room, which had become his room. Regardless, making love wasn't important—working through their grief together was.

Eliza went to the kitchen and came back with one of the bottles of white wine he had bought. She filled a glass and gave it Denver. He sipped, expecting her to go for a glass too.

Instead, she went for a bottle of water. They once loved to sip a glass of wine with dinner, sometimes before bed. It would leave them relaxed and playful, ending with kisses on the sofa and more than kisses in their bedroom.

After their blowup-become-laughter, Denver expected conversation while they ate. No such thing happened. He ate his final bite of turkey, mixed with mashed potatoes and gravy, and emptied the wine glass. "Whew, I'm stuffed. I really appreciate all this, Eliza."

Without looking at him, she continued to take tiny bites of her food. He took his plate to the kitchen, where her hearing aids were on the counter. That's right, she had let her hair down, so he thought she still had them in. He returned to the table. She was looking out the window toward the lake. He tapped her shoulder and raised his hands. "Want me to wash dishes while you shower? You didn't take one like I did after our canoe ride."

She raised her hands. "I'll take one in the morning."

Denver sat. "Want to let the dishes soak and share a glass of wine on the sofa like we used to?"

"I'd rather not."

Denver rubbed his chin. "I kind of hoped ..."

"You hoped we'd sleep together."

"That'd be great, and I mean just sleeping too. I miss you, okay? I miss how we used to be."

"Just sleeping?"

"That's all." Denver yawned. "It's early but I'm tired and sore from paddling the canoe. I'll clean up for bed and do the dishes in the morning."

Eliza stood. "I'll get ready in my bathroom. I'll sleep in my own bed."

Denver reached for her hand but she pulled away. "Can't you try, Eliza? How can we get close again if you don't try? It's been a great day so far, why can't you try?"

Her chest rose with a deep breath and fell with a soft sigh. "We'll see."

* * *

In her bathroom, Eliza brushed and flossed, washed under her arms, and dabbed perfume on her neck. Wear a skimpy nighty or not? Yes, it was time to see if she could make love to Denver. If she couldn't do that soon, their marriage would suffer more than it already had.

Instead of a nightgown, she undressed and slipped on a blue silk robe, cool against her skin. She had bought one for her and one for Denver for their honeymoon at the cabin in Occoneechee State Park. They had never worn them long that week.

Eliza touched her lips. She once loved Denver's kisses. He could be so sweet and gentle, touching her in all the right places until passion took them both into their own world of pleasure.

She brushed her hair while looking in the mirror. Although this night might well be their last chance, she hoped not. She shared a kinship with Denver, one strong enough to make her take this chance even though everything in her screamed to run.

She padded to his room—maybe to be their room soon—and climbed in bed beside him without taking off the robe.

Bare from the chest up, Denver rolled over to face her. "I love our robes you bought." He got up, revealing boxer shorts. "I'll get mine."

"Don't do that. I wore mine because the air conditioning is cool."

"I lowered it to sleep. I know how you hate to sleep hot." In bed again, Denver leaned over to look into her eyes. The bluest blue Eliza had ever seen, his eyes had drawn her to him almost from the moment they had met in Ohio at the sign language school. He leaned close. "Mind if I kiss you?"

"I … I guess."

Their lips joined—softly, oh so softly—and the overwhelming urge to vomit twisted Eliza's stomach into a knot. She ran to his bathroom, slammed the commode seat back, and heaved over and over. Thank goodness she hadn't eaten much for supper, or she'd fill the commode.

Water ran into the sink. Denver pressed a cool washcloth to her forehead. So sweet—so incredibly sweet—and she was breaking his heart without even knowing why. She stood and took the washcloth from him to wipe her sweaty face, her mouth, and flushed the commode. "I'm sorry I ruined things. I don't know why I got sick."

"Did you feel sick before you got in bed?"

Those blue eyes again, filled with love and caring. How could she keep hurting him over and over? "A little, and it's still there. I better sleep in my bed."

Denver followed her into his bedroom. As she neared the door, he gently turned her around. Now those blue eyes were filled with tears.

He cupped her cheek, a gentle caress she once loved as much as his kisses. "I hope you feel better. I …"

On a thread of hope as slender and fragile as single strand of spider silk, the words hung between them, words neither of them had said in so long a time, they didn't know how to say them now.

I love you.

Eliza took his hand from her cheek. "I'll be better in the morning." She closed the door behind her and went to the window to the sliding glass doors.

A full moon illuminated the lake, highlighting wavelets kissing the bank by the dock. So many memories here, too many.

Eliza went to bed.

* * *

In bed again, Denver pulled the cool sheets to his chin. He started to raise what had once been Eliza's pillow to his nose. Instead, he left it beside him, still and cold. Just one hint of her hair would set him on a crying jag to match those they had shared during their daughter's funeral.

Rolling over to face away from where she had lain, he closed his eyes. What would the morning bring? They had crossed so many barriers on this wonderful day, and he couldn't wait to cross as many more as possible.

* * *

Denver woke to a gray day. Low, black clouds scudded across the eastern horizon, visible through his window facing the lake. No aroma of breakfast nor of coffee. Everything quiet and calm. Maybe Eliza was sleeping in to get over her nausea. If so, she might be hungry for one of her favorites: french toast.

Shorts and T-shirt on, he went to the kitchen. Beside the coffee maker, a folded piece of paper made him stop in his tracks. He unfolded the paper.

Denver,

This will upset you, but I've gone home to teach sign language. Like Mama needed to get away from Kansas when my sister died, I need to get away from everything that reminds me of our daughter. I know you think we should fix our problems together instead of apart. If that hasn't worked since she died, it won't work now.

Another thing I know about you is how you enjoy going out on the canoe and hiking and taking the pontoon boat out to fish or just ride. I've kept you from doing those things. I don't mind you doing that with friends, even women friends, but don't do anything more than that because I expect you to honor our marriage vows, unless something changes that.

I'm sure you'll tell Mama and Papa, but wait until they get back from their trip. I don't want them coming to Ohio and telling me how I'm letting you down.

As far as women friends, I changed my mind. Tess will make a good companion for all the things you love to do. Since she's my sister, you know better than to do anything you shouldn't.

Don't call and don't come. I'm leaving my phone off and will call if I want to talk to you. Don't call Ethan either. Leave me alone for however long it takes. Only time can heal whatever is wrong with me.

Denver balled the note up and threw it across the kitchen. How could she do this to him? Tear his heart out? Rip it up? Stomp on it and shove it into his face by not even ending the note by saying she loves him or signing her name?

Ice picks jabbed his optic nerves.

Not no, *hell* no. Never, for as long as he lived, would he cry over Eliza again.

aftermath

Denver left the sliding glass doors. All day long, one after another, storms rolled over the lake. Lightning illuminated the insides of black clouds and thunder boomed, rattling window panes. Each crash and roll brought back the memory of the Jon's schoolhouse in Ohio, where Eliza had held Denver's hand to her chest one night during such a storm, saying she felt the thunder in her heart. Now that he thought about it, she must've been telling him how she felt the love in her heart for him. Well, that was shot to hell now.

He walked the house over and over. Every corner held a memory or a scent, both driving him near to tears, both causing him to swear he would never cry over her again.

Around three, he started toward the refrigerator for the wine, but the phone on the wall by the counter rang.

"Hey, you bigger doodlebug," Tess said. "Did you forget my ride to work?"

"This early?"

"I don't question the boss. You coming or not? I could always drive Mama's car and get a ticket for only having a learner's permit."

"Can't she or your dad take you?"

"Gone to Kansas, remember?"

"Be there in a minute."

In his pickup, Denver hit the accelerator, squealing tires as he left the paved driveway. The last thing he needed was a fun and sexy sixteen-year-old around him. A quick ride to work and a quick ride to take her home tonight and that would be that. He slapped the steering wheel. With Absalom and Oneita gone, and now Eliza, he and Tess would be alone the next two weeks. Whatever. He loved his home and the lake and he wasn't about to leave because of her.

When he pulled into the driveway, she ran to the pickup and got in. "What've you and Eliza been doing all day with those storms going on? At least they finally stopped."

Denver took off from the driveway, careful to not squeal tires and make her ask questions. "Nothing much."

"Did you comb your hair? Looks like a rat's nest."

"Didn't feel like it."

Mama and Papa told me how they told you and Eliza to teach sign language back at our old house. Given it any thought?"

Denver turned onto the main road. "No."

"You're not your usual talky self, brother-in-law. Bad night with Eliza?"

"We had a nice supper—turkey and gravy."

"Got any left? I just had a sandwich. I'll be starved by the time I get off work." She punched his arm. "Got a problem with picking me up at eleven?"

Denver cut his eyes at her. "Why so late?"

"Gotta clean up and stuff."

"I'll be there."

At the bed-and-breakfast, Denver stopped at the curb. "See you later."

Tess started to close the door but stopped. "Are you okay? You don't seem yourself?"

"Close the door. You don't want to be late for the first day of your new job."

Tess did so and jogged away. She wore tight black pants that fit entirely too well. She also wore a white blouse, and her auburn hair flowed down her back like a red waterfall. Slapping the steering wheel, he left for home. No Eliza. No Absalom and Oneita. No one else to keep him from ogling his gorgeous sister-in-law for two weeks. What a freaking mess.

Home again, he considered leftovers from last night but cooked a microwave dinner instead. All that stuff could rot as far as he was concerned. He considered wine too, and grabbed a bottle of red to go with the beef in his microwave meal. A glass? Huh, why use a glass when he could empty the bottle and be sober for his drive to pick up Tess by eleven?

On the sofa in front of the huge flat-screen TV, between bites and swallows of wine, Denver channel surfed until his thumb got sore. Meal done, he set his phone alarm for 10:40 and went to the dock, to sit and drink.

* * *

In her old room in Ohio, Eliza finished unpacking her suitcases. From the hall outside her door, the aroma of Ethan cooking supper rose up the stairs. He had mentioned fried chicken, including sliced tomatoes and fresh green beans from the garden he kept.

Eliza slid the empty suitcases under Tess's old bed and sat on hers. In the back yard, the old well pump whispered of days long gone, especially the day when Mama had slapped her. What a lesson for a deaf child of only five, but it had stopped Eliza from drinking water at the river.

She lay back on the pillow. When she had arrived and told Ethan what she was doing, he had asked about Denver. Good thing he had believed her lie about Denver needing to work around the house. The last thing she wanted was Ethan calling Mama and Papa and spreading gossip about her and Denver.

Footsteps clomped up the stairs. Ethan came to the door. "Ready to eat?"

"It smells great." Eliza got up and followed Ethan downstairs.

What once had been a huge family room was now divided into two by a wall with double doors in the center. Ethan and Timothy taught on one side while using the other for a living room, kitchen, and dining room. No more ice box or wood cookstove either; new electric appliances filled those spaces.

Ethan went to the sink and filled two glasses. "I sure don't miss carrying water from the well."

"I did my part of it for eighteen years." Eliza sat at the table and put a chicken leg on her plate.

Ethan placed their glasses on the table. "Wait a minute, okay?"

In the middle of spooning green beans to her plate, Eliza stopped. "What?"

He bowed his head. "This is what. Have you stopped saying the blessing?"

Eliza bowed her head, and Ethan closed his eyes. "Dear Lord, thanks you for this day and for this food. Thank you for all the plants and animals you provide to give us nourishment." He paused. "Whatever has my sister here, I forgive her for lying to me about it. Amen."

Filling her plate, Eliza let the comment go. Saying something about it would only make Ethan ask questions.

He passed her the tomatoes. "Nothing to say, huh?"

She took her hearing aids out, dropped them on the table, and took the tomatoes. Despite Ethan's question, her appetite had returned. As soon as the plane had left the airport, leaving all her troubles behind, a feeling of calm had washed over her. She salt and peppered the tomatoes and took a juicy bite. When had she last enjoyed food like this? She knew when, before the pain of losing her daughter. Leaving that thought behind, she crunched into the chicken leg and followed that with green beans and water, sweet and cold from the same source as the well.

Ethan raised his hands toward her. "I can sign almost as good as you can now. Don't think you'll get away with lying to me about Den—"

Eliza grabbed his hand and let go. She would see no peace until she told him why she was here. "Stop ruining this fine meal you cooked. We'll talk while we do the dishes." She finished the chicken leg and started on a wing. "Let's talk about your personal life."

"Like what?"

"You're nineteen."

"Meaning?"

"Are you dating anyone?"

"I was interested in a deaf Amish girl who lives on the other side of town. She started coming to class three years ago."

Eliza drank water. "And?"

"She's Amish and I'm not. I was dumb to think we could be together."

"Is she still coming to class?"

"She's too busy with her little boy, he's two." Ethan ate a slice of tomato. "Her husband comes once in a while. He wants to learn so he can teach her what she doesn't know."

"That's nice of him. Did you know Tess is working at a restaurant in Clarksville?"

"She called the other day. She said Denver will take her and pick her up after."

"Papa's doing well with his rocking chairs."

"He called yesterday to tell me about him and Mama going to Kansas." Ethan drank water.

Eliza tried the green beans, which were tender and seasoned with bacon. She took another bite of chicken, amazed at how just being in a different place had brought her appetite back. She faced Ethan. "How many students do you have?"

About to take a bit of chicken, Ethan lowered it from his mouth. "I thought we would have more, but some have moved. Jon's daughter, Ellie, is going to school now and learning there."

"How's Timothy doing with teaching?"

"He still has trouble with some of the more complicated signs. Since we only have a few students, we teach together."

Eliza let the conversation end so they could finish eating. They took their plates to the sink and wrapped the leftovers for the refrigerator. Ethan squirted dishwashing liquid into the sink and filled it with hot water. As much as she didn't want to talk about Denver, Eliza returned her hearing aids to her ears and went back to the sink. "Let's get this over with. What do you want to know about why I'm here?"

Ethan faced her. "Duh, sis, I want to know it all. Anyone who's ever seen you and Denver together knows you're perfect for each other. You should be working through your grief together instead of apart."

"It's not that simple. I need to get away from everything that reminds me of what happened. That means Denver too."

"Hey, it's your life. Just don't wait too long before you go home."

Eliza took a dish from him, rinsed and dried it and put it in a cabinet. "What do you mean by that?"

"You don't know? I'd think anyone could see it?"

"Would you please tell me and get it over with?"

"Tess has a huge crush on your husband."

"She's just sixteen. She doesn't know what love is."

"Wrong. Any time you and Denver were together before you lost your daughter, love was how you looked at each other."

"He's married. Besides, she's underage. He could go to jail if someone thought they were dating."

Ethan gave Eliza a soapy dish. "Whatever. You've still got Jan and Akina to worry about. If they find out you've left him, who knows what they'll do."

"He's an adult. He knows what he better *not* do." Eliza punched Ethan's arm. "I haven't left him. I just needed to get away to sort myself out."

Ethan said nothing, and Eliza let the silence continue. No, she hadn't left Denver, not in the way Ethan had meant it. Regardless, if Tess had a crush on Denver, and some woman wanted to date him, Tess would put an end to that right away. Her auburn-haired little sister could have an attitude when necessary, and any woman would catch that attitude if they tried to take Denver away from his wife.

* * *

Denver sat up from the dock. He had drunk half the bottle of wine and had fallen asleep, senses so dulled by alcohol and grief that he had stayed out here long enough for the dew to wet his clothes. His phone read 10:30, time enough to change and pick up Tess.

In dry clothes, he went to the kitchen and tossed Eliza's note in the trash. Tess had mentioned eating turkey. He couldn't deny her that, but he didn't want her to know Eliza had left. He could tell her Eliza was asleep if she stopped by.

At the restaurant, as he waited for Tess, lightning brightened the night, illuminating the old two-story home now transformed into a bed-and-breakfast. Seconds later, thunder rolled long and loud, followed by a downpour clattering on the pickup roof.

In the porch lights of the bed-and-breakfast, Tess ran across it and out to the pickup. Inside, she slammed the door and wiped rainwater from her face. "What a storm, I'm soaked."

Denver caught the sour aroma of something. "What's that I smell?"

"My clothes. I spilled some crab dip on the way to the oven."

"Did you get down in the floor and roll in it?"

Tess glared at him. "No, Denver, I spilled it on my blouse and pants."

"How'd it go other than that?"

"Not bad. Got some nice tips." Tess clicked her seatbelt. "Let's get home, I'm tired."

Denver steered the pickup onto main street. Good thing Tess hadn't mentioned wanting turkey. No need to risk her seeing how Eliza had left him.

When he turned into the subdivision driveway, Tess faced him. "Hey, I'm starved. Can I get some of that turkey and gravy?"

"Can't you get something to eat at home?"

"Not turkey and gravy. I love turkey and gravy. I'd fight over turkey and gravy."

"Okay, but Eliza's asleep. We have to be quiet."

"You really aren't yourself, are you, Denny?"

Denver cringed at Tess's nickname for him, which she started using right after he and Eliza were married. She had stopped using it a year ago and here it was, turning up like chewing gum on the bottom of a shoe. "I'm who I've always been, T-bone."

"Shut up. I can't help it if I like steak."

"Then don't call me Denny, T-bone."

"I thought you liked that name? Willow calls you Den and it's close."

"I'm not crazy about it."

"Okay, no more Denny. Still, you're not yourself. Eliza up and leave you last night like I said she would?"

Denver turned into his road and drove the short distance to his driveway. "Like I said, Eliza's asleep, so be quiet."

"Where's her car?"

"In the garage."

"You do realize I could run inside and scream and shout and she wouldn't hear me."

"I wouldn't try it."

"Does she sleep with her hearing aids in?"

"No, why?"

"That's why I've been telling you you're not yourself—she won't be able to hear me with her hearing aids out."

Denver left the pickup. At least the rain had slowed to a drizzle. Tess waited beside him while he unlocked the door. "Denver?"

"What?"

"Can I spend the night with you?"

He unlocked the door and shoved it in so hard, the knob almost slipped from his hand. "Look, Tess, I've about had enough of your teasing."

She closed the door and looked up at him innocently, green eyes blinking in the hall lights. "What're you talking about?"

"You know what I'm talking about, asking if you can spend the night with *me*."

"I *meant* here, with you and Eliza." Tess tilted her head to one side. "What do you think I meant?"

Denver said nothing. Either Tess knew what he meant and was trying to scoff it off, or she would crawl into bed with him if he said she could stay. He went down the hall and flipped the light for the kitchen. "Have at it. Everything's in the fridge."

Tess put her purse on the counter. "I meant what I said about spending the night. I left my house key on the kitchen table at home."

On the way to his bedroom, Denver whirled around. "You *what?*"

"Before you ask, I don't have one for the back door. Do you have one?"

Heaving a huge breath, Denver rubbed his chin. He had hoped to avoid telling Tess about Eliza being gone for as long as possible, but if she stayed, how could he do that? "You can sleep in the rocking chair shop. It has air conditioning."

"No bathroom and no bed, Denny. I'm your sister-in-law, show me some family courtesy. You can call a locksmith in the morning." She went to the sink and squeezed her hair until water dripped. "I need to get out of these wet clothes. Do you have something I can wear?"

Denver hesitated. Eliza was slimmer than Tess and he was larger, but a belt would hold his shorts up on Tess. "Be right back."

When he returned with a shirt, shorts, and a belt, Tess was gone. Must've needed the bathroom.

He went to the fridge for the leftovers and took them to the counter. The sooner she ate and went to bed, the sooner she would get up in the morning and get back home. No, he had to call a locksmith first.

The guest room door opened. Wearing Eliza's blue silk robe, Tess strode through the living room and into the kitchen. "Hope Eliza won't mind. I dumped my wet clothes into the tub in the guestroom bathroom and found this in the hamper." She turned around. "Think I need a larger size?"

Denver's mouth fell open. Yes, she needed a larger size, evidenced by how the clingy silk clung to all the right places perfectly, revealing curves and peaks and valleys and— He offered Tess his clothes. "Here. Eliza's robe is dirty."

"Your clothes are too big."

"Use the belt. Then the shorts won't slip down your hips."

Tess ran her hands down her sides and stopped at the flair of her hips. "I think my hips are too wide for my waist, don't you?" She raised the robe. "I wish my legs were smaller like Eliza's." She raised the robe more, showing smooth, muscular thighs. "My walking is paying off. See how toned my legs are?"

"Well ..." The clothes fell from Denver's limp hands. He snatched them up and shoved them at Tess. "Look, you need to put these on."

"I wouldn't need to if you would stop looking, Denny." She took a plate from the counter and added turkey, dipped a piece in the bowl of gravy and ate. "Mmm," she said while chewing. Another bite followed the first. "So moist."

Denver went to the sofa and plopped down. Tess brought the plate over and sat in the chair across from him, crossing her legs. The robe rode up her thighs, and it was all he could do to look away. They needed to get to sleep, like *now* get to sleep. Then he could get up early to call a locksmith and get Tess out of the house before she found out about Eliza.

She finished the food and took the plate to the kitchen. "I'll soak this in the sink. You want anything before I put it in the fridge."

Denver looked her way. Platter of turkey in hand, she was leaning over in front of the open refrigerator. The opening in the robe fell apart, revealing a single leg all the way up to her waist. He looked away. "No, I don't need anything."

"You sure?"

Denver said nothing. The refrigerator door thumped closed and Tess returned to the chair, tucking her legs under her. "Okay, brother-in-law, where's Eliza?"

"She's asleep. I told you that already, remember?"

"Bull."

"What do you mean?"

"There's a nightlight on in the garage. When we walked by on the way to the front door, I could see her car was gone."

Denver went to the kitchen trash container for Eliza's note. No need to keep lying. One way or another, Tess would find out the truth in two weeks, when Oneita and Absalom came back. He gave her the note and dropped to the sofa. "You should tell prophesies. She left me like you said she would."

Tess's eyes tracked the sentences. "I was just messing with you. I never thought she'd actually leave." She finished the note and returned it to Denver. "I can't believe she was gonna let you date other women and then changed her mind to only letting you date me."

"That's not what she said and you know it. She said going out on the canoe, stuff like that."

"With who? How many women friends do you have?"

"A few from college who moved here. I haven't seen them since the funeral."

"Other than that, I see nothing wrong with her going back to Ohio. I can see how she needs to get away for a while. Still …"

"*Still* what?"

"How long have you been sleeping apart? She told me that a while back."

"She shouldn't have."

"And?"

"*And* what?"

"Sleeping apart. No love. No sex. I bet you miss it."

"What I miss, Tess, is none of your business." Denver didn't add the unspoken part. *Especially with your gorgeous self sitting there in my wife's robe.*

She stood and sat again, crossing her legs. "It *is* my business. Eliza said in her note how she wants me to run interference against any women who might try to take you away from her. Since you're a man, you miss sex, and since you miss sex, you're vulnerable to some chick coming along and seducing you." Tess narrowed her green eyes. "Don't you dare call your old flame, Jan."

Denver crossed his leg over his knee and bounced his foot. "For someone who claims to love me and Eliza, you make it sound like all I married her for is sex."

"What about Akina? You two looked mighty friendly in Ohio when you came to get Eliza's paintings for her first art show."

Denver didn't regret many of his life choices, but he regretted sleeping with Akina—or did he? He was a mess at the time, still grieving over Mom and Dad's deaths from the car crash, confused about his feelings for Eliza. Akina had comforted him one night in the schoolhouse in Ohio, which began their short-lived affair. Honestly, he didn't regret it. He was a virgin at the time, and his experience with her had given him the experience to be a satisfying lover for Eliza. As far as Jan, he had admired her for wanting to wait until marriage for sex, but kissing until they were half-undressed on her sofa—and nothing more—had been one of the things that had led to his and Akina's affair.

He stood with the note and faced Tess. "Maybe you're right. Maybe Eliza just needs to get away a while. Can you keep it to yourself until your folks get back?"

"Are you going to call Willow?"

"Pretty sure I told you how she's working through the summer at college. I see no need to bother her."

Tess stood, raised on tiptoe, and kissed Denver's cheek. "No problem, Denny. With all my teasing, you might not think I want things to work out between you and Eliza, but I do. See you in the morning." She left for the guest room.

In bed, Denver rolled over to face the window. The storm had rumbled away into the night, leaving a brilliant full moon in the sky. What a day. His wife had left him, his seductress sister-in-law was only a few steps away, and he had absolutely no idea how all this would end.

He rolled over again. The main question was this: how did *Eliza* want it all to end?

a new day

Refreshed from her first full night's sleep in months, Eliza dressed in jeans and a sky-blue blouse, brushed her hair and met Ethan in the kitchen, where bacon sizzled in a pan. "Look at you," he said, turning to face her. "You must've had a good night's sleep."

"I did. That drive from Virginia wore me out."

"Miss Denver yet?"

Ignoring the question, Eliza took a carton of eggs from the refrigerator, cracked four into a bowl, and whipped them with a fork.

"Careful with that bowl," Ethan said. "You might break it."

"What I'll break is your head if you keep asking me about Denver."

Ethan plated the bacon and took it the table. "Want to go with me to church?"

"Church?" Eliza soaked the bacon grease up with paper towels and threw them in the trash.

"It is Sunday, you know."

"What church do you go to?"

"One on the other side of town in the country."

"I think I'll stay here and take a walk after breakfast, before it gets too hot. I feel like getting out." Eliza poured the eggs into the pan. Ethan gave her a spatula from a drawer.

"If you walk past Vernon's farm, you might see that family I told you about at supper."

"Who's that?" Eliza said, stirring the eggs.

"I didn't tell you their names. They're Joshua and Anna Allen. Their son's name is David. He's pretty calm for a two-year-old. Listens to his mom and dad well."

"What happened to you calling parents Mama and Papa?"

Ethan got a plate from a cabinet. "I guess not being Amish is changing me."

Eliza poured the steaming eggs into the pan. "How about toast?"

"It's in the toaster."

Eliza waited until the bread popped up and took it to table, where Ethan buttered it. She poured coffee and sat. Scars and gouges married the oak table's surface from countless family meals over the years.

Ethan said a short blessing. "Josh bought his farm right before he and Anna married. She makes the nicest baskets, sort of shaped like a ball with a flat bottom and a circular handle."

"What's Josh like?" Eliza had noted how Ethan had switched from calling Joshua Josh, so it must be okay.

"Quiet for the most part. Grateful for Anna and David. He's a great dad. Keeps saying he wants to take David fishing in the river when he gets old enough to hold a pole."

The phone on the wall near the door rang. Ethan went to answer it. "Hey, Tess. What's up?"

Eliza rolled her eyes. She should have told Denver to not tell her nosy sister how she had left him in the middle of the night.

"Yes, she's eating breakfast," Ethan said. "You want to talk to her?" He glanced at Eliza, who shook her head. "Sorry, Tess, she said no. Yeah, I know. How's Denver? Okay, I'll tell her, bye." Ethan cradled the phone and returned to the table.

Eliza swallowed her cooling eggs. "Tell me what?"

"She said she spent the night with Denver."

Eliza jumped to her feet, hitting her plate. Eggs and bacon spilled onto the table. "She *what?*"

"Chill, sis." Ethan turned her plate right side up and spooned her food into it. "She forgot her house key, that's all."

Eliza sat, cheeks hot. "That *better* be all. I'll throw her in the lake if she tries to take Denver."

"Huh, like you care."

Starting to sip coffee, Eliza lowered the cup. "I care."

"Then why are you here? Denver's a great guy. You better watch out, or some woman will snatch him up."

Eliza said nothing. Her reaction to Tess staying overnight had been nothing but emotion. Her sister wasn't a threat like any other woman wasn't a threat. Then again, Denver was an attractive man. Regardless, he wouldn't cheat on her like she wouldn't cheat on him. Still, he was the type of man who had more woman friends than man friends, although, as he had mentioned, most had moved away after high school. He did mention some girl he thought had liked him when he was seventeen. Eliza crunched bacon. Right. Whatever. To seventeen-year-old boys, any girl who paid the least bit of attention to them was cute. She had seen that enough with boys and girls nearing courting age in the Amish.

She and Ethan finished breakfast in silence. While washing and drying dishes, he told her tomorrow's sign language class would start at nine sharp and end at three. This allowed Amish families plenty of time to have breakfast together, perform morning chores, and return home for more family time and chores. He left, saying he was going to shower and dress for church. Eliza poured more coffee and took it to the back porch, where she sat on the steps.

Over the rolling hills to the east, the sun rose higher in the sky. Scattered clouds drifted by, shading her. No chickens scratched and clucked around the old coop. Buying eggs and having a chicken already cut up beat doing all that by hand.

Footsteps clomped to the screened door. "See you later. Need anything from the grocery while I'm out?"

"I used the last eggs."

"I get those from Josh. Enjoy your walk."

Ethan had bought a used pickup last year, after getting his license. Leaving the gravel drive, he beeped the horn and waved. Eliza returned the wave and sipped coffee, enjoying the fresh morning air. She hadn't felt this calm in months, and it scared her to think it was because Denver was several hundred miles away.

Coffee done, she rinsed the cup and left for her walk.

On the main road, she kept to the shoulder instead of the dusty gravel. In the tall grass filling the ditches, grasshoppers whirred and scattered. To her right, the green shoots of corn plants, each about a foot tall, covered a field.

Although she loved living on Buggs Island Lake, she also loved the simplicity of farm life. A person could lose their cares and sorrows with endless chores while surrounded by nature.

Still, growing up deaf, without the ability to communicate with anyone, let alone her family, had scarred her. Thank the Creator for sign language.

An unexpected surge of rage struck. She took a rock from the road and threw it into the corn. If the Creator—her name for God—created life in the form of nature, why did her daughter have to die? Was it punishment for falling in love with Denver, which had led to her family leaving the Amish?

Behind Eliza, horse's hooves *clop-clopped* on the hard-packed gravel. A buggy passed. An Amish man and his wife, all dressed in the black clothing, along with a boy and girl of about ten-years-old, were likely on their way to church. On the rear of the buggy, a triangular shaped sign of orange and red warned motorists of a slow-moving vehicle. The Amish started using these signs to prevent vehicles from hitting them at night, but the rare accident still happened.

The sun rose higher. Across a pasture filled with black beef cattle, the haze of humidity rose from the lush grass.

Sweat trickled from Eliza's underarms, leaving a cool trail down her sides. The nape of her neck grew hot from her hair. Should've tied it in a ponytail this morning.

A short way up the road, a buggy left a driveway and turned in the same direction as the other buggy. A man and his wife sat on the seat up front. Between them, a small boy turned to look at Eliza.

As she passed the family's house, she noted a sign with "Eggs for Sale" painted on it in brown letters. This must be where the Allen family lived. A few steps from the sign, a table with a jar and several cartons of eggs tempted Eliza to get them now and come back later to pay.

How wonderful to live where trust thrived, unlike out in the world where too many people failed to say please, thank you, and you're welcome. She had experienced this first hand in several cities during her art shows. Always the gentleman, Denver opened doors for her, including anyone else entering. Most people walked right through without the slightest hint of gratitude. At least the people of Clarksville weren't like that. With its small-town charm, its citizens would smile and nod and open doors and say thank you for each and every kindness. Gratitude: the only way to live.

A sudden pang of sadness brought the sting of tears. What did she have to be grateful for? Losing her daughter and wondering if she still loved Denver were the worst nightmares of her life.

Eliza turned to go home. Yes, Papa's farm, which Jon now owned, was home—not Clarksville, not Denver, not anywhere or anyone else.

temptation

Monday afternoon, tempted to throw his phone across the living room, Denver put it on the coffee table instead. Sitting in the chair across from him, dressed in her clothes that she'd washed and dried yesterday, Tess stopped reading a magazine. "Well?"

"The locksmith's phone has a message that he's on vacation. He'll be back next week."

"I thought you found two on your laptop yesterday."

"The other one is out of business."

Tess dropped the magazine on the coffee table and stood. "I've got a credit card."

"So?"

"Clothes, Denny. I can't wear my work stuff until a locksmith comes."

"I don't feel like shopping."

"The sooner we shop, the sooner I can wear something in the morning beside Eliza's silk robe."

Denver couldn't deny that logic. Like when he had slept with Akina while in a relationship with Jan, as much as he loved Eliza, he didn't know if he could trust himself around Tess when she wore that revealing robe, despite her only being sixteen. The last thing he needed was to be arrested for taking indecent liberties with a minor. Not only would Eliza divorce him, Absalom would kill him. At least that would put him out of his misery over his marriage falling apart.

"You're thinking mighty hard, Denny. You've got a little crease between your eyebrows."

Denver had lowered his head in thought. He looked up to see Tess pursing her lips at him. "You know," he said, trying to hold in a grin, "I wasn't crazy about 'Denny,' but I guess it works when you use it." He stood. "Let's find you some clothes."

On main street in Clarksville, toward the end of town, Denver parked beside the women's and men's clothing stores, both run by the same owner. He met Tess on the sidewalk. "Think I'll check out some stuff in the men's store. See you in a bit."

As he entered the door, he met a cold rush of air-conditioned air. He didn't need anything, but he didn't feel like watching Tess choose panties and bras.

At a rack of men's dress shirts, he glanced through them, then went to a rack of T-shirts. Comfort over dressy for Mr. Andrew's, thank you very much. He chose two shirts for this year's Lakefest, coming the third weekend in July. Maybe Eliza would be home then and they could take the pontoon boat out to watch the fireworks.

Nothing else caught his eye. He took the shirts to the register, where a cute brunette with brown eyes scanned the tags and rung them up. "I saw you looking around." She took his credit card. "Find everything you need?"

Denver tilted his head to one side. "Can I ask your name?"

Her cheeks reddened. "I was hoping you wouldn't remember me. Can't we pretend I'm just a cashier and get you on your way?"

Denver snapped his fingers. "Starts with an L, right?"

She touched his hand. "You're even cuter than in high school." She offered her hand. "Leah Hite. I had the biggest crush on you in the eleventh grade."

Leah's admission sent a little thrill through him. "Well, if I had known about your crush, I might've asked you out."

"I was shy back then. Acne and braces—my teeth and skin were terrible." She smiled hugely. "Lots better now."

Denver admired her cute smile. "If you don't mind me saying so, you look great."

Leah touched his hand again. "I'm not so shy anymore either. Think we can get together sometime and catch up?"

"Well ..." For some reason Denver couldn't explain, he wanted to say yes. No, that was as dumb as dumb gets. He wanted to say yes to get back at Eliza for leaving him. He held up his hand to show Leah his wedding band. "Any chance we could catch up as friends? My wife's out of town for a while. I wouldn't mind the company."

"You must have an understanding wife."

"You could say that."

"How long have you been married?"

Not that Denver felt like a celebrity from Eliza's art, but most everyone knew about their history. "I haven't seen you in here before. Have you been away?"

"I went to college and to work as an accountant. I missed small town life and the lake and moved back a month ago. I'm working as an accountant at the place by the post office and here part-time to earn money for a down payment on a house."

"I love the lake too." Denver started to tell Leah how his parents had died in a car crash, but he didn't want to get into that here.

Behind him, someone cleared their throat. Leah ran his credit card and returned it. "If you don't think your wife would mind, I'm free tonight. Where do you live?"

Denver took his credit card and stepped aside. "Let me get out of the way of your customer. I'll tell you when you're done." He turned to apologize to the person behind him—and dropped his wallet.

"Whatcha doing, Denny? Shopping for something special for tonight?" Tess pushed a shopping cart to the counter. "Don't mind me. I'm just this bozo's sister-in-law."

Leah's big brown eyes grew bigger. "Wow, if your sister is as hot as you, Denver scored a goddess."

Tess placed a packet each of bras and panties on the counter. "Actually, I'm hotter than my sister. She's kind of tall and thin without much shape." Tess patted Denver's shoulder. "I'm trying to get my brother-in-law to appreciate an hourglass like mine. You know, a girl with a little more meat on her bones."

"Don't pay any attention to her," Denver told Leah. "She's just a silly sixteen-year-old."

Tess pulled him aside. "Keep it up, Denny. I'll tell her how you gawked at this silly sixteen-year-old's hourglass in your wife's silk robe." Back at the counter, she gave Leah more clothing. "What's your name? I need to know it when I call my sister and tell her."

Leah looked around Tess. "I thought your wife didn't mind you having women friends."

"She doesn't." He logged into his cell phone and gave it to Leah. "Put your number in. I'll give you a call soon."

Leah did so and returned the phone. "Good. It'll be great to catch up."

Denver took the offered phone and went to wait for Tess in the pickup. Nothing wrong with talking to an old friend, nothing at all. Besides, he wasn't the one who had abandoned a spouse in this marriage, and Eliza would probably make new friends in Ohio.

Arms loaded with bagged purchases, Tess came out and shoved them into the back seat. She climbed in and slammed the door. "It's a good thing those stores have a walkway between them. I heard all that flirting between you and that mousy-brown brunette."

Denver cranked the pickup. "Then you heard how we know each other from high school."

"She won't like all that baggage you're carrying around, like a wife and why she left you."

"I thought you said Eliza just needed some time away?"

"I just said that so you wouldn't feel bad. I have no flippin' idea what she's doing. For all I know, she's gonna divorce you and marry some Amish guy." Tess crossed her arms. "Serves you right for cheating on her."

"Cheating on her? Really?" Denver let out an exasperated sigh. "You're the one showing off your so-called hourglass in Eliza's robe." He covered his eyes, then lowered his hand. "Look, I admit I'm attracted to you. That's why I told Leah we could catch up and why I said I'm married. That way she knows all we can be is friends, and I can get my mind off of you, you sixteen-year-old tease."

Tess fastened her seatbelt. "Forget it and drive."

As Denver checked for traffic, his phone on his belt holder vibrated. He checked the text. "That locksmith must've been checking his answering machine. He broke his leg waterskiing on his vacation. Maybe we should break a window to get you home and call someone to fix the window."

"Not happening, Denny. I'll mess up my parent's trip and tell them about Eliza leaving you if you do."

"Well, they'll know eventually."

Tess took her phone from her purse and waved it at him. "Sure, but I'll tell them how you were flirting with that brunette. Do you really want them to know about that?"

"Put your phone away."

Tess returned the phone to her purse. "Now, about you getting her phone number ..."

Denver checked for traffic again. Seeing none, he left the curb. "It's none of your business who I'm friends with."

"I get how you want to hang out with someone while Eliza's gone, but why couldn't she be a guy? Don't you have any guy friends? The only friends I ever hear you talk about is Jan and Akina."

"You forgot Jon and his family, and the women who came to the funeral."

"Jon and his family are in Ohio, and you haven't seen those women since the funeral. Now who's forgetting stuff?"

"Well, I was shy in high school like Leah was."

"Shy's one thing, Denny, an introvert is something else. Let's run by the grocery. I've got something planned for supper to get your mind off of my hourglass."

At home again, Denver helped Tess bring in several grocery bags. Unlike Eliza, she didn't want supper to be a surprise. She had grabbed a cart and wheeled it around, pointing at various ingredients. Clueless as to what she planned to cook, Denver had said nothing. He started to take a cabbage from a bag, but Tess took the bag from him. "It's sweet how you want to help, but you'll just get in the way."

"What're you gonna do with that cabbage? I can cut it up for you."

"I don't want it cut up."

"Chopped?"

"No."

"Sliced?"

"No."

"I like cooking," Denver said, leaning against the counter. "Can't you let me help? Eliza loved cooking with me."

"It's a traditional Amish recipe," Tess said. "You might criticize it when you see what I do with everything. Besides, don't you know I'm not my sister by now?"

"What're you gonna do with the pecans and flour?"

"Make a pecan pie."

"Okay, something I can do."

Tess shoved a bag his way. "Pecans and flour are in this bag, go for it."

Denver took a bottle of wine from the fridge and poured himself a glass. "Yuck," Tess said, making a face.

"Then don't drink any. You're long way from twenty-one anyway."

Saying nothing, Tess returned to emptying the grocery bags.

Denver admired how she sorted each item on the counter. He also admired her for wanting to cook for him and how she tended to take charge of a situation, like when she had accused him of trying to date Leah.

Then again, did he admire her because Eliza was gone and he had gotten used to having her around? No, what he had gotten used to was having a best friend around, as well as a wonderful lover. If she never came back home, his life would change drastically.

Between sips of wine and glances at Tess, he managed to get the pie ready for the pre-heated oven. As he started toward it, Tess, with a glass dish of rolled cabbage leaves, stepped in front of him and placed it into the oven. "Aren't you sweet, pre-heating the oven for me?" She took the pie from him and put it on the rack beneath the cabbage. "And our desert will be ready at about the same time."

Denver shook his head. "You're too much, you know that?"

"Does that grin mean I'm too much of a good thing instead of a bad thing? I've been wondering if you think my being here is a pain in your butt."

"Well, there's times."

Tess poked his arm. "Back atcha, Denny. I'll clean up and finish that magazine article I was reading before we bought clothes. Why don't you take a canoe ride?"

"I'll get all sweaty."

"If you haven't heard of it, there's this thing called a shower. I never knew what I was missing until I took one." She shoved him toward the sliding glass doors. "Canoe. Now."

Denver dragged the canoe from under the deck. Minutes later he was paddling away from the shore. Tess was a mess. She joked, teased, was intelligent, and her interest in building guitars intrigued him. If Eliza didn't bring herself home before Tess turned eighteen, she might lose her husband to her sister.

Denver stopped paddling. What a stupid idea. Since the moment he had realized he was in love with Eliza, she had been his entire world. Regardless of what might happen between them, he couldn't give up on her.

* * *

An hour later, hot and sweaty and feeling down from thinking about Eliza, Denver closed the sliding glass doors behind him. Tess was looking into the oven. She closed the door and faced him. "Thought I heard your big feet clomping up the steps." She gave him a bottle of water from the fridge. "Something cold for your shower."

Denver put the water back, shoved a carton of milk aside, and took out a can of beer. "Thought I had one more."

Tess took the water out. "This is healthier. Keep drinking like you do, it'll put you in the hospital."

"I don't drink that much." Denver popped the can open. On the way to the shower, he drank the cold, bitter beer. "Whoa, that's great."

"Water's better, Denny!" Tess yelled as he closed his bedroom door behind him. "Does Eliza know she married a drunk?"

Denver opened the door. "Does she know her sister is a busybody who needs to mind her own business?"

In the shower, he closed his eyes as the lukewarm water ran over his body. One more chug emptied the beer can. He crumpled the thin aluminum and tossed it over the shower doors. No way was he a drunk. In fact, he hadn't even gotten a buzz since the night he threw up in the lake.

Fresh from the shower, he found the cabbage and the pie on the dining room table, but no Tess. He knocked on the guest room door. "You mad at me?"

"Open the door and see."

"You're not wearing Eliza's robe, are you?"

"It's not my fault you can't handle my hourglass."

Denver rubbed his chin. Part of him—the part that missed making love to Eliza—definitely wanted to handle Tess's hourglass. Curious as to why she wanted him to open the door, he did.

With her thick auburn hair pinned up on swirls, wearing an emerald-green strapless dress fit for a Hollywood actress and black high heels, Tess turned around. "Not bad for an Amish chick, huh?"

Denver had to consciously keep his chin from dropping.

"You like? It looks like you like—your eyes are about to pop out."

He couldn't deny that statement at all. "You better be glad I'm married and you're sixteen. I might drop down on one knee and propose right now otherwise."

Tess strode by him to the table. "Compliments, Denny, won't get you anywhere. I bought this for my senior prom next year, and you won't be my date."

Denver pulled the chair out for her and she sat. "Aren't you the gentleman. Whoever I marry, I hope he's like you."

"He'll be a lucky guy." Denver sat. I see you found the good silver, what's the occasion?"

"Just getting used to the idea of having my own home." Tess looked around. "Not that it can be this one, but I'd love to have a place like this one day."

Denver raised a glass of ice water Tess had put beside his plate. "Here's to dreams, Tess. Never give up on them."

"I agree, like you shouldn't give up on Eliza." She put her hands together. "When's the last time you went to church?"

"Not since the—" The vision of a small, white coffin stopped him. His daughter's funeral had been at the same church where his parent's funeral had been, and she had been buried beside them. That was the last time he had attended any kind of church service. He turned away from Tess and stood. "Be right back. Got an eyelash in my eye."

In the bathroom, he jerked a towel from the rack and used it to muffle his sobs. God help him. What would it take to get him and Eliza back together again?

High heels clicked across the hardwood floor in his bedroom. Tess knocked softly on the bathroom door. "You okay in there?"

"Give me a minute. This eyelash is under my eyelid."

"I'm not stupid, you know."

More than anything, Denver wanted to open the door and let Tess comfort him. Ever since he had met Jan, he had known they weren't right for each other. Then, when he had met Eliza, she had filled his heart like he had never known was possible. Now she was gone and Tess was here. Would it be wrong to let her hold him while he cried for his dead daughter?

He hung the towel up, touched the doorknob, and let it go. No, he couldn't trust himself with Tess. He knew that as sure as he knew how much he missed Eliza.

"Denver?"

"Almost got it. Go ahead and eat before it gets cold."

The high heels clicked until they faded. Denver wiped his eyes and returned to the table. "Those eyelashes sure hurt. It's funny how they make both eyes turn red and water, isn't it?"

"Tell that lie to someone who doesn't know how much you miss Eliza and your daughter. When I heard she had been born dead, it broke my heart for both of you. Every time I went to bed, all I could see was that tiny white coffin. I cried for a week." Tess took a napkin from the holder and wiped her eyes.

The quietest silence Denver had ever heard fell between them. Either Eliza or her parents needed to get back here soon, before he fell in love with Tess. Sniffling, he cut one of the cabbage rolls. Ground beef and bits of green pepper and onion steamed. He took a bite, careful to not burn his mouth, and washed it down with water.

Tess did the same, apparently understanding how they should let the emotion of their shared pain pass. "Pretty good, huh? Mama taught me all kinds of Amish recipes over the years."

"She did a great job, this is perfect. What's it called."

Tess snorted laughter. "Cabbage rolls, you dummy, what else?"

Denver laughed too. "Tess the Mess. How's that for a nickname?"

She swallowed water. "Make you a deal—I'll stop calling you Denny if you don't use that nickname."

Denver clinked his glass to hers. "You got it. Any idea when you plan to make your first guitar?"

"The wood's kind of expensive. Papa said to see how his footstools sell before he buys any."

"That could take a while. What if I buy the wood for your first guitar?"

"You would do that for me?" Tess's tone was doubtful.

"Why not?" Denver said. "That's what family does, we help each other out." He ate another bite of cabbage. "I've got another idea, but I'm gonna keep it to myself."

"Then why tell me about it?"

"To make you curious, that's why."

"Whatever. Ready for pecan pie?"

"Sounds good."

They cleared the table, cut portions of pie, and Denver took his to the deck. It was still early, and the heat and humidity warmed the outdoors past comfort.

Tess came out with her pie. "I'm a little overdressed for the deck." She sat beside Denver in one of the chairs for the matching patio set and took a bite of pie. "Whoa, great job, Denver. This is as good as Mama's."

"It'd be better with vanilla ice cream."

Forks clicked plates. Lips licked pie filling. Tess stood, her plate empty. "Can we soak these for later? I'd like to try my new swimsuit I bought today."

Denver took the plate from her. "You swim, I'll wash dishes."

In the kitchen at the sink, as he washed the second pie plate, Denver heard the patter of Tess's bare feet on their way to the sliding glass door, which swished open and closed. He dried the last of the dishes and went to the doors. On the end of the dock, Tess was unpinning her hair. It fell down her back in stunning reddish gold waves. She lowered her hands. Denver moved so she couldn't see him. Her new swimsuit wasn't a swimsuit at all; it was one of the skimpiest bikinis he had ever seen. She turned and went to the dock's edge. The bottoms were hardly more than a thong.

He forced himself back to the kitchen. His sister-in-law—no, his *sixteen*-year-old sister-in-law—sure knew how to mess with his weak male mind. First that green dress that made her look like a princess, now a bikini that made her look like a swimsuit model.

After putting the dishes away, he got a bottle of wine from the fridge and went to the sliding glass doors again. Tess lay on the dock. The setting sun streamed through the trees and sparkled on the water beading her skin. Her wet hair was spread out around her head. One leg was up with her foot beside her other knee, while that leg was stretched out. A swimsuit model for sure.

He went to the living room sofa and took a long, cold drink of the wine. With any luck, he'd pass out before she came in. Otherwise, just the sight of her, and within arm's reach, might prove just how stupid he could be after not having the least bit of physical contact with Eliza for over a year and a half.

new friends

Tuesday Morning, as Eliza dressed, she considered how she hadn't done much of anything concerning sign language on Monday.

She had risen early to walk the farm and see the river. Around nine, she had stopped by the basket store, where Vernon, their neighbor who was such a good friend to Papa, and his wife, Abigail, were setting up baskets for sale.

At home again, when his son Timothy came from the classroom to help Ethan make sandwiches for everyone's lunch, he had hugged her and said how he was looking forward to teaching with her. He hadn't asked about Denver, so Ethan must've told him why she was here without him. Eliza appreciated her brother's tact and Timothy's understanding. Too bad Denver couldn't understand her as well as them.

Timothy also told her how his older brother, Hannes, was a papa now, including how his wife kept him out of her hair by making him do most of the chores while she visited the other mamas in their neighborhood, about five miles away.

Eliza appreciated the humor of the situation. After all, Hannes had teased her about her deafness since they were children, and when that had ended due to her kneeing his crotch one day at the river, she believed he deserved whatever he got in a wife.

After brushing her hair, she went downstairs, where Ethan had two bowls of oatmeal and two cups of coffee on the table.

"About time you got up, sleepyhead. We'll have students in thirty minutes."

Eliza sat. "Is it my fault I missed my old bed?"

"You worry me." Ethan sat and spooned oatmeal.

"Why's that?" Eliza asked.

"You're enjoying yourself too much for a woman who should be missing her husband."

"I can take me hearing aids out if you don't mind your own business."

"I see your words are clearer. Eat some oatmeal so I can hear what they sounded like when you got here Saturday."

Eliza spooned oatmeal and held the spoon as if she were going to throw oatmeal at him. "We'll see what you sound like with it all over your face if you keep on."

Ethan did the same with his oatmeal. "Food fight? I'm willing if you are."

Grinning, Eliza returned to her meal. As much as she understood the Amish way of life and how its members enjoyed their simple existence, she also enjoyed the changes in her family. They had never joked and teased like this before they left the order, and the refreshing change pleased her.

With breakfast done and dishes washed, Ethan took Eliza through a door in the new wall that separated the once huge family room. "This is the classroom." He pointed. "There's a chalk board on the far wall and books with photographs of different objects to teach signs for."

"How do you and Timothy teach at the same time?"

"He likes teaching the kids. He uses kid's books and takes them to the corner where the two tables are. If it's not too hot or raining, he sometimes takes them to the back porch."

Eliza picked up book from an adult sized chair. "How many deaf adults do you have?"

"Josh's wife is the only one when she can come. I have four adults now. Their kids are deaf, and that's who Timothy teaches. You know how much work the Amish do, so the men and women take turns when they can."

Eliza understood what Ethan was saying. Between planting new crops and gardens in spring, caring for cattle, chickens, and pigs, along with the housework required to keep a working farm running, not to mention cooking, family time, visiting neighbors, and attending church, making time for sign language showed how serious these parents were about teaching their children to communicate.

A horse snorted, and a buggy passed the window to the left. "Looks like the first family is here," Ethan said. "We start when they're all here. Let's go to the kitchen and introduce you."

A woman and her son came in. She wore a blue dress and a white bonnet. Eliza knew some of the different orders lived in Holmes County, so this woman must be from one of those orders who allowed colored dresses.

Ethan nodded toward Eliza. "Mrs. King, this is my sister Eliza. She's going to help teach a while."

"Nice to meet you, Mrs. King." Eliza pulled back her hair. "See my hearing aids? I lost my hearing from measles when I was a child."

"I see. My Ernst was born without hearing." She raised her hands toward Ernst. "Say hello to this lady."

Ernst removed his wide-brimmed black hat and saluted Eliza, the sign for hello, and ran into the classroom. Mrs. King followed.

"He must love learning sign language," Eliza signed to Ethan.

"Yeah, we need to sign, don't we? I forget sometimes until class starts."

Three more parents and their children arrived, one man and two more women, along with their children, two girls of about eight and the boy of about nine or ten, the same age as Ernst. Ethan repeated his introduction of Eliza, who enjoyed the interaction. These Amish spoke with a Dutch accent like most Amish. Papa had said some Amish were trending toward English, so he and Mama had decided early on to do the same, although they had spoken Dutch at church.

Ethan opened the screened door. "Morning, Timothy. Did your chores make you late?"

Timothy hung his wide-brimmed black hat on a row of pegs by the door. "The cow kept switching her tail in my face while I milked her. I'd much rather get milk out of carton from the grocery store like you do." He faced Eliza. "Are you ready to teach?"

"I'm not sure there's anyone I can teach. You two have it covered."

The door opened. The same man Eliza saw driving the buggy with his family Sunday morning came in. He hung his hat on a peg. "Good morning, everyone."

"Hi, Josh," Ethan said. "You should bring Anna and David sometime."

"She had a bad cold and now David has it. I had it first but I'm better now."

As Ethan introduced Eliza, she noted how Josh's black pants and white shirt hung on his thin frame. A strong wind might blow him away. His beard was trimmed neatly instead of hanging almost to his chest. He must be from the non-electric Amish order, who allowed more mechanical appliances and farm machinery than some orders allowed. "I saw your family Sunday," she said. "I almost got some eggs, but I didn't have any money with me."

Josh tipped his head toward her. "You must be Eliza. Ethan told me all about you." His cheeks reddened. "I hope you don't mind me saying so, but you are as beautiful as Timothy said you are."

"Come on, Josh," Timothy said. "You aren't supposed to repeat everything I tell you."

"I'm just me," Eliza said. "I'm nothing special."

"Oh, please," Ethan said. "A lot of people around here know about you and Denver and your art." He pointed toward a painting on the wall beside the staircase. "Remember that painting of a raccoon and her kits in the bowl of a tree? Jon bought it at one of your shows and hung it there."

"I remember. I painted that when I was about twelve."

Josh went to the painting. "I never noticed it, it looks so real." He came back. "Could you teach Anna how to paint? She wants to add farm scenes to her baskets."

"We'll see. It looks like I'll have time since there aren't enough people to justify me teaching sign language."

"Eliza could teach you," Timothy said. "Ethan and I can handle the rest."

Josh faced Eliza. "I would be honored, Eliza, if it's all right with you. I don't come very often, but I could if you …"

Eliza noticed Josh's cheeks reddening again. He seemed to admire her more than the average stranger, and she didn't know how to feel about it. Still, what harm could come from getting to know him, Anna, and David? "That should be all right. We can talk about painting lessons for Anna too."

Josh smiled bashfully. "We don't have much money saved, you know, with having a new family and all. Could I pay you in eggs and butter?"

Ethan patted his shoulder. "Throw in some tomatoes, you've got a deal. Eliza loves fresh tomatoes."

"I do too, especially with salt and pepper on one of Anna's biscuits."

"We better get to class," Timothy said. "Eliza, you want to take Josh to the back porch? It's nice out this morning."

Like yesterday, Eliza longed to be in the morning air. She agreed with Timothy and took Josh to the porch, where they sat in two of Papa's earlier attempts at rocking chairs.

"I love the outdoors," Josh said. He looked away.

Eliza waited. Since he hadn't come to class much, he might be embarrassed about not knowing many signs. Seconds passed. She touched his arm. "It's all right if don't know many signs or have forgotten what you learned. It's easy to do if you don't sign much."

Josh faced her. "It's not that."

"Can I ask what—"

"I'm not used to being around a woman other than Anna with her hair down. That and your English clothes—well, they're very distracting."

Since Josh had said she was beautiful earlier, Eliza could see how her appearance bothered him. Her long legs in blue jeans probably made matters worse, as well as her white blouse, unbuttoned past what Amish customs allowed. Regardless, she wasn't about to change her life to suit Josh, or anyone else.

"If you concentrate on our signs, that should help. Can't you do that?"

"Please, forgive me. My family is everything to me." His face reddened again, this time all the way to his forehead. "Like you, Anna is very beautiful. No other men were interested in her because she's deaf, but I know inner beauty is more important than outer beauty or hearing." Josh raised his hand to his chest. "Look at me—I'm too thin and my nose is too big. I have scars from acne too. Anna loves me in spite of how I look. I would die if I lost her."

Josh's heartfelt apology, including how much he loved his family, touched Eliza. "All right, let's get started. Sign something about the day."

Josh raised his hands. "Hello. It is a rainy day."

To keep from laughing, Eliza bit her lower lip. When the urge to laugh was gone, she raised her hands to sign but spoke at the same time. "Sunny day, not rainy."

"Oh, I see. What signs can I use for Anna and David's names? It's hard signing all the letters."

"It can be anything they like, as long as they know it when you sign it. It doesn't have to be their names. The main thing is for them to know it's how you address them."

"How do you sign 'beautiful?' I can name Anna that."

Eliza raised her right hand near her face and rolled her finger close. "Like that. Simple, huh?"

Josh repeated the sign. "It's much easier than signing all the letters. Now I need a name for her to use for David."

"Does she talk any at all?"

"She never tries."

"It's up to her, but she doesn't have to. It's important for the Deaf to understand how hearing people can't force them to talk if they don't want to. Besides, we can talk as well with our hands as the Hearing can with their voices."

"If Anna would try, I would love to hear her say mine and David's names. How do you teach that?"

Eliza recalled how Denver had taught her his name, by using words she remembered from before she lost her hearing. "How did Anna lose her hearing?"

"Her Papa said her neck swelled and she had a fever when she was six. When she got better, she couldn't hear."

Eliza bit her lower lip again, this time in anger. Some Amish allowed their children to get vaccinated against various illnesses like the mumps, which is what Anna must've had, and measles, which is what took Eliza's hearing. She understood the Amish ways of faith, but to let children suffer like she and Anna had suffered was wrong.

"I think Anna had the mumps. The high fever is what made her lose her hearing. If she lost her hearing at six, she might remember some of the words she knew before then. That's how I learned to talk."

Josh's expression brightened. "I hate to ask, but could you teach her? I'd rather you do that than teach her to paint."

"I'll be glad to. Now, let's see what signs I can teach you first." Eliza raised her hands.

What an amazing start to her stay here. Instead of sitting around the house at home, she felt useful again, especially since she might be able to help this couple fall in love even more than they already were through sign language, and possibly speech.

As the signs and words passed between her and Josh, one thing remained within her thoughts: Did Denver miss her? She didn't know if she hoped he did or not, because she had hardly thought of him since she had been here.

morning dream

Having drank most of the bottle of wine, Denver lay on the sofa, drifting in and out of sleep. Visions of Eliza crept through his mind—of her laughter, her kisses, her gasps of pleasure as they made love before their world had changed so drastically.

Sometimes she would get up from bed on certain mornings and cook breakfast and bring it back so they could talk and eat. Sometimes they would make love again after. Sometimes—

A cool sheet touched his chin. Warm lips kissed his cheek. "Do you have any idea how much I love you, Denver?"

He blinked. Sunlight poured through the windows and sliding glass doors. In a recliner beside the TV, Tess, wearing shorts and jeans, slept soundly, auburn hair a reddish gold mass around her head, face, and shoulders.

Had she covered him with the sheet and kissed his cheek and told him she loved him? No, no way. He had heard Eliza's voice in his dream as clear as the sun rising over the lake.

On the coffee table, the wine bottle was gone. Whether or not Tess had said she loved him, she certainly cared, or she wouldn't have covered him with a sheet, thrown the bottle away, or slept near him all night long. Every time Denver turned around, her sweetness factor rose by a few more degrees.

He knelt by her and brushed the hair away from her face. "I guess you're my guardian angel, huh?"

Tess groaned. "Only if you let me sleep some more while you make pancakes." She opened her eyes. "You worry me. Are you becoming a drunk over Eliza leaving you?"

"I don't drink that much."

"That empty wine bottle says you did last night."

"Well, I'll cut back for you."

"Nope, you'll cut back for Eliza. I'd hate for her to come home and find you dead from alcohol poisoning." Tess closed her eyes. "Pancakes. Hot. Butter. Lots of syrup. Coffee."

Denver didn't want to leave. Tess drew him like the lake drew him and Eliza. How would it feel to kiss her?

Tess opened her eyes again. "Why aren't you cooking?"

The hot rush of adrenalin burst into Denver's chest. No, not one kiss. One would lead to a hundred and a hundred would have them ending up in bed if she were willing. Only one thing would help get his urges for Tess under control, and he'd do that after breakfast.

He left for the kitchen. Tess's bare feet pattered after him. "Hey, why were you looking at me like that?"

"You drool in your sleep."

Tess slapped his back. "Shut up, I do not."

Denver turned around. "Thanks for covering me with a sheet and sleeping by me to make sure I was okay. That was sweet."

"About time you realized the full extent of my sweetness. You realize I'll only get better with age like wine, right?"

"I don't know, you're pretty sweet now."

"I'll be a lot sweeter with pancakes in me. Where's your flour?"

Denver opened a cabinet. "In here, but we've got mix."

Tess got the flour and shut the door. "Pancakes from a mix? Grab me some eggs and milk and salt and I'll show you *real* pancakes."

Denver gathered everything and put it on the counter. Tess got a bowl and a spoon. "Heat a non-stick pan and put some real butter in it, not that fake stuff. "I'm gonna fatten you up for when Eliza comes back and wants to start a family. Then she'll have some love handles to grab while y'all are going at it."

Denver didn't want to laugh—he tried his best not to laugh—but he did anyway.

Tess joined him. As her giggles ended, she punched his arm. "See how happy I make you?"

Rubbing his stomach that ached from laughing, Denver couldn't agree more. Unfortunately for him, her sex appeal was what worried him, not how she made him laugh. Then again, for him and Eliza, laughter was one heck of a turn on.

* * *

An hour later, Denver got up from the table. "Good grief, I'm about to bust. Those were the best pancakes I ever tasted."

Taking their dishes to the kitchen, Tess yawned. "I need a nap from watching over your drunk self."

"Asleep, not drunk. Want me to wash dishes while you take a nap?"

"And sleep on all that food and get fat? No way, I'm gonna take a walk."

"Good. You walk, I'll wash, and I'll get a nap myself."

Tess went to the guest room and came back with sneakers on. "See you later, you pancake lover."

Denver watched her walk down the hall. What a mess she was, full of youth and fun and more woman than he could handle, although if he were under eighteen, he'd sure like to try. Shaking his head at his idiocy, he went back to the sink and filled it with hot water and dish soap for their sticky dishes.

About to put the first dish into the sink, he went to his room for his phone instead. Time to get his mind on something else besides Tess.

He found Leah's number and dialed it. She answered after a few rings. "Hello?"

"Hey, Leah, it's Denver."

"Oh, I didn't recognize your number. I get those idiotic calls about car warranties all the time."

"Are you working? I don't want to bother you if you are."

"Listen to you, being so sweet. Do you know how rare that is these days?"

Denver grinned to himself. "Yeah, I'm sweet all right. I was wondering if you wanted to hang out sometime?"

"Doing what?"

"See a movie. Have coffee. Take my pontoon boat out on the lake. Whatever you like?"

"If you mean today, I can't. I'm visiting my grandma in the hospital in Richmond."

Denver sat on his bed. "Nothing serious I hope."

"She had her gall bladder out." Leah paused. "What are you doing Friday night?"

"Not a thing."

"What if I take you out to dinner? I've been dying to try the Mexican place on the west side of town."

"Sounds good, what time?"

"What's your address so I can pick you up?" Denver told her. "Got it," she said. "I hope you like hot and spicy. I plan to heat you up. See you at six."

"Leah, wait—" Denver dropped the phone beside him. Heat him up? He hoped she meant with Mexican food and not her cute self. His life was filled with too much female temptation already.

He fell back on the bed. What a mess. Not only did he miss Eliza to the point of dreaming about her, he had gotten so used to being married, he didn't like being alone. He closed his eyes. Whatever. Tess and Leah both needed to be friends *without* any benefits that would either get him arrested or divorced.

As he dropped off to sleep, gravel crunched in the road and a car engine cut off in the driveway. Eliza was home. He started to get up but didn't. Hopefully she would see him in bed and join him for a long needed snuggle.

The front door clicked open. Footfalls came down the hall and paused at his door. Then they came to the bed, which jostled as she lay beside him and snuggled into his shoulder. Eyes still closed, Denver wrapped his arms around her. If he counted all the reasons he loved her, he would count until the day he died. As he palmed her cheek and turned her face toward him for a kiss, she shoved him away. "Stop that, Denny. I was trying out your snuggle."

Denver jumped from the bed where Tess lay. "You're a pretty good snuggler," she said. "Want to try it again without you trying to take advantage of me?"

"What the heck are you doing?"

"I told you—trying out your snuggle."

"I meant what are you driving? And how? And where did you get the keys?"

Tess stood. "I walked home to water Mama's flowers and found a house key under a pot on the front porch. Imagine that, I could've been sleeping in my own bed instead of here with you lusting after my hot bod."

Denver covered his eyes. "You are too much."

"Uh-huh. Go to the kitchen counter. I've got another surprise for you in Mama's car."

Denver started to ask her about driving with only a learner's permit, but since they lived in a private subdivision instead of on public roads, her driving should be fine.

She came back with a thick magazine of some kind and opened it on the counter. "This is a catalog for all the guitar making stuff I need. Since you offered to buy this stuff, I'm taking. We can start a guitar together all next week, before Mama and Papa get back."

"Do we have to tell them about you staying here?"

"Good idea. We'll keep it between us."

Denver thumbed through the catalog. "All right, show me what we need. I don't know any more about building a guitar than I do about playing one."

"Something else we can learn together," Tess said, nudging his arm with hers. "Eliza better get her butt back here before I'm old enough to snuggle you for real."

Denver got a pad and pencil and noted whatever Tess said to note. He didn't know about guitars, but he did intend to get his mind off of Tess by catching up with Leah Friday night. Thank goodness she just wanted to be friends.

lessons

Friday morning, after a few days of rest and teaching sign language, Eliza walked toward Josh and Anna's home. She carried a basket of picture books she had bought in town, which she planned to use to teach Anna and David too.

Rain had fallen last night. She walked faster, relishing the aroma of clean air mixed with the aroma of cow manure. Some people might not like it, but Eliza considered the pungent aroma as part of the natural world. If she loved anything, it was nature.

She neared the home, a single-story wood-frame house with a front porch and a swing. Denver had mentioned hanging a swing from their porch, but he never had.

To the right, tomato, summer squash, cucumber plants, and a few stems and stalks she didn't recognize filled a garden. Somewhere behind the house, chickens clucked. Too bad the subdivision at home didn't allow chickens; the sound might soothe her fragile nerves while taking her mind off of losing her daughter.

Eliza stopped on the porch. No, her and Denver's daughter. She didn't care for how he seemed to be fading from her mind, almost as if he had never existed. No, he would always exist, even if he were tucked away in a small corner of her heart.

Footsteps pattered to the door, and a dark-headed boy peered through the screen at her. "She here, Mama!"

Wearing a blue dress of the same style as most Amish dresses, with a white prayer cap covering her chocolate brown hair that peeked from the edges, Anna came to open the door and gesture Eliza inside. Eliza came in and raised her hand to her forehead to say hello. Anna returned to sign, and so did David. "Papa, he get eggs."

Eliza knelt. David's eyes were similar to Anna's, huge and brown with long lashes. He wore dark jeans and a white, button-up shirt but no wide-brimmed hat, although a small one hung on a rack by the door. "Aren't you the smart young man? Cute as a button too."

David fingered one of his buttons. "Coot?"

"Hasn't anyone called you cute before?"

His eyebrows twisted into a knot. He looked up at Anna. "I coot, Mama. Like button."

Anna smiled softly. Josh was right about her beauty; it lived and breathed within her tanned cheeks, perfectly straight nose, and intense expression from wanting to know what David had said.

Eliza stood. Anna left for a doorway. Unlike most Amish homes, this living room was of average size with average furniture instead of hand made. With a deaf wife and a two-year-old boy running around, maybe Josh didn't have time to do any woodworking yet. Then too, tending a garden and chickens and making baskets could keep a couple busy as well.

David took her hand and led her through the same doorway Anna had entered, which opened into a spacious kitchen. The center of many households, it held a stove, likely natural gas since the Amish used that source as a rule in their ordnung instead of propane. A huge refrigerator filled a corner to the right, beside a sink, with a washing machine beside it.

Through a back screen door, Eliza could see Anna walking to a chicken coop. Beside it, two solar panels gleamed in the morning sun. Made sense. Many Amish used solar power these days, like the system Denver had designed for her old home, now Jon's second sign language school.

David pointed out the door. "Mama 'an Papa." He wiped his runny nose on his sleeve.

"I see." Eliza took a dishtowel from beside the sink and knelt to wipe his nose. "Your papa told me about your cold. You don't sound stuffy, so it must be better."

David touched her cheek. "You purty."

His simple caress touched her almost to the point of tears. If her daughter had lived, she would've touched her like this. She kissed David's hair, which smelled of a mix of fresh air and boy.

"You sad?"

Eliza looked out the door. Josh was giving Anna some eggs. Would they mind if she hugged David? She took him into her arms. So firm yet yielding, like a newborn colt. Would she ever have her own son or daughter to hold like this?"

David pulled away. "Mama 'an Papa."

Josh held the door for Anna. "I see you two are getting acquainted. David, this is Eliza."

David raised his brown eyes to Eliza. "'Liza?"

"That's me." She faced Josh and Anna. "He sure is a sweetheart."

Anna raised her hands. "Coffee? Tea?"

"Two of our morning drinks," Josh said. "Anna has a loaf of apple-nut bread in the oven if you can wait."

Eliza caught the aroma of cinnamon. "Maybe later with tea. I just had breakfast."

"Let's sit at the table. We'll have more room in here than in the living room."

Eliza placed the basket on the table and sat. "I just thought of something. David ran to the door when I crossed the porch and called Anna. How did she know to come?"

"She felt his little feet running across the wood floor. Anna's very sensitive to our movement in the house."

"I should've thought of that. I used to feel thunder in my chest." She took the books from the basket. "We've got one with farm machinery and one with animals and one with vegetables. Which would you like to start with?"

Anna touched the one with animals. "Me too, Mama," David said, climbing into a chair to sit on his knees.

"A fine choice," Josh said, moving his chair beside Eliza, who started the lesson on page one, with a chicken.

As the lesson continued, an unexpected picture formed in her mind, of her, Denver, and a boy like David swimming at the dock at home. If only that were true, or perhaps with a daughter too. They could take them out on the pontoon boat to watch the Lakefest fireworks, take them fishing too, and they could teach them how to sign. Then, when they got old enough, they could tell them the story of how they fell in love.

In the middle of raising her hands to show this family the sign for horse, she stood. "Do you have a bathroom?"

"Sure do," Josh said, smiling. "No outhouse for my family." He took her to a hall. "Last door on the right."

Eliza hurried down the hall and closed the door. She took a handful of toilet paper to her mouth to muffle her crying. Why do this now instead of at home where Denver could've comforted her? No, if he had held her, she would've pulled away like she did when they kissed on the night she had left him.

What a mess she had made of their lives. One minute she missed him, the next minute she didn't know if she loved him at all.

Someone knocked on the door. "Eliza, are you all right?" Josh's kind voice. All she needed was kindness, nothing more, no one expecting anything of her like Denver expected her to get over her daughter's death and make love to him again. She lowered the paper from her mouth. "I'll be out in a minute. Something I ate has upset my stomach."

"Just making sure. You sounded like you were crying."

Had he been waiting at the door for her? He couldn't have heard her from the kitchen. "Please, go back to Anna and David. I'll be there in a minute."

His work boots thudded down the hall. What a caring man, one who loved his family like Eliza wanted Denver to love her—simply, gently, patiently.

She wiped her eyes, blew her nose, and checked her face in the mirror over the sink. A fool with red eyes and a red nose stared back. "Hey, you," she whispered. "When will you start thinking about what you need to be happy instead of what Denver needs to be happy?" Eliza searched her memories for a hint of Tess's crush on Denver, like Ethan had said she had. Long glances. Joking and teasing. Laughter and smiles. Swimming at the dock and dunking each other. Eliza's lips tightened. Fine. Good even. If Tess wanted her selfish husband, she could have him.

At the kitchen table again, Eliza smiled at Josh. Too bad she couldn't teach his family the sign for jackass. She opened the book of farm animals. "Let's try the sign for donkey."

date

Combing his hair, Denver stopped to check his vibrating phone on the dresser. Tess had sent a text to remind him to pick her up from work after his date with Leah tonight. He threw the phone on the bed. What a hardhead. No dates, just friends.

The phone vibrated again. This time the text said the guitar making materials had come in two huge boxes, and she owed him for being so sweet. He shook his head. She sure ran hot and cold. Good thing Leah wanted Mexican instead of crab dip at the bed-and-breakfast. With his luck, Tess would wait on them and give him the evil eye the entire time.

A car engine neared and turned off in the driveway. He went to the door, but Leah wasn't there. "Hey," she said, waving from the corner of the garage. "I'm checking out your view."

She wore a red mini-skirt that fit like mini-skirts should fit, with her brunette hair in a ponytail, revealing the fine hairs on the nape of her neck. Denver swallowed. He was a sucker for ponytails and necks. Good thing this was a friendly date and nothing else. He joined her. "Mind if I tell you how great you look? I mean howling at the moon great."

She faced him. "Look at you, dress slacks and a button-up shirt." She unbuttoned the top button. "That's better. Let some of that sexy chest hair show."

"Ready to go?" Denver asked, trying to get his mind on eating instead of her fingertips touching his chest.

"Can I see your dock first? Looks like a great place to swim." She left for the dock, Denver beside her.

"Yeah, it's nice for swimming." He didn't mention how Mom and Dad had bought the sand to make a beach. No need to bring up sad memories.

Leah's high heels crunched in the gravel path. She grabbed his arm. "Oops, almost twisted my ankle in that gravel."

Denver put his hand around her waist. "Can't let that happen. Your skirt might split up to your hips."

Leah squeezed his arm. "Like you wouldn't like that." She laughed. "I'm just teasing. Can't have you cheating on your wife, can we?"

At the dock, Denver took his hand from around her waist. "Be right back." He jogged beneath the deck and plugged the LED lights in and jogged back. "There you go. You can see how the lights outline the edge of the dock"

"Oh, wow, I'd love to have place on the lake like this. Any chance your wife will divorce you?"

Denver went to the left edge of the dock, where the pontoon boat was tied. For a friendly date, Leah didn't mind making strange suggestions. "Nice boat, huh? Great for fishing and stuff, or just being lazy out on the water."

Leah joined him. "Or making out. You and your wife ever do that on the lake?" Denver faced her. The hint of a grin quirked the corners of her mouth upward. "Aren't I terrible, teasing you like that? Let's go eat, I'm hungry."

Instead of taking a left at the intersection for the Mexican place, Leah took a right. "Mind if we try the bed-and-breakfast. I've always wanted to try their crab dip."

Denver said nothing. Maybe Tess would be working in the kitchen.

"You don't mind, do you?" Leah asked, pulling into a parking place.

"It's fine. I like their crab dip."

Inside, Denver looked around for Tess. He didn't see her, so maybe his luck would hold out.

The greeter seated them, gave them menus, and asked if they would like something from the bar. Leah ordered sweet tea with lemon and so did Denver. With all her teasing, not to mention the way her mini-skirt enhanced her gorgeous legs, he didn't need anything with alcohol. The greeter left, saying a waiter would bring their drinks, and Denver held in a sigh of relief. Someone was looking out for him.

Leah pulled back the curtain over the window beside them. "Clarksville is quiet tonight." She let the curtain go and faced the room. "I love those old plank floors and how they're scarred. Who knows how many families lived in this old house before it was made into a bed-and-breakfast?"

The waiter arrived with their tea, took their orders of crab dip and salads, and left.

Just as Denver thought Leah wasn't going to talk, she touched his hand. "I'm sorry about your parents. I asked about you at work today."

"Thanks. Willow and I had a rough time of it for a while."

"I thought that was your sister's name. What's she doing now?"

"Working through the summer at college. She's going to med school. She wants to be a doctor like Mom."

"She doesn't mind you and your wife staying at that gorgeous lake house?"

"Mom and Dad took care of us with life insurance. All Willow wants of the house is a bedroom whenever she's in town."

"I think I remember seeing your family downtown during Lakefest one time. She's got curly red hair, right?"

"And a temper to match. She didn't get along with the woman I was dating before I met my wife. Then again, that woman didn't get along with Willow either. Some people talk about oil and water not mixing. They were like gas and an open flame."

The waiter returned with the crab dip and their salads, refilled the tea, and left again, saying to let him know if they needed anything.

Denver broke a piece of the bread from the half-loaf on his side of the plate. "I love this bread."

Leah did the same, spooned steaming crab dip on it, and took a bite. "Whoa, it's hot." She drank tea. "Think you can kiss my mouth and make it better?"

Denver grinned to let her know he was teasing her. "Sorry, not into crab breath."

"You could've fooled me, Denny."

Denver whipped his head toward the voice. "Tess?"

"It's me, it sure is. The waiter said a cute couple was enjoying the crab dip I made. I thought I'd come out and see who."

"Hi, Tess," Leah said. "I love how that flour brings out the highlights in your red hair."

Tess's green eyes cut from Leah to Denver and back. "Maybe you'd like to wear that crab dip instead of eating it?"

Leah faced Denver. "Teenagers, so childish."

Denver got up and took Tess by the arm to walk her to the hall. "You behave, okay?"

"*Me* behave? That mini-skirt's got tramp written all over it. I bet she had to oil her big behind with bacon grease to get it on."

Denver held in a laugh. "Look—"

"Go ahead, yuck it up. You know you'd rather have dinner with me than some woman who's after a married man."

Denver almost laughed again. Like Tess wasn't after him, what a joke. "I'm enjoying myself more than I have in a long time. I haven't been out to eat and talk with someone in over a year and a half. Eliza didn't care enough to stay and work things out, so what's wrong with me having a nice time with a nice person I knew from high school?"

Tess crossed her arms. "Nothing, but nothing about that mini-skirt and that stuffed bra says nice."

"Stuffed bra?"

"Shut up, you aren't blind. I should know from how you've been checking me out."

The greeter came from another room. "Is anything wrong, Tess?"

"Nothing, not a thing. This guy wanted to know if we have bigger breasts."

The greeter took a menu from a table by the front door and opened it. "That's funny, I don't see chicken on the menu."

"It's okay," Denver said through a grin. "I just wanted to thank this lovely young lady for her great crab dip. Y'all should give her a raise." He leaned toward Tess's ear to whisper, "Like a kick in the behind raise."

"Thank you, sir," Tess said, "but I'm too young for you to ask out." She whirled and stomped toward the kitchen.

At the table, Denver had to cover a grin. Leah, in the middle of drinking tea, lowered the glass. "Does your wife know her sister has a crush on you?"

"Naa, she's just a kid."

"Well, she's gorgeous for a kid." Leah tipped the glass toward him. "Tempted? You *are* home alone."

Denver tore another piece of the crusty bread from the loaf. "What I am is hungry."

Supper passed with small talk about college and jobs and small-town life in Clarksville, including Lakefest in three weeks. Denver mentioned working in solar engineering, and Leah mentioned accounting again. When the bill came, he took it before she could. "Nope, I really enjoyed tonight, so it's my treat."

Leah lowered her head and looked up at him from partially closed eyes. "I shouldn't say ..."

"Shouldn't say what?"

"I was thinking about desert."

"I could go for something sweet."

"Me too." Leah licked her lips. "As long as it's you."

Denver laughed. "You and your teasing." He stood and dropped money for the tip on the table. "What would you say to supper at my place tomorrow night?"

"Only if I can bring my bathing suit."

He glanced at his watch. "Whoa, I need to get home so you can get home. Tess's parents are on a trip. She only has her learner's permit and I'm taking her to and from work."

Leah stood too, pulling the mini-skirt down that had ridden up her thighs. "Had you noticed my behind about to hang out?"

Denver pushed his chair up to the table. "Nope, 'fraid not."

Leah took his arm for the walk to her car. "Liar."

During the drive home, Denver couldn't believe how much he had enjoyed the evening. Leah had taken a genuine interest in solar engineering and had asked him question after question about it. Aside from when he had designed the system for Eliza's old home in Ohio for Jon, she had never mentioned it again. Now she had left with orders for him to not call or not come see her. For all he knew, she was more than friends with some guy already. Whatever, two could play that freaking game.

As Leah parked in his driveway, he faced her. "Feel like a movie on TV?"

"I thought you had to pick up Tess?"

"That'll only take a few minutes." He got out and opened the front door and waved her inside.

She rolled down the window. "Maybe we shouldn't do this."

"It's just a movie. I like hanging out with you."

"Are you sure? What married guy asks a woman to his house while his wife is away and calls it 'hanging out?'"

"You could go inside and see. I'll be right back."

"Well …"

Denver ran his fingers through his hair. What a set of pouting lips and what a risk he was taking. No, Eliza took that risk by leaving him. "Hey, I understand if you'd rather not, Leah."

She got out of her car and joined him. "Do you know how rare you are? Any other man would be shoving me through that door."

"Then you'll stay?"

"Why not?" Leah closed the front door behind her and Denver left for town.

At the restaurant, Tess was waiting on the porch, arms crossed. She came to the pickup and got in. "Did you see Miss Mini-skirt off with a kiss?"

Denver puckered up and leaned toward Tess. "Come on, you know you want one."

She shoved him away. "Ask me again after Eliza divorces you and I'm eighteen."

"You know I'm teasing." Denver cranked the pickup and pulled onto main street.

"I'm *not* teasing. I called Ethan the other day and Eliza wouldn't even talk to me. That sister of mine has some serious soul searching to do about your marriage."

Denver said nothing. Like he had told himself earlier, if Eliza wanted to play that game, he could too.

When he stopped at Tess's house, she glared at him, eyes wide in the dashboard lights. "My new clothes are at your house."

"Your old clothes still fit, don't they? You can pick everything up tomorrow before work."

Tess shook her head. "I get it. You invited Miss Fake Boobs over tomorrow night and don't want me around when she seduces you."

"You sure forgot your Amish heritage. 'Fake boobs?'"

"Shut up. Is she coming tomorrow night?"

"None of your business."

"Then she is." Tess looked away and then back. "Don't you know by now how much I care about you and Eliza? Don't go doing something with Leah you'll regret."

Denver huffed a hard breath. "We're just friends, Tess."

She opened the pickup door. "And I'm running for president." She slammed the door and went to the house.

At home again, Denver found Leah on the sofa with her high heels off and her feet tucked beneath her. A bottle of wine and two glasses were on the coffee table, and soft jazz played from the TV.

"Hope you don't mind me making myself comfortable."

"Not at all." Denver sat at the other end of the sofa and took the remote from the coffee table. "Wonder what movie's on?"

"You have some nice family photos around. Your wife could be a model, tall and slender like she is. When do I get to hear how you met and why she's not here?"

Denver didn't care to talk about Eliza and their personal problems. He poured himself a glass of wine and sipped. "Let's talk about you. How is it that a gorgeous woman like yourself isn't married with a family?"

"I'm only twenty-five, like you. I could ask you about the family part too, but I don't see any photos of kids around."

Denver gulped wine. "Just haven't done that yet."

Leah ran her fingertip around the rim of the wine glass. "Are you likely to do that?"

"Honestly, I have no idea."

She took her feet from under her and slid closer. "That's a shame. You'd be a great dad."

Denver took her wine glass and put both on the table. Friends or not, this beautiful woman was right here and Eliza wasn't. Hell, she wasn't likely to be either. Might as well call a divorce lawyer and be done with it. He cupped Leah's cheek. "How in the world did I not date you in high school?"

Leah showed her teeth. "Braces and acne, remember?"

"Well, like I said, I was shy."

Leah eased toward him. "You're anything but now."

The kiss began soft and smooth, then grew firmer. Kissing his neck, she unbuttoned his shirt enough to kiss lower. Denver raised her chin and kissed her again, breathing in some sweet scent she wore—and stopped. "You hear something?"

Leah looked around. "I can't believe it."

Denver looked where Leah was looking, toward the sliding glass doors. Tess tapped the glass. "I forgot my key."

Leah got up, slipped on her heels, and took her purse from the coffee table. "I'm out of the mood now. Let's try this again

120

tomorrow night while your nosy sister-in-law is working." She strode down the hall, high heels clicking.

Tess tapped again. "Oops."

Denver let her in. "I bet you forgot your keys on purpose the first time."

Tess plopped on the sofa and sipped wine from his glass. "Not too bad. Let's get drunk and do what you and that bimbo were gonna do. That'll teach Eliza a lesson."

Denver sat. "Right, and put me in jail after your folks kill me."

"Just teasing, remember?"

"Why do I have the feeling you're not?"

Tess took a key from her pocket. "Durn, I forgot about the other key under the flower pot, imagine that. Do I get a ride home for my honesty?"

"What I should do is put you over my knee and spank your butt."

"Dangerous territory there, Denny, and you know it." She returned the wine glass to the coffee table. "I unpacked the guitar stuff before you took me to work. I can't wait to start on one."

Glad to change the subject, Denver turned sideways on the sofa to face Tess. "I'm looking forward to working with my hands."

"Want to come over tomorrow? I found some videos online that teach playing."

"No guitar yet, remember?"

"We can still check some videos out. I'll make breakfast."

Denver glanced at his watch. "It's almost one, let's make it lunch. I might surprise you with something."

"What, a mini-skirt? I bet I'd look better in one than Miss Fake Boo—"

Denver covered her mouth. "Don't. I like classy Tess better than trashy Tess."

She pulled his hand down. "I … uh. Well …"

"What?" he asked, still feeling the warmth of her lips on his palm.

"I think I just got an idea of what it feels like to get hot and bothered." She poked his chest and jumped up. "Just teasing! You couldn't turn me on if you had a key for it."

"Right, you nut." Denver stood. "Let's get you home."

second date

After a breakfast of scrambled eggs and sausage, Denver hopped in his pickup and drove to Clarksville. It was amazing how his appetite and energy level had risen since Eliza had left. He scratched his chin. Or was it because he and Tess had grown close or because Leah had been such blast last night?

When he had gone to bed for the last year and a half, his thoughts had churned in his brain like a sudden summer storm over the lake, turning calm water into whitecapped waves that crashed ashore. Last night, he hadn't given Eliza or their marriage a single thought. Good or bad, who knew? But it felt great to feel normal again instead of depressed.

He parked outside the indoor mall on main street. Inside, he strolled around, enjoying the view of books, crafts, photographs, clothing, and other countless items that vendors sold from various booths.

And then he saw it—an old guitar, strings tarnished, wood finish faded—hanging on a wall, along with new packs of strings and an instruction book. The book explained basic chords. Good. Great. Basic would work fine for Tess and his first lessons.

In his pickup again, he drove to the grocery and bought a birthday cake and some candles. Tess would be seventeen in a week—why not surprise her with whatever she was cooking him for lunch?

On the way home again, Denver lowered the pickup window and sliced his hand through the wind. Life was looking better and better all the time. He really, seriously, enjoyed making someone he cared about happy, like he used to do for Eliza.

He started to consider their times together, from the moment they fell in love until they lost their daughter but didn't. That would only bring pain and regret—pain and regret that would end his great mood.

About half a mile from the turn toward home, off Highway 15, he took the road to the right, which would take him to the country church and its cemetery where his daughter was buried.

When Eliza had stayed by her grave all that time, his tears had stayed inside him, concern for her holding them back like Kerr Dam held back the lake. But the first night of her stay at the mental facility, he had cried all night, soaking his pillow, until he finally got up and took a six-pack of beer to the dock to drink himself to sleep.

Sure, he drank too much. No, since Tess had come into his life, the urge to overdrink was gone. Nothing wrong with a beer or two or a glass of wine with a meal.

In a creek bottom, where a wildlife area for hunters and hikers beckoned, he turned around to drive home. Tess might like to visit her niece's grave with him.

When he parked behind Oneita's car, he caught a glimpse of Tess in the kitchen. Leaving the pickup, he sniffed whatever lunch was. Roast beef? Maybe potatoes and carrots and onions with it? A sudden gush of saliva filled Denver's mouth. He tried the front door and went in. "Hi, honey, I'm home!"

Wearing a blue apron, auburn hair up in a ponytail, Tess peeked around the corner, down the hall from the kitchen. "Hi, dear. Hard day at work?"

Walking down the hall, Denver laughed. "We sound pretty good together, huh?"

"That depends on if you compliment your lunch."

"Roast beef? Smells great." In the kitchen, Denver looked through the archway that led to the dining room and its huge oak table Absalom had made. "Wow, a huge porterhouse steak and baked potatoes and salads." He grabbed Tess's hands and spun her around. "You deserve a dance for that."

She pulled away and took off the apron, revealing jeans and last year's Lakefest T-shirt. "Tea okay?"

"Sure. Can I help?"

"I got it. I'm used to Papa and Ethan letting us women do the serving in Ohio."

"I don't mind helping, where's the glasses?"

Tess pointed to a cabinet. "How my sister could leave a sweet man like you, I'll never know."

Denver took the glasses to the table. Tess brought a pitcher of iced tea with lemon wedges inside and filled the glasses. She said a short blessing and sliced the steak; steaming juice filled the plate. "Want the tender part on the side?"

"You can have it."

"More sweetness." Tess put several slices on his plate. "We can share. You know, like happy couples do."

Denver cut his potato and filled it with butter and sour cream. Tess's sweetness factor kept rising and rising. "What kind of wood will you make your first guitar out of?"

"Adirondack Spruce top and sides and a rosewood back. Everything I've read says that's the best combination for volume and tone."

"What about the neck?"

"Mahogany with an ebony fingerboard." Tess took a bit of steak. "Do you see the sear marks? I cooked it on the grill."

"Must've been what I smelled when I got here, it's great."

"Did you know Papa's last rocking chairs have mother-of-pearl inlay along the arm rests?"

"The one we have is older."

"Right. I learned how to cut and install inlay for his chairs, so I can do the fingerboard on a guitar too."

Denver swallowed tea. "Aren't you the talented sister-in-law? You can cook and build furniture and maybe build guitars, what's next?"

Tess aimed a fork at him. "No 'maybe' to it. You'll see, it'll be a masterpiece." She split her potato. "No more talking, I want to eat while it's hot."

When they had done all the damage to the huge steak that they could, leaving half the equally huge potatoes on their plates. Denver stood. "You leave enough room for dessert?"

"Maybe a little. What did you bring?" Tess started to the sink with their dishes. Denver took them from her and led her back to the table.

"Cop a squat, pretty woman."

Tess crinkled her eyes at him. "Where'd that come from?"

"It's a movie with Julia Roberts in it. She had auburn hair like yours in it."

"Papa's careful about what we watch on TV. Does it have sex in it?"

"Not too bad. Be right back." At his pickup, Denver put the pack of new strings in his pocket, took the cake and guitar to the living room, and went to the kitchen. "Come to the dining room and sit. No looking, okay?"

"Is your surprise you naked? I wouldn't mind a surprise like that." Tess followed Denver to the dining room and sat.

"Close your eyes."

"Fine, Denny, they're closed."

Denver went to the living room for the cake and guitar. True to her word, her eyes were closed when he came back. He put the cake on the table and the guitar in the chair beside her, ran back to the pickup for the candles he had bought at the grocery, and stuck seventeen of them in the cake. In the kitchen again, he got a lighter from the junk drawer where he had seen Absalom get one when the grill lighter wouldn't work.

"You sure are doing a lot of stomping in and out of here," Tess said."

Denver lit the candles. "Open your eyes." As she did, he sang her the Birthday Song.

Tess snatched a napkin from the holder and wiped her eyes. "Durn allergies." She shook her head. "I know I've been saying it a lot, but you are so sweet."

"Too bad—" Denver cut the rest of his sentence—*Eliza can't see that*—off. "Make a wish, pretty woman."

Tess blew out the candles. "There. Now we'll see if it comes true when I turn eighteen."

"You and your teasing. Absalom will kill me if I marry you."

"I meant a new car. Papa said he'd buy me one on my eighteenth birthday."

"Think he'll buy you one of those?" Denver pointed to the guitar.

"Whoa, where'd you get that? There's no music store in town." She placed the guitar in her lap.

"I saw it at the indoor mall a while back." He took the strings from his pocket and gave them to her.

"Hey, this is supposed to be a good brand. Great job, my fellow guitar builder and picker."

"No picking yet. Oh, I left an instruction book in the pickup. Be right back."

When Denver entered the dining room kitchen again, Tess wasn't there. He found her in the kitchen, loading the dishwasher. "Too bad we didn't have one of these in Ohio."

Denver took a pair of snips from the junk drawer. "I'll put the new strings on and we can try the guitar out."

Rinsing a dish at the sink, Tess looked back at him. "Aren't you smart, knowing to snip the string ends after you tighten them?"

"Well, it's not solar engineering, but it's sort of mechanical."

Guitar strung, dishwasher humming, Tess joined Denver at the table and opened the instruction book. All right then, let's see if we can make a chord."

* * *

Showered and shaved and dressed in jeans and a pull-over shirt, Denver checked the salmon broiling in the oven. A light supper was a good idea after that huge lunch with Tess. He checked the asparagus sautéing in a pan, added some garlic and lemon juice, and moved the pan to a cool burner. Tess had insisted he take half of her birthday cake home, so that would be dessert.

Sitting at the table to wait, he glanced at his watch. Ten more minutes until Leah got here.

Funny how Tess hadn't mentioned her seventeenth birthday two weeks away, almost as if she didn't want to mention how they would be only a year away from their joke marriage date.

He checked his watch again. What guy was Eliza having supper with in Ohio? Some artsy-fartsy dude who had found out she was back home and wanted to hit on her? During their travels to art shows, she had mentioned men coming on to her when she was alone, but she had discounted them as overzealous art buyers. Still, Denver had seen a hand or two around her slender waist as they had walked with her to look at her latest paintings, and he didn't like it one bit. Huh. Like he had already told himself, two could play that game.

Hearing a car engine in the driveway, he went to open the front door—and considered closing it again as Tess took the guitar from the back seat of Oneita's car. "Hey, Denver," she said, coming toward him. "How about some guitar lessons?" She strode by him and went to the kitchen to raise the lid on the asparagus. "Mmm, aren't you sweet, cooking me supper." She opened the stove. "Broiled salmon, wow. We can have some of my cake for dessert."

Denver went to the kitchen. "Didn't I drop you off at your job at four?"

"You tell me, you were there."

"But how did you get here when I dropped you off?"

"My boss gave me a ride home and I walked here."

"Why would he do that?"

"I told him I didn't feel well."

Denver crossed his arms. "Some Amish chick you are, lying to him."

"I'm not lying. I didn't feel well because of what I saw you and Leah doing last night. Since I heard her tell you she was coming back tonight, I thought I'd see how round two was going." Tess waved a hand toward the stove. "That's who all that food is for and why you're dressed up, right?"

"I distinctly remember telling you she's none of your business."

"Bull. You're married to my sister. That damn well makes it my business."

"Don't curse."

"Don't *make* me curse. Don't you know you were going to do something you'd regret later?"

Denver went to counter and pulled a bar stool out to sit. Tess had a point. He was ready to throw his morals, not to mention his wedding vows, out the door. He checked his watch. "Leah's late. Wonder what's—" He glared at Tess. "What did you do?"

"Me? Why do you ask?"

"*Now* you go all shy Amish chick on me. C'mon, out with it."

Tess snickered. "You've got my number, don't you Denny?"

"Well?"

"I got Leah's number from your phone when you were busy one day."

"And?"

"I called her and told her all about Eliza and what happened with your daughter. She said— Wait a minute, let me get my tone right. 'Thanks for telling me, Tess. if I wanted man with *that* much baggage, I would date a garbage man."

Denver clenched his teeth to hold in laughter.

Tess dug her fingers into his sides. "C'mon now, let it out before you bust."

Shoving her away, Denver laughed so hard he thought his sides would split. Tess laughed too, holding her stomach. When they managed to stop, Denver shook his head. "Tess the mess, you *are* a mess." He kissed the top of her head. "There ya go, guardian angel. You saved me from doing something I never thought I would—breaking my wedding vows."

"Glad to do it, Denny."

"I already told you I'm not sure how I feel about that nickname, *Tessy*."

"Shut up and feed me supper, I'm hungry."

more lessons

Wednesday morning, Eliza carried an umbrella on her walk to the Allen family's home for their lessons. She could've driven, but she loved the gray aroma of the rain and the sound of gravel crunching beneath her shoes. Such things were simple, but simple things—especially now—were the best things, because they kept her mind off of Denver.

Although she had told him not to call, she had expected him to. Then again, he knew her ways, such as when she made up her mind to do something, he knew better than to tell her any differently.

As she walked the stone path to the front porch, Josh ran out with a larger umbrella and held it over her head. "There now, we can't have you catching cold. I wouldn't know what to do without you."

On the porch, Eliza shook rain from her umbrella and closed it. "And Anna and David too."

Josh closed the huge umbrella. "Especially David. Since you came the other day, he's done nothing but ask, 'When's 'Liza comin' back, Papa. She purty."

"He's talkative for two."

"Two and a half. Yes, he could talk an ear of corn off a stalk."

Eliza covered a giggle. "That's funny. I never heard that before."

Josh stared at her. "You certainly have a fine laugh. I'd give anything to hear Anna laugh."

"We didn't work on any words last time. Let's try some today."

Inside, as Eliza took some new books from her basket at the kitchen table, Anna came in the back door with a bowl of blueberries. An extremely bright woman, she had shown Eliza a leftover blueberry pancake during her first lesson, so the sign for that had been included. Josh had chuckled about it, saying how blueberry pancakes were his and David's favorite breakfast, plus how the previous owner of this farm had planted several bushes at the edge of the back yard behind the chicken coop.

As that first lesson had progressed, he had also told her how he was thirty-five and Anna was thirty. They had moved here from an Amish community to the north, about a day's buggy ride away. His father had died from cancer, and it had almost made Josh leave the Amish, because his father might've gone to the doctor earlier and caught it before it had spread otherwise. His mother *had* left the Amish. Although Josh was supposed to shun her, he would get a neighbor to drive him there to see how she was doing, buying baskets for Anna to use as patterns as a way to do so. His mother hated the split. She loved David and Anna as well as her son, and would sometimes cry over how they couldn't visit like normal people, but she couldn't get over how she blamed the Amish for her husband's death. Josh said he had come to terms with it. After all, many Amish did get medical care when needed. He had also said his father was like many men, stubborn about going to a doctor, and that would've contributed to his death as much as being Amish.

Anna put the bowl on the table near Eliza, popped a few blueberries into her mouth, and nodded to Eliza to do the same. Eliza signed, "Thank you" and tried the blueberries, a mix of sweet and tart tastes. Anna put the bowl in the

132

refrigerator and left for the backyard, where Josh had gone to get David. He was on his hands and knees by the chicken coop, drawing in a patch of dirt with a stick. Josh was kneeling beside him, pointing at the ground and grinning. He certainly loved his family, one of the finer Amish traits.

During a break in their first lesson, Josh had also told Eliza how Anna's parents were old-order Amish, strict and firm in their ordnung, even to the point of denying Anna treatment for her mumps as a child, which had led to her deafness. Like Eliza, since Anna was deaf, her parents had kept her from school to do farm work.

Josh and David came in. Anna shook her head and pointed at David's dirty knees. Josh took him outside to brush them off, visible beside the screened door. Smiling, Anna faced Eliza and raised her hands. "My two children."

Anna's perfect signs surprised Eliza. Josh must've taught her more than he had let on, although talking signs were different from object signs. Eliza raised her hands toward Anna. "How many signs you know?"

Anna took a small book from the pocket of her apron and gave it to Eliza. "All these."

Eliza thumbed through the pages. The signs in it were equivalent to two years of classes in many sign language schools. She returned the book. Anna put it in her pocket. "I am quiet with signs. I like watching my husband teach my son."

"He wants to know if you can learn to talk. Do you remember any words from before you were deaf?"

Anna tilted her head to one side. "Too many words."

Eliza signed again, using the minimum number of signs to communicate the meaning."

The screened door squeaked. Josh and David came in. "I see you signing. Did you start the lessons without us?"

Eliza faced him. "You didn't tell me about Anna's book."

"She looks at it a lot, why?"

"She knows all the signs in it. She's very accomplished, Josh, and you didn't know it."

A hint of pink tinted Josh's cheeks. "Are you saying she knows more than me?"

"No, I'm saying your wife is a wonderful and intelligent woman. You should be proud."

Josh rubbed his forehead. "I suppose she learned those signs while I worked outside. Have you—"

David tugged Josh's pants leg. "Papa, I want some water."

Josh got him water. "Go to your room and play with that wooden truck I carved you."

"But I wanna stay."

"Do like I say," Josh said, nudging David toward the living room. Josh came back. "Have you tried any words with Anna yet?"

"I was asking her when you came in." Eliza sat at the table and patted the chair beside her. Josh sat. "Josh, I meant for Anna to sit there."

"Oh." He moved to the other side of the table. "I can watch from here better anyway."

Anna sat, and Eliza asked her what words she might remember from her childhood. Slowly, haltingly, Anna said, "Dod … goad … hoss … baba … mama."

Josh frowned. "She never told me she knew those words."

"Did you ever ask her?" Eliza said, cutting the air with her signs.

"How could I?"

"I'm sorry, that's true." She faced Anna again. "Do you ever laugh?"

Anna tilted her head again. "Do not know sign."

Eliza smiled, patted her knee, and held her stomach, laughing without making any sound. Anna nodded.

"Sometimes, when David is funny."

"Why doesn't she laugh when I'm around?" Josh said. "We have fun together."

When Eliza first started talking after so many years of silence, she didn't care for how she sounded, like, as Ethan had said, she had a mouthful of oatmeal. Speech therapy and hearing aids helped, but if she didn't practice, sometimes to the point of Denver asking her to stop because it would scare the fish, her words got mushy in her mouth again. Luckily for them both, he enjoyed her laughter, which sounded low in her throat, almost like she was choking. Given the last year and a half, she hadn't had the chance to laugh at all.

Josh touched her arm. "Well?"

"She's probably embarrassed by how she sounds."

"Well, try now. I want to hear her laugh."

Eliza didn't like his demanding tone. She faced Anna regardless. During one of the recent lessons, she had taught Anna how she could use a letter for her name, and she had decided on A. "Anna, Josh wants to hear you laugh."

Anna shrugged. "Nothing funny."

Josh left and came back with David. Grinning like a loving father, he took him into his arms and tickled him until David burst out laughing. Anna shyly covered her mouth, allowing a low chuckle escape her throat. Josh jumped up to grab her arms and twirl her around. "Let's dance, Anna. That'll make you laugh." Anna did exactly that, throwing back her head, her laughter growing louder with each twirl.

Beads of sweat popped on Anna's forehead. She let go of Josh's hand and kissed him, cheeks turning red. Josh kissed her back. "I love you, Anna. More than I can say."

David tugged Anna's dress. "Twirl me, Mama."

Fanning her face, Anna got water for her and Josh and sat beside Eliza, while Josh returned to his seat. "What a fine day. My two favorite ladies in the world have given me a miracle."

David ran away and came back with his water. He put it on the table and climbed into Eliza's lap. "'Liza," he said looking up at her, "can you be my Mama too?"

Eliza hugged him. "No, you monkey. We can be friends like we are now, how's that?" His hair smelled of fresh air and sunshine, like her daughter's would have if—

She put David down and went to the living room to not cry in front of the Allens. What a treasure her daughter would've been if she had lived.

A hand touched her shoulder—Josh's hand. She went outside to the front porch. The drizzling rain trapped her there. Josh came out behind her. "What's wrong, Eliza? I've never seen you cry?"

She turned away. "It's … I can't talk about it."

"I hate to see you this way." His hands circled her waist. His cheek touched hers. "Please don't cry."

A vehicle engine's noise came from the opposite direction. She didn't want anyone seeing Josh holding her and getting the wrong idea. She pulled his hands from around her and stepped away, wiping her eyes. "I miss my family in Clarksville, that's all."

"That's not something you can talk about?"

"Maybe another time. I need to leave."

Josh went inside for her basket and umbrella. "We'll work on the new books until next time. I hope you feel better."

Eliza opened the umbrella and walked into the rain.

She had no idea when she would ever feel better.
If ever.

guitars

Thursday afternoon, Denver parked at Absalom's house. Tess climbed from the pickup while he got his new guitar, bought from a shop in Henderson, North Carolina, and followed her into the house. Inside, she got her guitar and brought it to the living room. A laptop sat on a coffee table, where her and Denver had been learning chords from both the internet and the book he had bought with her guitar. She left the guitar on the sofa and looked at her fingertips. "Well durn, I'm getting callouses."

"Me too," Denver said. "No work, no reward." With the guitar case across his lap as he sat on the sofa, he unlatched it and took the guitar out. "This is okay, but when you get your skills down, I'll pay you to build me a nicer one."

"It'll do for learning. Maybe I should experiment on you for my first guitar build. I won't charge much."

"Since I don't know when Eliza's coming back, I might have time to help with it. Then you can charge half."

Tess took a pillow from the sofa and faked throwing it at him. "Typical man. Doesn't appreciate a woman's work."

Denver set the case on the floor beside him. "You know I'm messing with you."

"What if we messed around in Papa's shop and checked out all that stuff we ordered?"

Denver ignored Tess's teasing about messing around. "Have you heard from either him or your mama since they left? Tomorrow's two weeks, and they should be on the way back."

Tess dropped the pillow on the sofa. "Didn't they say something about seeing Mount Rushmore and making a circle to the Great Lakes?"

"True." Denver stood. "Let's check out that guitar stuff like you said."

In Absalom's shop, Tess opened two reinforced cardboard crates and took out three flat cartons about a foot wide and three feet long. "This is what I want to see."

She gave one to Denver; he set it on a workbench. "Is this the wood?"

"Can't you smell it?"

"That could be the sawdust in here."

She came over with the other two cartons and used a knife from a tool board to open one. "No way. This is an entirely different smell." She took a piece of thin wood out, dark and streaked with grain, and sniffed it. "Mmm, it smells like oak but more intense." She held it toward Denver. "See?"

He sniffed the wood. "You're right. The inside of the guitar I bought you smelled like that—aged and stinky like you." Grinning, he took the wood from her and wacked her bottom with it. "You deserve a spanking for teasing me and telling Leah about Eliza."

Tess jerked the wood from him. "Saved your behind from sleeping with her, didn't I?"

"I guess."

She put the wood on the workbench. "Can I ask you something?"

"Sure."

"When's the last time you and Eliza slept together?"

Denver didn't know whether to be surprised about Tess asking about his and Eliza's sex life or not. Still, they had gotten close the last two weeks and he didn't mind. "About six weeks before …"

"Before you two lost your daughter."

"Yeah."

"I guess you miss sex or you wouldn't have almost slept with Leah."

"You could say that," Denver said, a sad tone slipping into his voice. "I was gonna drive out to the cemetery the other day and thought you might like to go. Wanna go now?"

"Can I drive? I need the practice."

He took his keys from his pocket and tossed them to her. "All right. I get a chauffeur."

In the pickup, she adjusted the seat and the mirror. "You and your long legs." She turned the key and steered into the road. "Sweet. Does it have four-wheel-drive?"

"Yeah, not that I use it much."

They left the subdivision and continued until Tess turned into the narrow country road leading to the cemetery. They passed a few houses here and there, drove through the creek bottom and over the small bridge. Oaks, maples, and hickory trees lined the road but opened onto farm land during the drive.

Nearing a sharp right curve, Tess pointed. "I didn't know we have a winery this close."

"Well," Denver said, turning her way, "you probably didn't notice it during the funeral procession."

At the church, Tess pulled into the drive and parked. Headstones of all shapes and sizes nearly filled the cemetery, with space near the back for more. They got out and walked to the grave, set beside his mom's grave. He wanted it there because he planned to be buried beside her one day, and Eliza beside him. He stopped. Plans likely to never happen now.

Tess knelt to brush some leaves from the tiny grave. "I thought you would've put a headstone here by now."

Wind rustled the leaves of an oak grove behind the cemetery. A tractor roared past, several round bales of hay on a trailer.

Denver rubbed Mom and Dad's stone, cut from dark granite. "We had a lot going on. We never even—" Emotion filled his throat. "We never even named her."

Tess stood. She slipped her fingers into his and lay her head against his shoulder. "Remember when you and Eliza came to get her paintings to sell for her first show and Papa told her about losing their first daughter?"

Denver nodded. "I'll never forget that. Your mom apologized for how she treated Eliza most of her life. If your dad hadn't insisted on that talk, who knows if she and Eliza would've ever made up."

"He told Ethan and me about that before we moved here. He told us in the barn away from Mama because just talking about Lily's death made her cry.

"Lily was her name?"

"Lily Eliza Gray. Papa made Mama name Eliza Eliza because he wanted a small part of Lily with them always."

Tears seared Denver's eyes. He knew exactly how Absalom felt. "I love the name Lily. It's got a sweet and innocent sound to it."

"Me too." Tess let go of Denver's hand and turned to face him. She slipped her hands around his waist and held him tight, placing her head just below his chin. Soft sobs escaped her. Soft sobs escaped Denver.

The wind blew through the oaks again, warm and gentle, exactly like Tess. As much as he loved Eliza, if she never came home, could he find someone to love as much as he did her?

The question shocked him, because the answer was yes, in the wonderful young woman he now held within his arms. He rubbed a circle between her shoulder blades. Their sobs faded. "Tess?"

She pulled away to wipe her eyes. "I didn't mean to cry. I bet a look a sight."

Denver thumbed a tear from her cheek. "You look great."

Tess turned away. "Don't look at me like that."

"Why not?"

"It's how you used to look at Eliza."

"Is that so bad?" He placed his palm on the back of her neck, bare from a ponytail. Saying nothing, she reached up to hold his hand. Time fell away—time and worry and angst and pain—but it came back in a rush. Loving Tess was wrong in every way, the least of it being her age, not to mention how people would talk about him and her after the notoriety of being with Eliza in her art shows. Then there was the fact that Absalom would kill him, and Denver wouldn't blame him one bit, as he would do the same in his shoes.

Still holding his hand, Tess turned to face him. "I know I tease you a lot about us getting married and stuff, but I should stop."

"I love your teasing. It's kept me smiling when I could be depressed over Eliza leaving me." Denver kissed her forehead.

Tess took a few steps way. "Don't do that." Her cheeks flared red.

"I didn't mean anything by it."

She looked up at him, green eyes wet again. "I don't want to come between you and Eliza. If I—" She turned away, and Denver knew why. Despite all her teasing, she was falling in love with him. It showed in every minute they had spent together for the past two weeks, in how she covered him with a sheet and slept near him when he had drunk too much, in how she cooked for him, in how they laughed together, in how they shared so many things in common, like their love for the lake, their interest in guitars, and the complicated simplicity of his daughter's grave needing a headstone. Truth be told, he could love Tess too, and it wouldn't take much to push him over the edge of that complication.

He placed his hand on her shoulder and turned her around. "You mean a lot to me, okay? I don't think either of us wants to mess that up."

"You are so sweet."

"I'm just me."

"Don't."

"Don't what?"

"I already told you to not look at me like that."

"I can't change how I look at you."

Tess came close enough to place her palms on his chest. "Can I kiss you? I'll never ask again if you do." She stood on tiptoe to wait.

Inside Denver, his heart filled. Yes, he could love her as easy as diving naked off the dock to swim in the moonlight. What a life they could have together. She closed her eyes. He closed his. As the warmth of her breath joined his, a car horn blared and they jerked apart. Driving down the road, the minister waved.

Tess sputtered laughter. "Saved by the car horn, huh?"

"You're telling me," Denver said, grinning so hard his cheeks ached. "Maybe he thought we were getting emotional, but not exactly *how* we were getting emotional."

"Hope so. If it got out that I was trying to seduce my brother-in-law, Papa and Mama would kill you *and* me." Tess knelt to pat the tiny grave. "What if we name her Lily? It isn't like my bonehead sister is here to object."

"I like it." Denver knelt beside Tess and touched the metal grave marker the funeral home had left. "See you later, Lily. Daddy loves you."

"Sheesh, Denny, you're gonna make my cry again." Tess stood. "Let's get back and learn some more guitar chords. Those sounds you make will have us laughing again for sure."

During the drive back, Denver looked out the window but saw nothing. After falling in love with Eliza, he never expected to have feelings for anyone else, let alone serious feelings. Good thing the minister had stopped that kiss. If not, he and Tess might've played something besides guitar when they got home.

"Huh," Tess said, "pulling into the driveway. "Mama and Papa are back."

"Maybe they got homesick." Denver touched Tess's hand. "Here it comes, I've got to tell them about Eliza leaving."

As they started up the porch steps, Ivy ran out, red curls bouncing. "We're back, Tess! Did you miss me?"

Tess picked her up. "Hey, yourself. You have fun on the trip?"

"My seat hurt my butt."

"I bet it did," Denver said.

Oneita came into the living room from the kitchen. "I see someone bought some guitars." Her tone was flat instead of upbeat, as if something were bothering her. She went to the kitchen and came back with Absalom. "Well," he said. "I understand Eliza slipped off in the middle of the night and drove to Ohio."

Denver glanced at Tess and back to Absalom. "I thought about calling you but I didn't want to ruin your vacation."

"Ethan called us," Oneita said. "I just couldn't believe it."

"Come now," Absalom said. "Maybe she needed some time to herself."

"That's not what—"

"Tell me about your guitars," Absalom said, going to the sofa to sit."

Ivy climbed onto the sofa. "Can I try?"

Denver faced Oneita, whose lips made a hard, tight line. "Did you talk to Eliza? She left me a note saying not to call or go there."

Oneita's mouth fell open. "I'm sorry, Denver. If I could, I'd turn her over my knee like I used to. How she can be so ungrateful for having a man as good to her as you, I'll never know." She sat beside Absalom. "Isn't that right?"

He placed a guitar in his lap. "Show me a chord, Tess."

"How'd it go in Kansas, Papa?"

"It went well. We saw some old friends and went to the cemetery. Oneita and I cried, of course."

Denver took a chair across from Absalom's end of the sofa. "Tess and I just got back from visiting—" He looked up at Tess. "Oneita, would it bother you if I named my daughter after your daughter? Tess told me her name. I think it's beautiful."

Oneita covered mouth for one quick sob, then lowered her hand. "I'd love that, Denver." She got up and kissed his cheek. "Thank you for thinking of her."

"It was Tess's idea. We've spent a lot of time together while you were gone. If you haven't been to the shop yet, there's two big cartons of guitar building stuff out there."

Absalom and Oneita looked at each other. "You've spent a lot of time together?" he asked.

"Learning guitar and eating supper." Tess crossed her arms. "Do you expect us to not see each other for two weeks? After all, we *are* related."

"I'm glad," Oneita said, cutting her eyes toward Absalom. "You could do much worse than spend time with Denver." She went to Denver and kissed his cheek again. "You're a wonderful son-in-law, despite my ungrateful daughter. Want to stay for supper? We stopped by the grocery for a pack of chicken for the grill and greens for salads."

Denver checked his watch. "Sure. Then I won't have to go home and eat by myself."

He glanced at Tess, who was placing Absalom's finger on the guitar neck to make a G chord.

And he got to stay near someone who really cared about him, since Eliza didn't.

apology

Eliza left her room for the back porch. Rain had drizzled since Wednesday, and she had used it as an excuse to keep her away from the Allens and their lessons. She could've driven, but Thursday, when Josh had stopped by to ask, she told him she needed time to catch up on laundry.

The truth of the matter between her and Josh was how his holding her on his porch had made her as uncomfortable as her and Denver's near kiss on the night she had left Clarksville, and she didn't go back to teach his family any sooner because she wanted to give them time apart. When she looked back at her and Josh's time together, small things hinted at stronger feelings toward her than he should have, especially being a married man with a child.

On the back porch, she sat in one of Papa's rocking chairs and crossed her bare feet at the ankles. Or could she be imagining Josh's interest in her? He certainly adored Anna and David, so maybe the concern was overreaction.

Eliza breathed in the aroma of the crisp air, ushered in by a cool front after the rain, so the weather station on her phone had said. She rarely turned it on, not caring if Denver called or not.

Behind her, the screened door squeaked open and Ethan came out. "I enjoy the sign language classes, but I'm always ready for Saturday."

Eliza turned to look at him. "Going to town to find a wife?"

"You've got nerve, joking like that when you're here. You left Denver two weeks ago. Aren't you ready to go home yet?"

"Am I not welcome here?"

"It's Jon's school, not mine."

"What's he doing these days?"

"Don't change the subject."

"I'm not, I really would like to know."

"Jon's doing something you should be doing—painting and enjoying your family." Ethan sat in a rocking chair. "I called Papa and Mama and told them what you did."

"They were going to find out anyway." Eliza turned away.

Ethan tapped her shoulder. "Mama said, and I quote, 'that ungrateful daughter of mine doesn't know how fine a man she has in Denver. It would serve her right if he fell in love with someone else.'"

"Denver's an adult. He can do whatever he wants."

Ethan got out of the rocking chair to stand in front of Eliza. Like with Papa, tiny lines at the corners of his eyes betrayed anger, except Papa's lines were deeper. "I agree with Mama, I'm ashamed of you. When you fell in love with Denver, we moved to be near you, and you've left them too."

"I didn't ask them to move," Eliza hissed. "They did that on their own."

"Listen to you," Ethan said, his tone like Papa's would be if he were here. "You talk fine when you act like a spoiled brat."

In the past, when either Mama or someone had mistreated her, either about being deaf or housework done wrong, Eliza had gone to the river to escape. Time to do that before she punched her brother in the nose and kneed him in the crotch like she did Timothy's brother, Hannes, which, along with the measles and her deafness, had set her on a path she could've never foreseen. Now she was married to a man she might not love, let alone care for, and she didn't know what to do about it.

Without a word or a sign, she got up from the chair, took her hearing aids out, and left for the path to the river. She could imagine Ethan glaring at her back, possibly yelling despite the hearing aids in her hand. He could glare and yell until he ran out of breath. She would leave and find somewhere else to go if he kept treating her like a child instead of an older sister who deserved understanding.

Over the path, oak, hickory, and maple limbs joined like fingers slipping into each other. The thick foliage, lush and green, catching and shining what sunlight penetrated the woods, created a shadowed tunnel. Leaves from last year's autumn surrounded tree trunks with a carpet of dingy brown.

Eliza stopped to put the hearing aids in her pocket and raise a handful of leaves to her nose. Water from the rain combined with dirt from the ground to smell rich and earthy. How many times had she done this as a child, one who spent hours here and at the river to escape the trials of being a deaf Amish child? The number would take more fingers to count than on the hands of her loved ones. She dropped the leaves, brushed dirt from her hands, and continued along the path.

When she reached the rolling water, somewhat swollen from the rain, she stopped at the bank instead of dipping a toe in. She had last been here with Denver, shortly after she became pregnant and—

What else had they done that day besides check the solar system he had designed for the house and have lunch with Ethan and Timothy? Eliza tapped her chin with a fingertip. Did they see Jon? No. Did they see Vernon and Abigail at their basket stand? No. Did they—?

The dark tunnel in the woods beckoned her, then a dream of love, now a nightmare of doubt.

She had taken a blanket to the woods while Denver was working and had led him there to make love to him. Although she could remember that, the memory of their kisses and caresses and joining drifted within her mind like the ghost of—

Eliza shoved tears from her eyes with the palms of her hands. Hard cheekbones. Wet skin, cool from the moisture. Yes, she was an icy star, insulated from the warmth of Denver's love. She should drive to town and see an attorney about drawing up divorce papers and be done with it. Then she could get on with her life, shunned by her family who was ashamed of her for leaving the man she once loved, who she was now unable to love.

The irony of the situation struck her, yet she turned from it as if it were the pain of knowing she would never make love to another man for as long as she lived, because Denver had stolen the last remnants of her desire like—

No, no one had stolen her daughter. Not God or, as she called the deity who created the whole of Nature, the Creator. If she gave into doubt, any hopes she had of being happy again would fall from her heart like snow during an Ohio winter.

She took the hearing aids from her pocket, placed them into her ears, and closed her eyes.

The breeze in the branches. The river whispering near her feet. Birdsong in the woods. The *crunch-crunch, crunch-crunch* of a squirrel bounding in the leaves.

"Hey, 'Liza."

Eliza opened her eyes and faced the path. Josh and David stopped beside her. Josh carried fishing poles and a tackle box. David carried a crooked limb over his shoulder as if it were a pretend fishing pole. Leave it to this cute little boy to make her smile in the middle of all her worry about her future.

Josh touched the brim of his wide-brimmed straw hat. "I'm glad to see some sunshine. This boy has worried me to death about going fishing."

David narrowed his eyes. "Who die, Papa?"

"No one, Son. It's just an expression."

"Spression?"

"Something that has a different meaning that what it sounds like."

David faced Eliza. "Who die, 'Liza?"

Eliza knelt to look him in the eye. "Like your papa said, no one died." She touched the limb over his shoulder. "I like your fishing pole."

He offered it to her. "You have it. Papa got two."

Eliza took the limb. "Aren't you sweet?"

David nodded hard enough to lose his straw hat. "Mama say I fweet."

Josh chuckled. "He mixes up S and F sometimes." He gave David one of the poles and pointed. "See that log? Take your pole there and sit and wait for a me a minute. Can you do that for me?"

David nodded again. Josh brushed dirt off the straw hat and put it on his son's head. "That's a good boy. I'll be there in a minute."

As David reached the log, Josh faced Eliza. "I want to apologize about putting my arms around you the other day. If I made you uncomfortable, I didn't mean to. I'm just grateful for you bringing Anna out of her shell about talking and laughing. She's remembering more words from before she went deaf too."

Eliza didn't know what to think about Josh's apology. It made sense, but when he held her that day, she sensed something other than gratitude. "Please don't let it happen again. I don't want people to get the wrong idea about why I'm going to your house."

Josh looked down and back up. "If I remember correctly, you haven't mentioned your husband since you've been here. I asked Ethan, he said it was personal."

"It is."

"I'm not trying to pry, but everyone around here knows how you met and how you paint. Did your artwork interfere with you having children? No one ever mentions you having any."

As much as Eliza hated to talk about this subject, she wanted to get it over with. "My daughter was stillborn a year and a half ago. It strained our marriage, and I wanted to come home for a while."

"But you're not separated or divorced ..."

"Not at all."

"Will you go back?"

"You've passed the point of what I want to tell you, Josh."

He looked around her toward David, who had found another limb and was shaking it at the river as if he were casting a line. "I'm an only child. Anna's parents were killed when a wheel came off their buggy and it tipped them over into the path of a car. With help from the Amish near where she lived, she raised a garden and learned how to make baskets to sell for things like flour and milk."

"I'm sorry to hear about her parent's," Eliza said. "How old was she then?"

"Twenty. I told you how no men ever courted her because of her deafness."

Eliza had no idea why he was telling her these things, but Anna's history interested her. "Does she have any other relatives close by?"

"Her parents moved here when they were young. If any relatives are near, no one has ever mentioned them."

"Do you have any other relatives besides your mother?"

"No, and she's in poor health. Except for Anna and David, I'll be all alone soon." Josh picked up a rock and threw it in the river. "You might wonder why I'm telling you all this."

"Yes, I was."

"My point is if you feel alone, you're strong enough to handle it like Anna did." Josh shared a slight grin. "Although if something happened to her, they might as well dig a grave beside hers for me. I'd be lost without her."

Eliza started to touch his arm but didn't. Just the thought of touching a man repulsed her. "But you'd still have David."

Josh smiled fully. "I was only joking."

"What's Anna doing?"

"Picking more blueberries. I bought a recipe book in town the other day. She's got the pages with blueberry desserts dog-eared."

"She can read?"

"Not long after we were married, I got out all the measuring cups and spoons and showed her the words for them in a cookbook. I did the same for numbers and fractions, like half a teaspoon. Between that and her cooking experience with her mama, she can make most anything she wants in the kitchen."

"You're a very loving husband, Josh."

"Anna makes it easy, Eliza." He nodded toward David. "Would you like to fish with us? You can use my pole while I watch. Anna doesn't like fish slime on her hands and how it smells."

"You go ahead. I'm just here to enjoy the day."

Josh left to Join David. They followed the river bank to where a huge log lay in the water, creating a calm spot. Josh took a can from the tackle box, baited their hooks with what was likely worms, and cast them into the water. As the red and white corks floated in the calm water behind the log, they sat on the end laying across the bank. David waved at Eliza and she waved back, then left for the path.

Strolling along to enjoy the sun dappling the leaves beside her, she stopped at a white stone beside the path. She had placed the stone here to mark the place to go into the woods, where she and Denver had made love. Picking her way through the thick foliage brushing her arms, she found the spot where she had left the blanket: a small clearing where a tree had died and fallen, leaving a sunny spot that day so she could see Denver's features clearly as they undressed, kissed, caressed, and finally, had joined with their familiar rhythm. She loved his kisses, loved the way he could make her feel, as if they were one beating heart. Heat surged within her at the thought of their joined bodies, slick with sweat, heaving with completion.

Eliza touched her lips. Could her time away from Denver have eased her anxiety about them making love? On the nights after she had first arrived here, just the thought of him touching her had filled her throat with the urge to vomit, like it had on the night she left when she attempted to see if she could make love to him.

The possibility filled her chest with anticipation. Still, she needed to be patient and see if she felt differently.

On the path again, as the sun dappled her with light, she touched her lips again and prayed to the Creator to give her a sign, one that might end her troubles and send her home to Denver and the family who loved her.

fireworks

Lakefest Saturday. Hot and humid. Main street blocked for traffic. Craft and food vendors setup in parking spaces. People filling the street.

Denver took a deep breath. Grilled chicken. Roasted turkey legs. Popcorn. French fries. Worn out deodorant. Faded aftershave and perfume.

"Hey, Denver!"

He turned to look for the voice's owner. Taking an ice cream cone from a vendor, Leah waved. Not looking forward to her asking about Eliza and their troubles, he turned as if he hadn't seen her.

"Want some ice cream?"

Denver turned around. "Oh, hey."

"I've been hoping you'd call me."

Bring up what Tess had said or not? "I thought you didn't like baggage?"

"I thought about it for a while and decided to take the chance."

"What about all that with my wife?"

"Is she back yet?"

"No."

"Do you expect her anytime soon?"

"No."

Leah licked ice cream from the cone and raised it toward Denver. "Want some? I don't have germs."

He took a step back. "Look, Leah, as much as I appreciate your interest, I'm still married, and I don't want to do anything I'll regret."

"We could start out as friends. If it doesn't work out with your wife, we could be more than friends."

"I don't know how long that might be."

Leah licked ice cream again. "I'm not patient with melting ice cream, but I can be patient with you. I didn't keep a crush on you all these years to just give up."

Denver noticed some people watching him and Leah. He and Eliza were well known in Clarksville. "Let's walk while we talk. It's hot in this crowd."

Leah pointed. "How about the shade from that tree?" She left for the shade, Denver beside her. Although no breeze blew through Clarksville, the shade was better than standing in the sun.

Leah offered him the cone. "Go on and have some. You know you want to."

He licked ice cream and returned the cone. "A little subtext in what you just said?"

"You have no idea. I wanted you that night. I mean I *really* wanted you."

Sweat trickled into the hollow of Denver's back. "Well, I have to admit I wanted you too."

"Like I couldn't tell. I asked around town about you and your wife. I wanted to verify what Tess told me."

"My sister-in-law should've minded her own business."

"I'm sorry about your daughter. I can't imagine what you and your wife went through."

Denver scanned the crowd. Tess had said she was coming downtown with the family. Absalom had mentioned renting a pontoon boat to watch the fireworks from tonight. Since that was the case, why not do the same from his pontoon boat with some company? He gave up looking for Tess's auburn hair in the sea of blonde, brunettes, and darker shades and returned to Leah, who frowned. "Looking for Tess? Whether you know it or not, that girl's got a thing for you."

"Naa, we just hang out a lot. Her dad makes rocking chairs and she's getting into building guitars. We're going to start making one after all the Lakefest stuff is over."

"Do you play? I love guitar music."

"We're learning that together too."

Leah's melting ice cream ran down the cone. She licked it. "You two have an awful lot in common."

Denver leaned toward her for more ice cream. Either that or sweat to death. "Hey, we don't choose our in-laws. Still, she's fun to hang out with. What do you think about going out on my pontoon boat to see the fireworks tonight?"

"Something I always wanted to do. Any chance we can make some fireworks of our own?"

"What happened to being patient?"

"I can be patient and tease. What time?"

"Come around eight-thirty. That'll give us time to cruise up to the bridges and get a good spot."

"Eight-thirty it is."

As Leah left, Denver rubbed his chin. Short shorts. Killer figure. Cuter than cute. Better carry an extra dose of willpower during the fireworks tonight, or he and Leah might end up back on the sofa.

* * *

At seven, Denver heated some grilled chicken and cabbage he had bought from a vendor. He had also run by the grocery for some beer. Nothing wrong with a cool brew with supper. Sitting on the bench on the dock, he enjoyed his meal as early fireworks watchers cruised up the lake toward the bridges in pontoon boats, ski boats, fishing boats, and houseboats.

He glanced at the window where Eliza used to sit. Almost a month and not a word from her. He would've never believed that before they lost their daughter. Well, it was her life to do with as she saw fit. If she didn't want him, that was that.

Finishing his meal, he turned to the sound of gravel crunching in the path to the dock. "Hey, Denver." Tess sat beside him. "You didn't save me any?"

He offered her the empty plate. "You can lick it if you want."

She shoved the plate back. "We already ate. Are you going out to watch the fireworks?"

"You aren't working at the restaurant?"

"I asked off."

Not wanting to give away his plans with Leah, Denver had no choice but to lie. "I'm too tired from walking that hot street today."

"I looked for you. When do you want to start working on a guitar?"

"Playing or building?"

"Both."

"How about Monday? That'll give us a month and a half until you go back to school in September. Are you looking forward to your senior year?"

"I'm not going back."

Denver could hardly believe it. "What about your prom and college?"

"I told you how I'm going into business with Papa. His foot stools are selling well, and he's thinking about building a line of outdoor furniture. The people who come by to pick their stuff up love his Amish craftsmanship. He says it's a good selling point."

"What about driver's ed? You want to drive, right?"

"I'm not in a hurry. I'll get my license in a year when I turn eighteen."

"I'm sorry I missed your birthday."

"I didn't mind, we did the family thing. When you didn't come by or call after we almost kissed at the cemetery, I thought it might be better to not see each other for a while."

A huge deckboat, similar to a pontoon boat but with a fiberglass bottom, cruised by. At least ten people crowded it.

Denver didn't know what to make of the change in Tess—more adult without her teasing. He missed the old Tess, but maybe she was trying to keep her feelings for him in check.

She looked at him. Green eyes. Auburn hair framing her heart-shaped face. Full lips with a hint of pink lipstick. Green blouse unbuttoned to her cleavage. One year until she turned eighteen. If Eliza never came back, what then? Divorce her and marry her sister? If Tess would have him, and if Absalom and Oneita approved, he could see spending the rest of his life with this amazing young woman.

But as the thought hit him, the pain of losing Eliza hit him also. No, he had sworn to never cry over her again.

Tess stood from the bench. Without a word she held his head to her chest. He wrapped his arms around her and cried for all the loss he and Eliza had suffered, cried for their daughter, cried for the man he had become during his wife's absence—a man on the verge of alcoholism, a man who was falling for his sister-in-law, now seventeen.

He pulled away from Tess and wiped his eyes. "Tess, I—"

She kissed his forehead. "Shh, I would hate myself if you and Eliza didn't get back together because of me." She palmed his cheek. "I could love you so easy, Denver, and I don't mean love from physical attraction either." Grinning, she tapped his nose. "Although that has it's perks."

Denver shared her grin. "Tess the Mess. What would I do without you?"

"Want to come with us to watch the fireworks?"

"What about not seeing each other for a while?"

"Dumb, huh? We can't build our guitar if we do that."

"Or learn how to play either."

"You got it. Let me get home. Papa parked the pontoon boat at the community dock, and we've got to get up the lake for a good spot."

Tess left, and Denver faced the lake. She was right about spending time apart to give their feelings a break after their near kiss at the cemetery. Sure, they needed to be together to build a guitar and learn how to play, but he needed to get his mind off of her some other way, and that way could be with Leah.

He took his plate to the kitchen to wash and returned to the pontoon boat. Tanks filled with gas. Lifejackets in their compartments. Red and green running lights on the bow and white on the rear working. Cooler filled with ice and water. Beer or wine would be great, but state law prohibited drinking and driving on the lake like on the roads.

On his way back to the house to wait for Leah, he heard a car engine turn off. Better not be Tess, like when she had supposedly forgotten her keys.

Wearing powder-blue shorts and a yellow blouse, Leah rounded the corner of the house. "I thought you might be back here."

Denver kissed her cheek. "You look great."

Leah returned the kiss. "You too. You love cargo shorts, don't you? You've been wearing them every time I see you."

"Hey, I'm the outdoorsy type." A bass boat zoomed up the lake. "Ready to go?"

"Sure. I remember the boats from last time I was here. They practically fill the lake."

Minutes later they were cruising toward the bridges. Unlike the first time Denver took Eliza there, he and Leah were early enough to find a spot between the bridges for a good view. He killed the engine and dropped the anchor. Opposite him, Leah raised her tanned legs and lay back on the long seat. "Wow, I could get used to this."

On the business bridge, workers checked the canisters where the fireworks would get the electrical signal to fire. To the west, the sun sank lower, coloring distant clouds orange that intensified to red. The sight usually calmed him, but since he had shared many a lake sunset with Eliza, it saddened him. The sooner the fireworks were over the better. Eliza had abandoned him for an entire month without so much as a word or a phone call. When he got Leah back home, he was sure she would suggest something that would lead to kissing on the sofa and he was ready—*more* than ready.

Behind him, a boat idled into place, evidenced by a gurgling exhaust and the *plunk* of the anchor hitting the water.

"Well, well, look who we found, Oneita."

Denver whirled. Absalom, standing in the front of a pontoon boat, waved. In the back, Oneita and Ivy waved also. In a seat like where Leah sat, opposite the driver console, Tess waved as well. "Small world, huh?"

"I don't believe it," Leah grumbled. "We can't get a break."

Oneita joined Absalom. "Who's this young lady, Denver?"

"She's a friend from high school."

Leah lazily flopped a hand toward Oneita. "I'm Leah." She faced Denver, lips a tight line, and whispered, "I hope your in-laws don't follow us back to your place after the fireworks. Tess told me they live near you."

Denver rubbed his cheek to cover his mouth. "Don't worry, they won't."

The sun dropped below the clouds. "Mama," Ivy whined, "I don't like the dark." She ran from Oneita to the front of the boat. "Denver, can you hold me?"

Absalom threw a rope. "Pull us together and we'll tie up."

Denver didn't care to act like a jerk, so he did as Absalom said. "All right, doodlebug, come on over."

Absalom picked her up and gave her to Denver. "She misses you since you haven't come over lately."

Denver returned to his seat. Ivy hugged his neck and kissed his check. "Can I spend the night wif you?"

Leah turned toward the bridge. "I cannot believe this." Like before, she kept her voice to a low grumble.

"Not tonight," Denver told Ivy.

"Then when? I want to swim at the dock."

"Another time, okay?"

Ivy pointed. "What's that fire?"

Denver faced the bridge. "That's the fireworks."

The single rocket arced into the night sky on a trail of red. At its apex, it exploded loud enough to make Denver's ears ring.

"Noooo!" Ivy screamed, "I'm scared!"

Leah crossed her arms. "At least *someone's* getting held."

"Give her back to me," Absalom said, reaching over the boat railing.

Denver did so. "The noise won't hurt you, Ivy. Look," he said, pointing at more trails of fire. "Watch all the colors they make. These will be quieter."

The following fireworks exploded into brilliant balls of red, blue, or green sparks.

Ivy clapped. "Oh, they're pretty."

Tess came to the front of the boat and climbed over the railing to sit by Leah. "What's up?"

She glared at Denver. "Nothing. Not a thing." Crossing her arms, she faced the bridge. "I'm just watching these fireworks. They're about all the fireworks I'll see tonight."

Tess winked at Denver. "Any idea how we found you in all these boats?"

"I haven't thought about it, why?"

"I bought you a present at Lakefest today. I can't believe you haven't noticed it." Tess pointed over Denver's head. "Don't you like that flag with the big A on it for Andrews on the flagpole on the aluminum roof? One of the craft vendors had them."

Denver went to the front of the pontoon boat, out from under the roof. A huge red flag with a blue A stitched into it hung from the flagpole. "When did you put that there?"

"Before you got back home from Lakefest. Like it?"

He returned to the console. "Thanks. I think."

Leah faced Tess. "How thoughtful," she said, her tone icy.

Tess winked at Denver again. "That's me, Miss Thoughtful."

The fireworks ended. Tess climbed back over the railing to the other pontoon boat. "See y'all later."

Absalom pulled the anchor up. "Guess we'll cruise on back."

Oneita waved. "Nice to meet you, Leah. My son-in-law expects his wife home anytime now."

"Bye, Denver!" Ivy yelled.

Absalom cranked the engine and idled the boat away. When the running lights mixed with the rest of the other boats, which left the aroma of bitter gas exhaust, Denver faced Leah. "Sorry about that."

"They're nice, but too much of a good thing's still too much of a good thing." She paused. "If looks could kill, your mother-in-law would have me dead and buried by now."

Denver waited until the night quieted from all the boats whining into the darkness, and only his overhead lights illuminated the circle of lake around the boat. Then he pulled anchor, cranked the boat motor, and headed home.

Leah got up and sat beside him. "You were sweet with Ivy."

"I'm a sweet guy."

"This thing with your wife ..."

"What about it?"

"I know we said we'd see each other as friends, but you know I want more than that."

Denver lowered the throttle into a slow idle. "Look, Leah, I have no idea what's gonna happen with my marriage. To be honest, I've gotten used to having someone around."

"So I'm just a fill in."

"No, I really do need a friend right now. Someone not a relative, know what I mean?"

"What if I want more than that when we get back to your place?"

Denver couldn't deny the attraction of sleeping with this cute woman. After all, that's what he had intended to do tonight, regardless of how he had just said he wanted Leah as a friend only. "Can we take it slow and see how it goes?"

Leah kissed his ear. "I didn't bring a swimsuit."

"I didn't know you wanted to swim."

"The point is" —Leah kissed his ear again— "I don't need a swimsuit."

Imaging the sight of Leah diving off the dock nude made Denver shove the throttle to full speed. He didn't need a swimsuit either.

At the dock, he tied the pontoon boat to its cleats. "There's some water in the cooler. I forgot all about it."

Leah hopped from the boat onto the dock, tanned legs shinning in the LED lights lining it. "Do you have any of that wine left? That'd be great after our swim."

"Sounds good, I'll get it."

"I'll come with you. The restroom's calling."

At the top of the steps, Denver opened the sliding glass doors and went to the kitchen. He pointed toward the far corner of the living room. "Bathroom's in that door, Leah." As he opened the fridge door for the wine, someone knocked on the front door. Not Tess again—she should be home by now. He opened the door. "Hey," Jan said, pushing by him. "Mind if I come in?" She turned the kitchen lights on. "Let's brighten it up in here. Looks like you're getting ready to cheat on Eliza." She nodded toward the sliver of light beneath the bathroom door. "Huh, I was joking, but that car out front and that light right there say I might be right."

The bathroom door opened. "Denver, who—"

Jan strode toward Leah. "Hi, I'm Jan, the woman Denver jilted for Eliza."

Leah ignored Jan. "Denver, who is this?"

Denver opened his mouth but nothing came out.

Jan got a bottle of water from the fridge. "I was out on the lake with friends to watch the fireworks and we didn't have anything to drink." She opened the bottle and swallowed water. "Oh wow, that hit the spot."

Leah tapped a sandal on the hardwood floor. "I cannot believe this."

"Believe it," Jan said.

Denver sat at the bar. What a night, one that wasn't going to end the way he wanted it to. "You could've gotten water on the drive to Raleigh, Jan."

She tipped the bottle toward Leah. "And miss telling Leah here how you'll never stop loving Eliza? No way."

Leah kissed Denver's cheek. "I don't believe a word of it. Call me when you know no one's coming over."

The door slammed behind her, and Jan laughed. "She's stubborn like me. Except for what I probably interrupted, is she good for anything else except sleeping with my ex who's married?"

Denver covered his eyes. It was almost as if all these interruptions with Leah were planned. He lowered his hand. "Are you going now?"

"I just got here." Jan emptied the bottle and put it in the trash. "Jon told me about Eliza leaving you."

"Who told Jon?"

"Duh, Denver, your brother-in-law told Jon. They do talk, you know."

She took Denver's hand and led him to the sofa. "Spill it. How can the marriage of two people who love each other as much as you and Eliza love each other fall apart?"

"How about we sleep together? It's not like we ever did."

"You don't mean that."

"No, I don't. You were at the funeral, so you know about our daughter. It's pretty much devastated us."

"Jon told me about everything—from Eliza staying at the cemetery to her stay at the mental health facility. If I had known about it then, I would've been here for you. You know that, right?"

Denver appreciated Jan's offer. Their breakup hadn't gone well, but they had eventually put it in the past. Jan had handled Eliza's shows as her agent and she had been great at it, gradually understanding how much he adored Eliza. "I know you would've been here for me."

"Good. Now, are you dating Leah or just sleeping with her?"

"I'm doing neither."

"Tell that to someone who kept you in a constant state of arousal while we dated."

"Well, I miss Eliza. We haven't been together since before Lily was born."

Jan's eyes softened. "That's a beautiful name."

"Tess thought of it."

"Yes, she told—" Jan started coughing.

Denver sat up straight. "Tess told you what?"

"That's not who I meant." Jan cleared her throat. "Sorry, had a tickle."

"Whatever. Who told you—"

"During one of the art shows when Absalom and Oneita came, she told me about Lily."

"Oh."

Jan yawned. "Mind if I stay over? I'm too sleepy to make that long drive back to Raleigh, and I'd like to visit the cemetery with you."

"Sure." Denver stood. He had put clean sheets on Eliza's bed, so Jan could sleep there. He showed her the way. "You might not believe it, but I'm glad you stopped by."

"Listen to you," Jan said, "as sweet as ever. Don't you worry about a thing. One way or another, we're gonna get you and Eliza back together."

In his room, Denver dropped to his bed. What a night. If Jan wasn't here, he could use a beer—or a dozen.

accident

On the morning after her walk to the river, Eliza woke to one of the best night's sleep she had ever had, which included several dreams.

Still in the hazy afterglow of the last one, she rolled over to see the sun filling the window with light.

Each dream had begun and ended with Denver: his smile, his blue eyes, his kind and gentle touch as they made love during the first days of their marriage. With each dream she could feel her aversion to his kisses drifting away. Now, with the sun filling her room, she felt whole again—whole enough to take a chance on love one more time.

She got up and took a quick shower, packed her suitcase and found Ethan sitting at the table in the kitchen, a cup of coffee before him. He looked up with bloodshot eyes. "Sometimes I envy you."

"What do you mean?"

"Since you answered me, you have your hearing aids in. Do you ever sleep with them in?"

"Not here, why?"

"I envied you last night because you didn't hear the ambulance picking up Anna."

"What?" Knees giving way, Eliza dropped into a chair. "What happened?"

"You showered and went to bed around nine—the ambulance came around 9:30 and stopped down the road, between Josh and his neighbor's place. I ran up there to see what was wrong. They were loading Anna into the ambulance. The neighbor said she had come to borrow flour for a blueberry cobbler for Josh and David. They know each other pretty well, so she did that from time to time."

"But what happened?"

"He was on his porch watching Anna walk down the road and one of those huge eighteen-wheeled milk tanker trucks hit her. She was wearing a dark blue dress. The driver said he never saw her, just heard a thump."

"Oh no, that's— Is she ..."

"Josh called this morning. The neighbor drove him and David to the hospital. Josh wants to know if you can take care of David for a while."

Eliza started to ask why Josh's mother couldn't take care of David, but she remembered him saying her health was bad. Those trucks went by often, on the way to a dairy a few miles down the road. She couldn't imagine one hitting a person. "How bad is Anna hurt?"

"She's got severe internal injuries and is in a coma from brain swelling. It was all Josh could do to tell me. Poor guy was crying like I never heard a man cry." Ethan sipped coffee. "I couldn't sleep because of it."

Eliza got cereal and milk. She would eat and unpack. She poured milk and sat, hardly tasting the cereal. How ironic that Josh had just told her how he wouldn't know what to do without Anna, and now he might find out.

Cereal done, she went upstairs where she had left her suitcase. How stupid to think her dreams of Denver had meant she was ready to go back to him. Death happened all the time. People lost loved ones all the time. Josh and David needed her more than her selfish husband did. She unpacked. Leaving her room, she almost bumped into Ethan, who was yawning. "I'm going to bed. Are you going to get David?"

"Do you mind if he stays here? Tess's old bed is still in my room."

"Not at all, but he might be more comfortable at home."

"We'll see, it depends on what Josh says. How do I get to the hospital?"

"It's the Holmes County hospital. You can find it on your phone." Ethan yawned again. "Want me to take you?"

Eliza rubbed his shoulder. "We don't need any more accidents."

"True. Wake me up when you get back."

Eliza found the hospital on her phone. Fifteen minutes later she had parked and was on her way to the main entrance, where she asked the directions to intensive care. As she neared it, she passed a waiting room, saw Josh and David inside, and went in. David was asleep on a sofa. Josh sat with his son's head in his lap, fingers slipping through his hair with his eyes closed. On an end table at the end of the sofa, a pile of balled up tissues showed how Josh had been crying like Ethan had said. She touched Josh's arm. He opened his eyes. "Eliza."

David sat up. "'Liza," he wailed, holding his arms out.

Eliza picked him up and sat to rub his back. "How bad is Anna, Josh?"

"They operated to stop the internal bleeding. They just took her in again to relieve the pressure on her brain."

"I'm so sorry this happened." Eliza considered asking about Anna's chances but didn't. No need in speculating about that and upsetting Josh even more.

He leaned forward to place his elbows on his knees and hold his head. "I wish I had left the Amish when my mama did. My Papa died because he didn't go to the doctor when he started getting sick from his cancer. Anna is deaf because of mumps, something a simple vaccine could've stopped. Now she's in here because she couldn't hear that truck coming behind her." He raised up to look Eliza in her eyes. "And you lost your hearing because of measles. Don't you hate the Amish?"

"I try not to hate anyone. People make choices. Those choices lead to more choices we have to deal with. Anna didn't get hurt because she's Amish. She got hurt because the driver couldn't see her walking when it was almost dark."

"Doesn't matter now. My bishop came by earlier and I told him to take his Amish lies and go to he—"

"Hush," Eliza said, using the harshest tone she could manage. "David doesn't need to hear that kind of talk. Anna is important now, not your anger."

David raised his head from Eliza's chest. "Where's Mama? I'm hungry."

Covering his ear, Eliza pressed his head to her chest, and whispered, "Josh, you haven't told him about Anna?"

"He's tired. I told him she was hurt but she'd be better soon. Will you take him home for me? I can't—" Josh swallowed. "I don't know how long I'll be here."

"Can he stay with Ethan and me? We have room."

"No," David whined. "Wanna go home."

"All his toys and books are there," Josh said. "He's potty trained, so you don't need to worry about that."

"You want me to sleep there?" Eliza said, hardly believing it. "Can't your mother come and stay with him?"

"There's a room beside his. Besides, part of my mama's medical problems keep her in a wheelchair. She can't watch him like that." Josh placed his hand on Eliza's. "Please? I would do it for you. I need you. We all need you."

The pain in Josh's voice touched Eliza. He would come home in a day or so and it would work out. "I would be ashamed of myself if I didn't help your family, Josh." She stood with David. "Do you have a phone to let me know how Anna is?"

"My neighbor went back for an old phone of his and David's car seat for when you take him home. I really appreciate this. There's plenty of food that Anna canned and the freezer is full. If you need anything from the grocery, I'll pay you back."

"Do you mind if I take David out? I don't care to stay there all the time."

"I understand. I'm not ready to go back myself … you know, because it'll hurt to not have Anna there."

Eliza put David down. "Tell your papa bye. I'm going to take you home and stay with you for a while."

"Really?"

David's bright eyes and huge grin made Eliza grin as well. "That's right, really."

Josh went across the room to a chair and took a car seat from behind it. "I'll take this and show you how it works. They can be difficult if you've never had one. I bought it for when David stayed with my mama before she got sick."

At Eliza's car, he buckled David into the car seat. "Be a good boy for Eliza. I'll call you soon as I can."

"What 'bout Mama?"

"The doctors will fix her up. I told you already, remember?"

"Okay, Papa." David held his arms out to Josh, who hugged him and kissed his cheek. "I love you, Son."

Driving away, Eliza watched Josh watching her in the rear-view mirror. Yes, helping this family through this tragedy was much more important than her selfish husband.

gift

In his pickup on the way to the cemetery, Denver glanced at Jan. "Thanks for that veggie omelet. It was great."

"Not great enough to get you into bed the last time you came to my house. Then again, little did I know you were falling in love with Eliza."

"I'm glad we got through all that."

"Had to. You know how I love my commissions from acting as her agent and selling her art."

Denver turned left on the narrow country road to the church. "Met anyone special yet?"

"I *thought* that was you."

"I *thought* you were over me."

"For the most part. I still think you're the sweetest guy I ever met."

"Water under the bridge, Jan. Water under the bridge."

"I know, I know, but I'll always regret you." She looked out the window and back. "Regardless, I'll do whatever I can to help you and Eliza get back together. You two are perfect for each other."

Braking for the right-hand turn at the road to the winery, Denver glanced at Jan. "Too bad she doesn't know that."

"What if you talked to her?"

"She's a grown woman. She made her choice and now she has to live with it."

"Oh, please, Denver Andrews, don't use that excuse for wanting to sleep with Leah. You're still in love with Eliza and you know it."

At the cemetery, Denver parked in the driveway like before with Tess. As he and Jan got to Lily's grave, his mouth fell open.

"That's a beautiful headstone." Jan knelt to run her fingers along the pink granite, speckled with white. "I love the paint brush and palette and the canoe paddle to represent you and Eliza." She touched the letters inscribed into the stone. "Lily Andrews. We Love You, Sweetheart, And Always Will. Mommy and Daddy." Jan stood. "Why no date?"

"I …"

"What's wrong? You look like you're about to faint."

"I …" Denver's vision hazed. Jan's voice faded. He squatted before he *did* faint."

Jan knelt beside him and took hold of his arm. "Whoa, now, I got you. Deep breaths, okay?"

Denver took several deep breaths; his vision cleared and Jan's voice grew louder. "Jan, that headstone wasn't there when Tess and I came here two weeks ago."

Jan lifted his arm. "Can you stand."

Denver stood. "Yeah, I'm okay now."

"Do you think Eliza had the stone made?"

"If she did, she didn't tell me about—"

Jan grabbed his arm. "What? You're turning white again."

Denver said nothing. Let Jan think Eliza had the stone made, because he wanted to see who did and thank her.

He started toward his pickup, and Jan caught up. "Why the hurry?"

"I thought you'd like to get back to Raleigh."

"What about the stone?"

"I'm gonna call the funeral home to see who makes those stones and see if Eliza did it."

"It means a lot, don't you think?"

Denver got in the pickup, and Jan joined him on the other side. "Are you gonna answer me? You could go to Ohio and ask Eliza. I bet she'd love to see you."

Denver left the cemetery. "I'll think about it."

At home, he hugged Jan and thanked her for stopping by. She returned the hug, kissed him quickly, and told him again how she thought he was the sweetest guy she had ever met. Denver waved as she left. He didn't know about being the sweetest guy, but he knew who the sweetest woman was, and he was going to make sure she knew it right now.

Inside, he called Absalom's home number. After a few rings, Ivy picked up. "Hey, doodlebug. What's your sister doing?"

"She's making noise with her guitar."

"Can you give her the phone?"

"Okay."

"What's up, Denny? You're interrupting my practice."

"Since I missed your seventeenth birthday, I'd like to make up for it by taking you out to dinner."

"How about steaks here? Mama's thawing some for supper and we've got plenty."

"Just me and you, okay? I want to take you someplace special where you can wear that amazing green dress again."

"Sounds intriguing. How special?"

Denver paused. He'd never get away with his plan without asking Absalom and Oneita. "I better come over and ask. We won't get back until Friday around noon. I'd like to keep you longer but you need to get back in time for work."

"Are you nuts?" she whispered. "They won't let me spend the night with you."

"Just let me handle it. Be there in a few minutes."

Denver hopped in the pickup, squealed tires out of the driveway, and pulled into Absalom's driveway in record time.

Tess met him on the front porch. "Look, I thought about it. I appreciate whatever you want to do for me, but I'm not eighteen yet and you're still married to my sister. Mama and Papa will never let—"

Denver covered her mouth. "Let me handle it. Can you let me handle it? Believe me, I can handle it."

"Fine," Tess said, going to the door. "It's your face Papa's gonna smash, not mine."

She led him to the kitchen, where Oneita was washing a head of lettuce and Absalom was sharpening a butcher knife. Denver touched his throat. He better word this just right, or he might not live through the next few minutes.

Absalom fingered the knife blade, then shaved hair from his arm. "How'd you'd like a haircut, Denver?"

Oneita turned from the sink. "He looks handsome as always. How's that so-called friend of yours? Leah, right?"

"I guess she's okay. We haven't spoken since the fireworks."

"I should've taken a picture of you two kissing and shown it to Eliza to make her jealous and come home. That daughter of mine is—"

"Oneita," Absalom said, his voice stern, "you'll do no such thing. Denver's a fine young man. He wouldn't dare see someone romantically while he's still married to Eliza."

Tess cut her eyes at Denver. "Papa, Denver wants to ask you something."

Absalom was shaving arm hair again. "What's that?"

"Let me have the knife first." Tess held out her hand.

"What are you two up to?" Oneita said.

Denver took a deep breath. It was now or never. Maybe someone would make *him* a nice headstone.

"Go ahead," Absalom said. "He put the knife on the counter. "I'll leave this here in case I need it."

"I'd like to take Tess out for her birthday. I feel bad about missing it and—"

"*And* what?" The corners of Absalom's eyes deepened into intense chevrons. "You're still a married man and my daughter isn't eighteen yet."

"It's not like that, Absalom."

Oneita smacked Absalom's arm. "Hush. If Eliza doesn't want him, Tess might, and I'd like some grandchildren one day."

Tess's face reddened. "Mama!"

Ivy came in from the hall. "When's supper?" She faced Denver. "Hi, Denver. Want a steak?"

Denver picked her up. Time to try cute and innocent and see what happened. He kissed Ivy's cheek. "Hi, doodlebug. Maybe another time."

"See that?" Oneita said to Absalom. "Denver and Tess would make wonderful parents, not like that ungrateful daughter of mine."

Denver put Ivy down and knelt in front of Tess to take her hand. "My darling, Tess, I've loved you ever since we met, when you were thirteen and I was twenty-two. Will you marry me?"

Absalom slapped his leg and roared with laughter. "I always enjoyed you and Eliza teasing each other. What do you want to do with Tess?"

Tess jerked her hand from Denver. "You people have lost your minds."

Denver put his arm around her shoulders. "Absalom, Oneita, despite my joking, Tess means a lot to me. She kept me from going crazy when Eliza left and while you were on your trip. A friend of mine has a plane parked at the airport. He flew Eliza and me to some of her art shows and said to call whenever I needed him again. I want to take Tess to the mountains, to a cabin where Eliza and I stayed one weekend. It's a great place for hiking and the views. I'll have her back in time for her job Friday."

Absalom's eyes chevroned again. "I agree with Tess—you *have* lost your mind."

Oneita shoved his arm. "Don't you trust our daughter? I'm sure the cabin has plenty of bedrooms."

"It does," Denver said. "It's on the side of a mountain and the view is great."

"It sounds very nice," Oneita said. "When do you want to leave?"

Tess crossed her arms. "Don't I get a say in this?"

"Sure," Denver said. "Just say yes."

She grabbed his arm. "Let me talk to this knothead a minute."

"Go ahead," Oneita said. "But If you don't want to go, I will."

Denver and Tess left to the sound of Absalom and Oneita laughing. They may have been Amish for most of their lives, but they sure weren't Amish now.

Tess pulled him to the front porch. "Look," she said, keeping her voice down, "we both know we don't need to be alone in any cabin in the mountains, much less anywhere else."

Denver grinned. "Afraid you'll let yourself go, little Amish chick?"

"Shut up."

"I really want to do this for you."

"Why? I'm not anything special."

"That's the thing, you *are* special, in a million ways and I want to make sure you know it."

"You know how we've almost kissed twice. I want kids one day, but not until I'm married."

"Do you trust me?"

"After what I saw you and Leah doing on your sofa, no."

"That was dumb, I'll admit it. "I'll put it this way—the last person in the world I want to break my wedding vows to Eliza with is you. That's how special you are to me."

"Well …"

Denver leaned down to look into her eyes. "C'mon, say yes."

"What's this about my green dress?"

"Don't worry about that until you have to."

"I guess."

"Good, go tell your folks. I'm going home to call my pilot friend and make sure he's available Wednesday at noon. That'll give you a few days to get used to the idea."

On the drive home, Denver tapped the steering wheel as if it were a drum. Tess had pulled him from the depths of near-depression and near-alcoholism over Eliza, and she deserved this trip.

He pulled into the driveway and got out.

As long as they behaved.

settling in

Sitting at the kitchen table with David, Eliza pointed to a picture in a book she had bought him. "What's that animal. You don't have a TV, so I doubt you've seen one of those."

He crinkled his eyes. "A cow?"

She touched the picture. "Not a cow. Cows don't have horns growing from their mouths, do they?"

He crinkled his eyes again. "A bull?"

Smiling, Eliza kissed his head. "It's an elephant. Can you say elephant?"

"El …"

"You can do it. El-uh-funt."

"Elphant."

"Very good! Ready for some lunch?"

"I want some more pitchers."

"After we eat." Eliza got up to make David a peanut butter and jelly sandwich, his new favorite over tomato.

"Is Papa coming today?"

"I'm not sure, he hasn't called."

"Can we go fishing?"

"It's raining."

David turned a page in the book while Eliza got everything for his sandwich.

Except for the August heat and the lack of air conditioning, Eliza enjoyed watching David. Like Josh had said, Anna had canned plenty of vegetables from their huge garden. Eliza had learned that skill from Mama, and she had canned several quarts of tomatoes and green beans from the garden here. For fresh taste and a delicious crunch, cucumbers off the vine didn't last long around her and David.

Eliza glanced at her phone on the table. Poor Josh, dedicated to his wife, rarely called or came home, except to shower and change clothes every few days. When he did, he hugged David, thanked Eliza for helping with him, and went to his room or the bathroom. Even after a shower and fresh clothes, which normally brightened anyone's outlook, his face never changed from its haggard expression, eyes downcast with no hint of happiness whatsoever.

Since the home had solar power, Eliza was tempted to buy a window air conditioner for the kitchen and her room. Cooking and sleeping were priorities, so why not avoid sweat and wet clothes while doing those things?

She spread homemade blueberry preserves onto bread and added peanut butter, poured a glass of milk and set everything on the table in front of David, who ignored his meal for his book.

For the first few nights after coming home, he had endlessly asked Eliza when his mama and papa would be back. The only answer Eliza could give him was the same one Josh had used: when the doctors made his mama better.

She started to make a sandwich for herself and stopped when her phone vibrated. David, pointed. "Phone, 'Liza."

"I bet it's your Papa." Eliza swiped the screen to see a strange number. She stopped the call and returned to her sandwich.

"Not Papa?" David asked.

"It's not his number." The phone vibrated again. The screen had the same strange number. "Hello?"

"I guess you didn't recognize my number," Josh said, his voice flat. "My neighbor wanted his back. Since I told my bishop I was leaving the Amish, I got my own phone."

Eliza hated how Josh blamed the Amish for Anna's accident. Still, it might be to an advantage. "Do you mind if I buy two window air conditioners? It's hot in the kitchen and in my room."

"I'm thinking about getting central heat and air."

"How's Anna?"

"The same. Her doctor says it's impossible to tell when she'll wake up."

Josh's denial of the situation disturbed Eliza. She had researched the type of brain injury Anna had suffered. Most patients never woke up. The usually ended up in a long-term care facility on a feeding tube until they passed away. Ethan had mentioned this also, when she told him why she was staying at Josh's home.

"Are you there?" Josh said.

"Are you coming home today? David would like to see you."

"Not today. I— I need to go, someone's calling me and I'm trying to get used to this phone. I'll call you back." The call ended. Eliza left her phone on the table. She couldn't stay here forever. Josh needed to make arrangements, like moving his mother in. Wheelchair or not, she could take basic care of David.

"What did Papa say?" he asked.

"He's going to call back in a min—" The phone vibrated; the screen showed Josh's new number. "I'm here, Josh."

"Eliza …"

"I'm here."

"I don't know why this is happening. God must hate—" Josh sniffled. "God must hate David and me."

"Don't say that, Josh, what's wrong? Did something happen to Anna?"

"That call was from one of my mama's neighbors. She stopped by to check on her this morning, but she wouldn't answer the door. The neighbor called the police. They broke the door in and found her in bed dead."

Eliza dropped into a chair. What did this poor man and David have to go through next? Except for Anna in the hospital, they were alone in the world, even more so since he had left the Amish, who helped each other through times like this. "I'm so sorry, Josh."

"I've got to go. They found her will in a desk drawer. I need to see if she made any arrangements for a funeral."

"Do you need me to drive you?"

"My neighbor's taking me. I suppose I need to buy a car and learn how to drive." He ended the call.

Eliza put the phone on the table. Josh hadn't said to not tell David about his grandmother, but she would regardless. She didn't want him coming home to tell him, still filled with hate and blame for the Amish, not to mention God. She finished her sandwich, poured milk, and sat beside David to eat.

How to tell him about his grandmother? Life and death were hard enough to understand as an adult, but he needed to be told so his young mind could accept it, and that included accepting Anna's death when it happened.

She waited until they finished their lunch and David asked her to show him more pictures in the book. Instead, she took him into her lap, imagining how it would've have felt to hold her own daughter, who would've been two this December had she lived.

As she held him tight, David snuggled into her chest. "'Liza?"

"What, sweetheart?"

"I miss my mama."

"I miss her too. She loves you bunches and bunches."

"You 'member when I asked 'bout …" He stuck his finger in his mouth.

Eliza kissed his hair. He knew more words than the average boy his age, but stringing long sentences together could be difficult. "Do I remember what?"

"When—when I said could—could you be my mama."

"I remember."

"Not my real mama. Just … just pretend." He sat up, dark eyes peering at her. "Can I call you Mama?" He hugged her neck. "'Cause I love you."

Eliza rubbed his back. Fresh air in his hair from playing outside before the rain. A slight sour smell from his damp neck. Before she met Denver, hearing her child call her mama had been a fantasy. Then, when she was falling in love with him, it had become a dream. Marriage and pregnancy followed, and her dream neared reality until—

David pulled away. "Can I?" He raised a small fingertip near one of her eyes and gently wiped. "Are you sad? You got tears."

His gentle touch and the tiny knot of concern between his dark eyebrows combined to make Eliza smile. What a joy to have a son like— No, David belonged to Josh—get that thought under control. Still, caring for David as if he were her own child was as close as she would likely get, considering her problems with Denver. With that being the case, she could easily care for David as long as Josh needed her help.

She kissed David's cheek, catching the aroma of peanut butter on his breath. "Yes, sweetheart, you can call me mama if you want." Eliza paused. Josh might not like that, thinking she was trying to take Anna's place. "But only when we're alone, okay?"

"Like a secret? I like secrets. Papa got a secret but—" Wide-eyed, David covered his mouth.

"Don't worry," Eliza said. "You don't have to tell."

"Good. Can we look at the book now?"

Eliza still wanted to tell him about his grandmother. "What if we sit on the front porch first? It'll be cooler with it raining."

David grabbed the book from the table and ran from the kitchen, his shoes pattering on the wooden floor. "Can't catch me, Mama! I'm fast!"

Eliza ran after him, swept him into her arms at the door, and spun him around. He held his arms out. "I'ma airplane, Mama!"

"You sure are," she said, putting him down. "Whoo-wee, I'm dizzy." He took her hand and led her to a chair on the porch, shoved another chair close and climbed into it. She took the book from him and placed it in her lap. "When's the last time you saw your grandmother?"

"Who?"

"Your papa's mama."

"That's Meemaw."

"Okay, when did you see her?"

"She rides in a chair with wheels. She makes noises like she hurts."

Thankful for an opening she could use, Eliza sent a prayer to the Creator. "When I was a little girl, before I lost my hearing, we had an old hen. A fox caught her and hurt her very badly. My papa ran the fox away, but she made noises like she hurt too."

David stuck his hands under his arms and flapped them like wings. "Er, er, errrr. Like that?"

Eliza grinned. "Not quite like that, but she was in very bad pain and died that night. Then she didn't—"

"I know. The man at church—he said—he said." David swallowed, excited at whatever he was about to say.

"Slow down," Eliza said, patting his back.

"Okay, 'Liza—I mean, Mama. He said we don't hurt no more then." David paused. "I mean when we die."

"That's exactly right."

The cute bundle in her arms grew quiet, the knot between his eyebrows forming again. "Mama?"

"Yes?"

"Did Meemaw die?"

"I'm afraid so. Your Papa told me when he called. Are you sad?"

"She made fried chicken like Mama's. An' cookies. An' mashed taters." David paused. "She hugged good too, but … but she don't hurt no more, right?"

"That right."

Saying another prayer to the Creator, Eliza opened the book. If Anna passed away, Heaven forbid, at least David would be prepared. Josh, on the other hand, might not. She pointed at a giraffe. "Have you seen one of these?"

"That's a goose, he got spots."

"What about feathers?"

"Well … is fedders on his belly?"

Eliza held in a giggle. "You're a mess."

"Mama said that when I, when I—"

"Slow down, okay? What did your mama say?"

"I a mess in a puddle. Like a pig."

"I'm sure you—"

A blue pickup stopped at the mailbox. Josh climbed out and waved at Jim, his neighbor, then checked the mail and shuffled to the porch. He sat in the chair David had pulled close to Eliza. "Son, I need to tell you something."

"Is it 'bout Meemaw?"

Josh face Eliza. "I didn't say you could tell my boy about my mama."

Eliza couldn't read Josh's flat tone. "I just—"

"Meemaw not hurt no more, Papa."

"Well, that's true." He faced Eliza again. "Sorry. I didn't know how to tell him. That's as good a way as any."

Eliza caught the hint of alcohol on Josh's breath. Could this be the secret David had mentioned? She had never seen any bottles around the house, so Josh might keep whatever he drank hidden in his room. Since he had never seemed drunk in anyway, maybe he drank to deal with all the tragedy in his life, not that it would help.

Josh stood. "Let me get a shower and some clean clothes. Jim's taking me back after I get a bite to eat."

Eliza led David inside behind Josh. "Is there any change in Anna?"

"The doctor's talking about putting her in a long-term care facility. Thank goodness it's not far from the hospital so I can still stay with her."

"I cooked a roast last night, with carrots and onions and potatoes. I can heat that for you when you finish cleaning up."

On the way to his room, Josh turned. "I can't thank you enough for taking such good care of my boy, Eliza." He started to reach out to her but stopped. "It means the world to me."

"He's a real sweetheart, Josh. He means the world to me too. It's almost like—" As Eliza hesitated, the vision of her daughter burst into her mind. The day she and Denver went to see her for the first time at the funeral home had nearly killed her. How would she feel when she eventually had to leave David, who filled her with the same love with which her daughter would have filled her?

"I understand." Josh gently touched her hand. "The day David and I went fishing, Ethan walked down to the river. We got to talking and he told me about your daughter."

"You've known that long?"

David took the book from Eliza. "Y'all talk. I'll look at elphants in the kitchen."

Josh smiled, mostly with his eyes. "A new book with elephants?"

"I got it in town."

"Like I said, you mean the world to me." He started to turn and Eliza touched his shoulder.

"I need to tell you something."

Josh faced her. "Do you need anything for the house, or for David?"

Eliza braced herself. She didn't know how Josh would react, but he should know in case David called her Mama when he was here. "David asked if he could pretend I'm his mama. He misses Anna so much, I couldn't tell him no."

"Pretend how?"

"Well ..." Eliza lowered her head. "He wants to call me mama."

"Eliza, please look at me."

Not knowing what to expect, Eliza raised her head. "If it bothers you, I—"

"It doesn't bother me one bit. If it makes him happy, I'm fine with it."

"Do you think he would like to see Anna when she's moved?"

"I'll think about it. I'd hate for him to see her with a feeding tube in her nose. She's still bruised too, and her head's bandaged. Maybe when that's off and the bruises get better."

"I agree, that sounds like a terrible thing to see."

Josh left for his room. Eliza went to the kitchen to sit beside David at the table. What a nightmare for this sweet family: the loss of Josh's mother and David's grandmother, with Josh's wife and David's mother in a coma, which could end her life at any time.

She kissed David's head. Whatever it took, she would keep this sweet little boy happy.

mountain trip

At the cabin, Denver unlocked the door and went inside. Tess followed him in with her suitcase. "Wow, this place is awesome." She went to the huge stone fireplace and ran her fingers along the thick oak mantle." Too bad it isn't winter, we could have a fire."

Denver said nothing. He had rented a different cabin than the one he and Eliza had stayed in because of the memories of him and her making love on a quilt in front a fireplace similar to this. Still, it was close enough to make him turn away and go to the open-plan kitchen, which the internet rental site had touted. He opened the fridge, stocked with food as well, including red and white wine but no beer. Good thing. Beer tended to go down in gulps when wine went down in sips.

Tess went to a pair of sliding glass doors. "Wow, what a view of the mountains."

Denver took his suitcase and found one of the three bedrooms. "Come here and tell me which bedroom you want?"

Tess's flats tapped across the heart-pine floors. "Does one have a fireplace? I'll turn the AC down for a fire if I have to."

Denver opened a door to a bathroom. "Hot tub anyone?"

Tess came over. "Don't think so. Who wants Tess soup?"

Denver laughed. "Don't tempt me."

Tess opened a door between the bathroom door and the bedroom door. "Cool, a walk-in closet." She sniffed. "With cedar walls." She went to a set of tall curtains and pulled a string to open them. "Another deck and a view to die for. I could get used to this."

It was all Denver could do to keep his mouth from falling open. With Auburn hair in her familiar ponytail, shapely figure accentuated by snug faded jeans, Tess drew him like fish to bait. He left the room to find the other bedrooms, opened a door and set his suitcase on the double bed. The other room, with its king-sized bed, hot tub, and mountain view, must be the master bedroom instead of this one. No fireplace though.

He unpacked and checked his watch, went to Tess's room and tapped her shoulder as she still looked out the sliding glass doors. "We need to change into our fancy clothes."

Tess turned. "You never said where we're going."

"It's a surprise."

"Surprise or not, you know as well as I do how we're too attracted to each other to be here all alone in this romantic cabin."

Denver winked. "I'm not the one who wants to turn the AC down for a fire in the huge fireplace."

Tess took her suitcase to the bed. "Out. Unless you want to see me naked."

Denver went to his room. No doubt about it, she drew him like fish to bait.

* * *

Denver parked the rental car at the end of several filled parking places near the restaurant. "Sit tight." He got out and hurried around to open Tess's door. "How's that for sweet, gorgeous?"

Tess turned sideways. Keeping her legs together, she stood. "You just wanted to see if this tight dress would split up to my butt when I got out." She adjusted the thin strap of the silver-sequined purse on her shoulder and ran her fingers through her hair, which fell loose across her shoulders. "Do I look okay?"

"Denver closed the door. "You've got to be kidding."

"Too much eyeliner and red lipstick? It's awful bright."

"It's perfect, not that you needed it."

She adjusted Denver's tie. "Dress shirt and slacks and shoes instead of cargo shorts and a T-shirt—you dress up nice for a Buggs Island Lake guy."

"Thank you, ma'am." He offered her his arm. "Let's go." As they strolled the sidewalk, beside the cars lining it, Denver noticed how Tess's high heels brought the top of her head to his chin.

She looked up at him. "Don't look at me like that."

"Can't help it."

"Whatever. What's so special about this restaurant?"

"I saw it when Eliza and I were here."

"I hope you ate there. That way you can think about her instead of me."

Denver didn't tell Tess they hadn't eaten here, which is why he had chosen it instead of the other restaurant down the street. The last thing he wanted to think about tonight was Eliza.

The sound of soft-rock music grew louder. "Hear that?"

"Sounds like some of the older music that station in South Hill plays. I like it a lot better than anything else on the radio." Her head tilted up. "That sign up ahead says Romantics. Is that it?"

"That's it." They arrived beneath the sign and Denver opened the door. "After you, gorgeous."

Inside, Tess faced him. "You can stop calling me that any time now."

Hand in the small of her back, Denver walked her to a greeter. "Reservations for two for Andrews."

The greeter ran a finger down the list on her podium. "Corner booth, very romantic." She took two menus from a table. "Follow me, please."

With his hand still in the small of Tess's back, Denver walked her through the crowded restaurant. Round tables with red tablecloths were the theme, along with photos of classic rock entertainers on the walls. It also included dim lighting and a dance floor to the right, in front of the band playing the music.

The greeter stopped at the booth, tucked into a corner like she had mentioned. Tess slid into one side of the huge booth. "Sheesh, this dress is tight."

The greeter set the menus on the table. "I love it. You look great in it."

"Thanks."

Denver sat across from Tess. The greeter said a server would be there in a moment and left. He opened the menu and looked over it to see Tess glaring at hers. "Whoa, this place is expensive."

"You're worth it, Tess."

"Uh-huh, this ex-little Amish chick is pretty simple, really. I'm not up for all this whoopdy-do, fancy-shmancy stuff. Give me blue jeans and my family and the lake and I've got everything I need to be happy."

Denver touched her hand. "What about a husband?"

"I'd like to get married one day, do the children thing, make guitars and keep a small garden like Mama has with her containers."

"Sounds like a life I'd enjoy, Tess."

"The life you'd enjoy is with Eliza and you know it."

"Like I have a choice in that." Held out his hand, palm up. "Hold my hand."

Rolling her eyes, Tess plopped her hand into his. *"And?"*

Denver closed his hand over hers and rubbed her knuckles with his thumb. "Couldn't you get used to that?"

"I— Oh, you make me so mad."

"Because?"

"Like I already told you, I could love you so easy."

"Then why not try? You'll be eighteen next year at this time."

"A lot can happen in a year."

"I'm not going anywhere. Are you going anywhere?"

"I mean with Eliza."

"What if I don't want that to change?"

"You don't mean tha—" Tess took her hand from his. "Thank goodness, here comes the server."

A young man wearing a white shirt and black slacks came to the table. "Good evening, I'm Sean. Would you like to start with something from the bar, or an appetizer?"

"Iced tea with lemon," Tess said.

"Make that two." Denver said. "Do you have prime rib?"

"We certainly do. It comes with mashed potatoes and grilled asparagus."

"Prime rib of what?" Tess said.

"That'll be fine," Denver told the server, who left.

Tess smacked his hand. "What's prime rib, something from some animal I don't know about because I've been Amish most of my life?"

"You like steak, right?"

"Does a cow mow?"

Denver covered a laugh. "You're hilarious."

"Right, I'm an Amish comedian. What's prime rib?"

"It's slow-roasted beef, juicy as can be."

"Fine. Look, I was about to tell you how you don't mean what you said about not wanting things with Eliza to change."

"Eliza who?"

Shaking her head, Tess looked toward the band. The lead guitar player, identified by his six-string electric guitar instead of a four-string bass, stepped to the microphone. "The dance floor is empty. Any requests?"

Denver trotted to the stage and pointed at Tess, told the guy his request and trotted back to Tess to offer her his hand. "Cool," she said, rising, "Lets rock."

Denver gawked. "What do you know about rock?"

"I watch people dance on the internet. Let's bust a move." Tess took his hand and led him to the dance floor.

"I didn't ask for that kind of song," Denver said, stopping her.

Tess went to the stage, said something to the guitar player, and came back. "Too bad, Denny."

The guitar player approached the microphone. Overhead spotlights shined into his eyes. "Denver?"

Denver waved. "Right here."

"All right. That hot young lady of yours made a request just for you. We'll play yours after hers." He nodded to the drummer, who thumped the bass drum, followed by the guitar player strumming a sizzling riff. At the microphone, he sang the first line of ZZ Top's *Sharp Dressed Man.*

Several dancers gathered on the floor, whooping and hollering. Tess bopped a circle around Denver, hair flying as she turned her head back and forth, hips gyrating to the intense beat. "C'mon, Denny baby, show me whatcha got."

Denver joined her to dance like she did, doing his best to keep up. Sweat soon slickened his underarms, and the song ended just as he was about to give out of breath. "Good grief, I need to paddle my canoe more often."

Tess shoved his chest. "Poor old guy, can't keep up with me."

"Don't give me that old crap, I see sweat on your forehead." He nodded toward the guitar player, who started the slow and sultry love song *I Only Have Eyes for You.*

Tess frowned. "Leave it to you to pick some draggy old mess like that."

Denver grabbed her by the waist and pulled her close. "Put your arms around my neck and hush."

She did. After a few lines, she hummed along with the tune. "Well, I admit, tonight I only want you to have eyes for me instead of my dumb sister." She lay her head on Denver's shoulder. As they swayed slowly with the music, he rubbed slow circles between her bare shoulder blades.

"Not too bad, huh? Gives me a chance to catch my breath."

"It's a pretty tune."

"How about the words? Eliza ran off to Ohio and abandoned me. That means I really do only have eyes for you."

Tess squeezed his neck. "You realize I could get used to this."

"That's what I've been trying to tell you. Do I feel like an idiot for having feelings for my sister-in-law? Yes, but—"

"Don't, okay? I know I keep saying you and Eliza need to get back together, but I don't want to think about her right now. I don't think I've ever been this happy in my entire life."

They continued swaying. Denver breathed in the floral aroma of her shampoo, nuzzled her silky hair, lowered his hands to the dip in her back.

Tess pulled away. Green eyes. Soft smile. Shimmering red lipstick. She leaned forward, cheek to cheek, her breath in his ear. "Ja maakt me gek."

Denver chuckled. "I've always like your family's Dutch accent. What did you say?"

"You're driving me crazy."

"Vice versa, mijn kleine mandje."

Tess snorted laughter. "Learned some Dutch while you were in Ohio, huh?"

"Why do I have a feeling I got it wrong?"

"You called me 'your little basket.'"

"Oh. What's the word for flower?"

"Bloem." Tess lay her head on his shoulder again. "What am I gonna do with you?"

"We could always eat, our food's on the table." Denver waited until she slid into the booth and sat. "Wow, this looks great."

"Does it ever," Tess said, picking up a knife and fork.

Denver did the same, allowing her to enjoy her food and the soft rock music coming from the band.

Her dancing had left her flushed and her eyes bright. Between bites of food, she glanced at couples dancing. She sipped tea and licked her lips. "Why aren't you eating that meat on your fork?"

Denver blinked. He had been looking at Tess for longer than he thought. Although it was the truth, to tell her he only had eyes for her would be as cliché as cliché got. Maybe tell her something else about himself to see what she thought about it. It was extremely personal, so it would give him good idea of how she might handle his past. "Just thinking about something."

"Like what?"

"Have you ever wondered about my history with women?"

"Before everything happened with Eliza, and after we moved to Clarksville, she told me about you and Jan." About to cut a stem of asparagus, Tess dropped her knife. "She said you had never slept with Jan, why?"

"Sisters talk. Did she say anything about our honeymoon?"

"She said she had a great ti— No, how could she have a great time at her honeymoon if that was your first time too? One of you needed some experience to make it great."

Denver aimed his knife at her. "What do you know about so-called experience, Miss Amish chick?"

"I'm not stupid."

"I didn't say you were."

Tess's cheeks turned pink. "Well, you can find anything on the internet these days."

"Huh, my little flower is a little pervert."

"And you love it, don't you?"

Denver cut a huge slice of beef and stuffed it into his mouth.

Tess kicked his shin. "You'll have to swallow eventually. Then you can tell me whatever it is you're hinting at."

As Denver chewed, he felt the unmistakable sensation of A warm foot sliding up his pants leg to his calf. Tess blew him a kiss. "How's that for a little pervert?"

After swallowing the beef, Denver washed it down with tea. "Don't start something you can't finish, little flower."

"*We* can't finish, not just me." Tess wiped her mouth with a napkin. "Did you see anything in that cabin fridge for dessert? I'm about to pop now."

"Some wine, not that you're old enough. You'll blab to Ivy and she'll tell your folks and I'll get my face smashed anyway."

"Mama bought some one time and let me taste it. When they left the Amish, they left the Amish."

"Half a glass, that's it." Denver waved to the greeter, who brought the bill. With it paid and a nice tip added, he stood. "Let's see what kind of mountain sunset we get at the cabin."

During the drive back, Denver glanced at Tess every so often as she looked out the passenger-side window. She never faced him, as if she had something on her mind.

He watched the rising, curving road. The setting sun shone in his eyes, and he had seen a deer cross as they started up the mountain.

Tess still faced the window. What could she be thinking?

Inside the cabin, she went to her room and came back a few minutes later, dressed in jeans and a powder-blue blouse, padding to the living room on bare feet.

"No shoes?" Denver said.

She pushed a button on the AC. "I want cold feet for that fire." She came to him at the sliding glass door, where he was watching the sun turn reddish-orange while it sank over the next mountain to the west. "Don't feel like getting into your old clothes, sharp-dressed man?"

"I guess."

"You seem sad."

Denver let the quiet settle between them. "I was wondering what Eliza is doing."

Tess wrapped her hands around his arm. "If she weren't my sister, I'd hate her for what she's doing to you."

"Part of me does."

"But part of you doesn't."

"I guess it never will. What we have—had—whatever, I guess it'll always be with me." Denver turned toward Tess. "You wouldn't ever hurt me like that, would you?"

"There's still a chance, Denver. It's not like she's divorcing you."

"It sure feels like it."

The sun lowered into the horizon, coloring distant clouds orange and red. Denver left to change into jeans but left the button-up shirt on. He also came back barefooted, went to the kitchen and poured himself a glass of red wine—red for the bloody mood that had settled over him like that bloody sunset.

Tess came over. "Can I taste it? Mama had white wine."

"It's sweeter than most reds." He gave her the glass.

"Mmm, might pour me one too."

Denver was tempted to tell her not to but didn't. She was the most adult seventeen-year-old girl he had ever known—a woman really.

He found wood outside in a covered box and had a fire going in a few minutes. When he finished, Tess was sitting on the sofa. He joined her at the other end.

She sipped wine, which stained her lips redder than the lipstick she had taken off. "Now, what's this about you being experienced for your honeymoon?"

Denver regretted ever mentioning it. He also regretted it happening to begin with, but considering how it happened, he understood why. "Will you think any less of me because of it?"

Tess tucked one foot beneath her. "I could ask you the same thing. I might not be the innocent little ex-Amish girl you think I am."

Of course, she was speaking hypothetically. "You know my parents were killed by a drunk driver just a few weeks before I went to Jon's school to teach sign language."

"Eliza told me it. I can't imagine."

"I had dealt with the worst of it. It still came and went at times, and it came one night at the school."

"No, you didn't."

"'Fraid so."

"You slept with Akina, the other teacher?"

"Like I said, I'm afraid so."

"I remember her from when you and Papa and Eliza came for her paintings for her art show, and then, when she and Dan came to the wedding. She was something."

"She was 'something' enough so that we slept together for several weeks, and that was while I started having feelings for Eliza. I was upset about Mom and Dad one night. A hug led to a kiss and a kiss led to—well, you know."

"She comforted you. I can see that."

Denver sipped wine. "I'm glad. I'd hate for you to judge me for it."

"Good, because I sort of did the same thing once. A friend from school invited me to her birthday party. I still had long hair and some kids at school teased me about being Amish. She invited me so they could do the same thing. I left to walk home, not thinking how to find it, and one of the boys followed me to apologize. The next thing I know, we we're kissing and stuff. All I could think was how nice he was. Like you said, one thing led to another. Thank goodness I didn't get pregnant."

To think of Tess with someone else set a burning rage into the center of Denver's chest. She slid close to look into his eyes. "Your face is red, are you mad at me?"

"How old were you?"

"Fifteen. Young and dumb and thinking something as simple as boy being nice meant something."

"Like you understand about what I did, I understand about what you did." The fading rage hit Denver again. "But I could beat that kid for taking advantage of you."

"Good thing he moved away the following year." Tess slid back over to sip wine. "Not bad."

Denver sipped wine also. He left the glass on the table and took Tess's hand in his. "I know what you did, and it means more than I can say. That's why I wanted to bring you here and take you out to a nice place."

Tess pulled her hand from his. "What do you mean? I didn't do anything."

"Jan came by after the Lakefest fireworks."

"Oh, really," Tess said, smiling and nodding. "Did she interrupt you and Leah in the middle of something?"

"We hadn't started anything, thanks to Jan. Leah took off and hasn't called since."

Tess clapped. "Yay, Jan. Way to go, girl."

After another sip of wine, Denver faced Tess again. "Jan was tired and didn't want to drive to Raleigh. She wanted to go to the cemetery the next morning. That's when I saw the headstone you had made. I almost fainted when I realized you did that."

Tess lowered her head. "Maybe Mama and Papa did that. Or maybe Eliza."

Denver cupped her chin. "Why are you giving anyone else the credit? You even came up with the idea of naming my daughter Lily."

She looked up, tears in her eyes. "I'm so stupid. I hoped you would think Eliza did it and you would go to Ohio and ask her to come home."

"But she would've said she didn't do it, Tess."

Tess downed the entire glass of wine, went to the kitchen to fill the glass, and came back. "I should get drunk. What an idiot I am."

Saying nothing, Denver got up to prod the dying fire with the poker. If anyone understood the need to drink to get over pain, he did, although it never did anything but numb the pain until the morning came, with its inevitable hangover.

Behind him, Tess's bare feet pattered to the kitchen again. "Not too much," he said. "You don't want to get sick." With the fire flaming again, he returned to the sofa. "Look, you might want to act like you did that to get Eliza and me back together, but it's still one of the nicest things anyone has ever done for me."

Tess emptied the glass. "Uh-huh. Is this the part where we sleep together? I sure would like to know what I missed that first time because it hurt like hell."

"Don't curse. That's not you and you know it."

Holding her forehead, Tess fell over onto the sofa. "Why in the world do people drink if it makes their head feel like it's filled with mud?"

Denver rubbed her back. "Not gonna get sick are you?"

"Just walk me to bed, I'll be okay."

Denver stood her up but she slipped out of his arms. "Grab my neck, my little wino. I need to carry you."

At the bed, he sat her on the end while he turned the sheets and blanket back. "Gonna sleep in your clothes?"

Tess fell back onto the bed. "Good idea."

Denver slid her up to the pillow, tucked her legs beneath the covers, and pulled them to her chin. When he turned the lights out, she was lightly snoring.

In bed by himself when he would rather be with Tess, he closed his eyes. What a mess his life was. Yes, despite Eliza leaving him, he still loved her. But despite loving her, he loved Tess too.

He rolled over.

Even though he understood why Tess had slept with that boy, it had shocked him to think of this innocent young woman, not long from being Amish, to come to an entirely different world and be treated like that.

Thank the good Lord above it hadn't scarred her, or, like she had said, gotten her pregnant. Talk about a nightmare.

He rolled back over to face the ceiling.

Where would all this end? As of this very minute, he couldn't see anything good coming of it. If he, Eliza, and Tess weren't careful, they all would end up with broken hearts worse than they already had.

brother

In town after sign language class, Ethan took a grocery cart from the row and rolled it to the produce section. He loved tangerines. Too bad he couldn't grow those in Ohio. Over by the lettuce, a woman in a nurse's uniform said hello to another woman. As Ethan looked through the tangerines for a bag of larger ones, the nurse mentioned Josh. Although Ethan had found what he wanted, he kept looking. Maybe the nurse worked where Anna had been taken. If so, he'd like to know her condition.

"Such a shame," the second woman said. "Does her doctor think she'll ever come out of the coma?"

"The chances are pretty low," the nurse said. "Her husband brought his son to see her for the first time the other day. They came in while I was checking her vital signs and feeding tube.

The first woman shook her head. "That poor family. I understand the deaf woman is watching the boy while his father visits his wife."

"That's what he told me." The nurse moved closer to the woman. "If you ask me, there's more between him and that deaf woman than it seems. She's been there over two weeks now."

"Didn't his mother die recently? Maybe he has no one else to watch his son?"

"It's still strange. I wouldn't be surprised if he hopes to marry her when his wife dies. The way he goes on about her, it's obvious he has feelings for her."

The first woman's mouth fell open. "Really?"

"I'm afraid so." The nurse picked up a head of lettuce. "Have you seen how the prices are rising?"

Josh left the cart by the tangerine display. He hadn't thought much of Eliza watching David while Josh visited Anna, but it was time they had a talk. If he were married and his wife had left him like Eliza had left Denver, then moved into some man's house, he would want to know what her intentions were.

He drove by Josh's house first. He, Eliza, and David were in the garden. Ethan parked behind an oak beside the road and rolled the window down, but he was too far away to hear anything but muffled voices.

David was attempting to hoe weeds from between the tomato plants. Eliza pointed at him and smiled at Josh, who smiled back while placing his arm around her shoulders.

Ethan slapped the dash of his pickup. Denver would give anything for Eliza to smile at him and let him hug her like that.

At home again, he went to the barn. Too bad the house had central heat, or he could split wood to ease his anger. He sat at Papa's old workbench. No, he should give his sister the benefit of the doubt and ask her about her and Josh when Josh was gone. Although he had stayed with Anna every day and night the first week after her accident, Ethan had seen him at home more afternoons than not. Wait until the morning, when Josh might be gone.

* * *

During sign language class the next morning, Ethan pulled Timothy aside. "I need to run to town for a minute. Can you teach without me until I get back?"

"I can," Timothy said. "What do you need? Papa might have it."

207

"I forgot my tangerines."

"Can't you wait until later?"

Ethan paused. He hadn't thought of this, but it could explain his need to leave. "I'd like to teach the sign for them."

"Not a bad idea," Timothy said.

Ethan hurried to his pickup. Time to get to the bottom of this Eliza and Josh thing.

As he neared the oak tree, he slowed. Josh's neighbor was picking him up. They left, and Ethan parked in Josh's driveway. At his front door, he knocked. The door opened to reveal Eliza in a robe. "Josh, did you forget something? Oh, Ethan. I thought—"

Ethan pushed past her. "What? Did Josh forget his goodbye kiss? I'm ashamed of you Eliza. You abandoned Denver and come here to live with a married man?"

"Keep your voice down, David's still asleep." She went out on the porch, and Ethan followed.

"I saw you in the garden yesterday, smiling at Josh and him hugging you. Denver would give everything he has to have that with you."

Eliza's jaw worked. "Nothing I do is any of his business. I'm my own person—I don't need the likes of him or you telling me how to live."

Ethan turned away, disgusted at how the gossip was true. He faced Eliza again. "As much as you and Denver loved each other, why are you throwing it away? When you got married, all I heard people saying was how you were the perfect couple, and how they'd give anything to have what you have."

"Had, Ethan, had. I love it here. No one expects anything of me. I love David and he loves me. I'm not giving that up—not for you and not for Denver."

"Ah, so you've replaced your daughter with another man's son. Isn't that nice while you break Denver's heart. I talked to Tess the other day. He's trying to get over you by dating some girl he knew in high school. That's how desperate he is for you to come home."

"Good for him," Eliza said, baring her teeth. "Maybe she can give him children like I can't."

"Did you try?" Ethan knew the answer to his question. Since Eliza had done nothing but sit in the rocking chair or on the dock for the last year and a half, she probably hadn't slept with Denver, much less try to get pregnant.

Footsteps pattered to the door. Behind the screen, David rubbed his eyes. "I'm hungry, Mama."

Ethan pulled Eliza to the side of the porch. "'Mama'? Really? Not only are you living with a married man, you've stolen his wife's child and have him calling you mama?"

Eliza jerked her arm from his hand and slapped his face. "You know nothing about it." She shoved him away. "Leave before I call Josh and—"

"What?" Ethan rubbed his stinging cheek. "You'll have him come to the school and hit me like you just did?"

Eliza raised her hand. "I don't need him to do anything for me."

"Mama? Why are you fussin' at Ethan?"

Ethan shook his head. God help that little boy.

At home again, he went to his room and took a picture of his red cheek with his phone. Despite his sister's rage he loved her, and he wanted her to be genuinely happy again.

Ethan brought up the picture on the screen. Her fingers had left four red streaks evenly across his cheek.

If she ever did something as stupid as forget how she had treated Denver—and now her own brother—this picture would come in handy.

rain.

Denver woke to darkness. The sound of crying came from Tess's room. He checked his watch—4:35—and put a robe on over his boxers. In her open bedroom door, he turned on a switch that lit a lamp on the dresser. "Are you sick?"

"Sick people don't cry, you idiot. Can't you come and hold me?"

"Why are you crying?"

"Does it matter? I need you."

Stepping to the bed, Denver stopped. "Your clothes are in the floor."

"I woke up hot." Tess sobbed again. "Please, okay? Don't you care about me?"

Her crying tore at Denver's heart. Despite the risk of what might happen, he took off his robe and got in bed. Tess snuggled into his shoulder and continued to cry. All he could do was wrap his arms around her and hold her close. Good thing her sadness overrode the feel of her warm body next to his, along with her silky hair lying across his chest.

She gradually stopped crying and fell asleep, evidenced by her even breathing against his cheek.

No doubt about it, broken hearts were coming their way, and he had no idea what to do about it.

Eliza.

She hadn't broken his heart; she had ripped it apart and spit on it, while her sister was doing everything in her power to put it back together again.

Denver kissed Tess's forehead. She snuggled deeper into his shoulder.

So young. So innocent. So loving. So thoughtful.

Then again, he had thought the exact same thing about Eliza only a few short years ago.

Like he had said on the day she had left him after he admitted to loving her, God help him … God help him.

* * *

"Oh, my head."

Denver opened his eyes. Tess was sitting up in bed, her bare back facing him. He took his robe from the nightstand and put it by her. "Cover up, okay?"

She turned look at him, auburn hair scattered around her face. "Look all you want. I don't care about stuff like that." She slid out of bed and went to the bathroom before Denver could look away.

The sink ran. The commode flushed. She returned to crawl under the covers. "Thank goodness for mouthwash. If I look like my mouth tasted, I'm rotten grapes."

Tempted to tell her how great she looked anyway, Denver rolled over to face her instead. "I've got ibuprofen if you need it."

"It's not that bad. I *am* looking forward to a cup of coffee, hint-hint." She raised the covers. "Nice boxers. I bet you've been raising the covers to check me out too, haven't you?"

"Nope. Slept like a baby."

"Uh-huh, because it's raining. What were you planning to do before we go back home tomorrow?"

"I thought about hiking a trail to a waterfall a few miles from here."

Tess pointed toward the sliding glass doors, where rain streamed down them. "I'm not hiking in that." She shoved

Denver toward the edge of the bed. "Get your blue-striped boxers up and make us coffee."

As Denver measured the gourmet roast the rental agency had stocked the cabin with, Tess peeked around the hall entrance. "Didn't I see bacon and eggs in that fridge?"

Denver opened it. "Yep. How many eggs?"

"None."

He squinted at her. "Then what—"

"Pancakes too, with my recipe you watched me make." Tess strode past him to open cabinets. "Do we have syrup?"

Denver turned away. "Sheesh, Tess, put some clothes on."

"Found it." Something clunked to the counter. "It's beside the stove." Small hands with slender fingers joined at his navel. Warm skin pressed against his back. Soft hair lay against his neck. "Remember how I told you I could get used to this when we were dancing?"

"What about it?"

"Could you get used to this?"

"Do you have to ask?"

Tess popped his behind. "Just checking. Time for a shower."

Denver turned in time to see her bottom bouncing away. Opening cabinets to find the flour, he shook his head. "Sheesh is right. I've become a dirty old man before I'm even an *old* man."

By the time Tess returned, hair in a ponytail, dressed in faded jeans and a yellow blouse, still barefooted, Denver had dressed too. He waved a hand toward the dining room table beyond the sliding glass doors, where diners could see the mountains. "Your cuisine awaits, mijn kleine bloem."

"Your pronunciation sucks." Tess sat and added sugar and cream to her coffee, stirred it with spoon and sipped. "Mmm, not bad. You get a point for decent coffee."

"You've had my coffee before."

"Just teasing."

As they ate, Denver realized how Tess often used teasing to bypass serious subjects, which meant she thought he was going to ask why she was crying last night. He sipped coffee and swallowed eggs, watched the rain splatter against the sliding glass doors, and turned back to his plate to try the pancakes. Not as good as hers but tasty regardless, especially when he added a bite of crunchy bacon with it.

"You're so obvious," Tess said.

Denver sipped more coffee. "About?"

"You're giving me the silent treatment so I'll tell you why I was crying."

"Crying?" Denver crunched more bacon, followed it with eggs and pancakes, and washed it all down with more coffee. He filled his cup from the carafe, filled Tess's too, and set the carafe on a potholder on the table. "I didn't hear any crying."

"I could always eat naked until you admit you want to know about it."

"About what?"

Tess covered her eyes. "And I thought *I* was bad."

"Okay, love of my life," Denver said while holding back a grin, "tell me why you were crying to the point of asking me to hold you in your birthday suit."

Tess growled. "Don't call me that. You should be calling Eliza that."

"In case you haven't noticed, she's not here. Besides, like my performance at your house, when I asked you to marry me, your folks knew I was teasing."

"Do you want to know or not?"

Denver sipped coffee. "My coffee's better than your coffee."

"My behind's tighter than yours, old man."

"You really went anti-Amish when y'all moved here, didn't you? Skimpy bikinis. Your mom drinking wine. You running around in front of me naked."

Tess rolled her eyes. "Don't forget me sleeping with that guy as an innocent fifteen-year-old."

About to drink coffee, Denver lowered the cup. "Don't tell me that has anything to do with you losing your Amish ways in only a few years."

"I didn't know it at the time, but I was trying to fit in. Teenagers do that, you know."

"But you figured it out."

"Well, not that long ago. After what that jerk did, I just got to where I didn't care anymore."

Denver stood. "If you're through, let's take this conversation to the sofa."

Tess refilled her cup and joined him. "I called him a jerk because I found out later he only apologized and gave me a ride home to see if I'd do what I did."

"You were fifteen. One of your folks was supposed to pick you up, right?"

"I told Mama my period had started and I didn't have anything with me."

Denver cringed. "Just blurt it out."

"Stop being a prude, Mr. Slept with Akina Guy." Tess drank coffee. "I found out later at school. He told his friends I was no good at sex and they spread it around."

Silence fell with her words. Denver didn't know what to say. Well, he *did* know what to say—he'd like to beat that punk senseless.

"So now you know why I lost my innocent Amish ways so fast. After all that, I just stopped caring."

"But you changed, right? You've been taking care of me really well since Eliza left."

"I changed because I remembered the first time I saw you and Eliza walking in my yard back in Ohio. You were holding hands and smiling at each other like I wanted a boy to smile at me one day." Tess lowered her head. "And now she's ruined all that."

Lighting brightened the room. Thunder rumbled. The rain fell harder, thudding against the sliding glass doors.

Denver took her coffee cup from her and put it on the coffee table with his. "Tess?"

"What?" she said, head still down.

He slid over and took her into his arms. "I'm sorry about what that jerk did to you, but I'm glad Eliza and I helped get you over it."

Tess pulled away. She cupped his cheek with her hand. "I know I say it a lot, but you are so sweet. I love Eliza but I hate her too. I never thought she would let anything break you up."

Lightning flashed, reflecting in Tess's green eyes, followed by the low echo of thunder rolling through the valley between the mountains.

"Denver?"

"Hmm?"

"Could ..."

"What, Tess?"

"Could you show me how it feels to make love to a woman and mean it?"

"You know I can't do that."

"Please? I care about you so much. Just for a little while, can't we make everything bad go away and let it just be about us?"

Denver took her hand from his cheek and kissed it. "I'd be worse that that guy if I took advantage of you."

Those amazing green eyes blinked until a tear ran down her cheek. "Can I at least kiss you?"

"I wouldn't be able to stop." Denver gently eased away. "Believe me, Tess, I want you worse than anyone I've ever known, and that includes Akina and Eliza. Doesn't that mean more than actually sleeping together."

"Only if you mean it."

"I mean it." Denver hated to lie, but despite everything Eliza had done to him, she still held his heart in the palm of her hand, although who knew what she was about to do to it.

He sat back against the sofa. "Turn around and sit back against me and listen to the rain."

Tess did so, wrapping his arms around her and holding his hands.

Denver let the silence fill the room, a silence of a million miles between them, while their heartbeats joined together as a living testament as to how great they would be together if it were possible.

"Tess, don't ever let anyone make you forget to care again, okay?"

"I won't." She twisted her head around to look at him. "As long as you'll keep reminding me."

a son

Eliza opened the oven to check the ham Josh had bought from one of his Amish friends. Butchering Day had come and gone a few days ago, and many Amish sold their extra meat. Not only did the roasting ham smell delicious, the oven's warmth felt wonderful on her face. December was here, and although she enjoyed the crisp mornings with frost glistening in the yard, Ohio winters could be brutal. She went to the thermostat in the living room and lowered it a few degrees, as the warmth in the kitchen, where two pots simmered on the stove, one of green beans and one of potatoes, would soon heat the space past comfort.

At the kitchen table with a toy wooden truck Josh had carved, David stopped rolling it. "Supper almost ready, Mama?"

"Not quite."

"Is Papa coming home to eat?"

"He said he would."

David started to roll the truck again but stopped after a short push. "Do you like Christmas? Mama used to cook a turkey. And sweet taters. And pecan pie. I like pie."

Eliza sat beside him. The bright youngster, talkative as well as inquisitive, was learning his sentences faster than most three-year-olds, possibly because she worked with him and his books every day. She kissed his head. "I'm sure you miss your mama very much."

"She's sleeping. She doesn't hurt like Meemaw hurt."

Eliza hugged his shoulders. Through tears, Josh had told her how David had reacted when he saw Anna on their first visit, asking about the feeding tube in her nose and the beeping heart and blood pressure monitor. Josh only visited her twice a week now, saying how seeing her like that took away his hope of her coming back to him and David. Eliza kissed David's head again. "Your mama loves you very much."

"I know," he said, rolling the truck across the table. "She said she was ready to go to Heaven. She said you could be my mama for real, not my pretend mama." He stopped rolling the truck and faced her. "Is that okay?"

"When did she tell you that?"

"Last night in my sleep."

"Oh, you dreamed it."

He nodded. "Uh-huh. She kissed me and hugged me. She told me to be a good boy for you."

Eliza envied his dream. The rare times she dreamed, nightmares of her daughter's tiny pale body in the tiny white coffin caused her to jerk upright in bed, sobbing terribly. Still, something about David's last statement bothered her. "David?"

"What, Mama?"

"Didn't your mama tell you to be a good boy for your papa too?"

"No, just you."

Discounting his dream as nothing more than the stress of missing Anna, Eliza checked her watch. Along with the time, the aroma of sizzling pork meant the ham should be ready soon. At the stove, she stirred the green beans and potatoes and inserted a thermometer into the ham. Just a few more degrees to go.

She took glasses and plates from the cabinets for her and David. Josh usually came home by now. Since he hadn't, he would drive his used pickup to a fast-food place near the long-term care facility and take his meal back to eat while watching Anna.

At the refrigerator, she checked the banana pudding she had made to surprise David, who said he loved bananas but never tried them in pudding. Frowning at her first attempt at meringue, which had turned out flat and yellow instead of brown and fluffy, she placed it on the counter beside the sink to remove the plastic wrap.

Through the window, movement caught her eye: Josh walking to the small barn behind the chicken coop, a brown bottle in his hand.

Although Eliza didn't care for his drinking strong alcohol, he never showed any signs of drunkenness like Denver had. Since that was the case, she let it go. Except for the one time he had held her on the porch and apologized for it at the river, he was a perfect gentleman and father to David. She didn't even mind his occasional signs of affection by giving her shoulders a quick hug. Such a thing was natural from anyone who appreciated her. Denver, on the other hand, expected her to fall into bed and have sex. She swallowed. Just thinking about her last attempt to kiss him caused gorge to rise in her throat.

She took out a plate and glass for Josh. "David, wash up for supper. Your papa's out back and we'll eat soon."

"Okay, Mama." David pattered from the kitchen as Josh entered the back door.

"Mmm, that ham smells wonderful." He lifted the lids on the steaming pots. "Green beans and potatoes, much better than a cold hamburger and soggy french fries."

Eliza took plates and silverware to the table. "How's Anna today."

Josh hung his coat on a rack by the door. Sitting at the table, he heaved a huge sigh. "The same."

Curious about his drinking, Eliza stopped stirring the green beans. "You don't say much about how all this is affecting you."

"As you know, I was a mess the first few weeks. Part of me wishes she could move on to where she's meant to be."

Eliza went back to the oven to check the ham. Although Josh had gradually gotten over his rage at the Amish, he still wouldn't mention any belief in God or Heaven. Saying that about Anna moving on to where she's meant to be was an improvement, which would help him and David through her death when it happened.

Josh came over to face her. "I saw an attorney today. Anna won't last much longer and I want you to adopt David."

Along with the shock of the idea, the shock of his saying it like a demand instead of a request made Eliza whirl toward him. "How can you just tell me something like that without asking, Josh? That's a serious thing to expect of me, and more responsibility than I'm ready for."

"You're practically his mother now."

"Not legally. Besides, Anna might come home one day."

Josh's eyes softened. "We both know that's not going to happen, Eliza. David loves you. I care about you. Just knowing you're here to come home to takes away the sadness of knowing Anna's not coming back to me." He opened the oven, closed it, and faced Eliza again. "Please think about." He slipped his fingers into hers. "It would mean the world to me if you did."

Just the touch of his hand filled Eliza's throat with nausea. She eased her hand free. The effect of Anna's accident was clear: Josh's feelings were growing into something past the simple act of appreciating Eliza for taking care of David.

She took the ham from the oven and placed the pan on a potholder.

And she didn't like it one bit.

Like a man who knew he had crossed an invisible line between them, Josh wordlessly took a fork and knife from a drawer and sliced the ham.

David came to Eliza and tugged her apron. "All clean, Mama"

She looked down to see his raised hands. "Aren't you a good boy?"

He nodded vigorously, dark bangs flopping back and forth over his forehead. "I am, Mama."

"Are you good enough to say the blessing before we eat?"

He climbed into a chair and folded his hands. "I'm ready."

While Eliza drained the steaming potatoes and buttered them, Josh took the sliced ham to the table. At the stove, he leaned close. "Can we talk after David goes to bed? I think I upset you and I don't want you to think bad of me."

The caramel hint of bitter alcohol rode his breath. Still, he didn't seem the least bit intoxicated. "That will be fine. Let me get everything on the table so we can eat."

The meal passed with talk of the coming Christmas, including how David wanted new books and for Josh to carve him a tractor. He also asked Eliza what she wanted, and she said just a hug from him would be fine. When the plates were cleared, and the banana pudding eaten, David and Josh remarked at how they had never thought of making pudding with bananas.

After washing dishes, with Josh drying, Eliza settled on the sofa with David to read him the Bible story about David and Goliath. When she got to the part where David was about to battle with Goliath, David snuggled into her side and told her how he would always protect her like David was protecting his friends. He grew quiet after that, yawning until Eliza took him to the bathroom to help him wash his face and brush his teeth. He then knelt by his bed and said his prayers, ending with "God bless my mamas and God bless my papa, amen."

Eliza tucked him in and kissed his cheek. "I love you, David. You make me happier than I've ever been in my entire life."

"Really?" he said, dark eyes crinkling.

"Yes, really." She turned the lamp on his nightstand off. "Goodnight."

In the living room, Josh stood by the open door. The porchlight illuminated snow falling in the yard. She went to the window to watch. Whatever he wanted to say to her about adopting David wouldn't matter, especially since he was having romantic feelings for her. She needed to put those thoughts out of his head right now. If not, she might be forced to leave David, and that would break her heart.

The snow grew heavier, huge flakes glistening in the porchlight. Like those snowflakes drifting sideways when the wind blew, a memory drifted to her from the hazy recesses of her past with Denver.

Two weeks before her labor started, a snowstorm struck Clarksville. They called her family to make sure they hadn't lost power and had enough food, then settled down in front of the TV with a bag of popcorn and a glass of iced tea to share. She had forgotten what show was playing, because they ended up making love despite how she shouldn't, being so close to her due date. Denver's gentle touch and tender kisses had thrilled her beyond control. Satisfied, she returned his love in kind, and they fell asleep on the sofa beneath the throw they kept there in the winter, snug and warm with the snow falling and the wind moaning.

Like the night of their failed lovemaking, when she had left him later, Eliza touched her lips. They had been so in love, even to the point of knowing each other's needs without speaking. How could she find that time with him again, including a love so deep and pure it made her ache for nothing more than his blue eyes gazing into hers?

Josh shut the door. "You're thinking about your husband, aren't you?"

Eliza faced him. Here it was—Josh's profession of love and proposal of marriage for when Anna finally passed away.

He went to the sofa. She sat in a chair across from him. "Josh, I—"

"Me first. You know I appreciate you helping with David, but you think I want more than that."

"I … well, to be honest, I don't know what to think. Living here is strange, but it would break my heart to leave David."

"Is that because you lost your daughter at birth?"

Eliza's lips slowly parted. "Who …?"

"I asked Jon in town today. He says Ethan is upset about you staying here. Jon didn't say so, but I got the feeling he didn't approve either. I think they should mind their own business."

"I agree, especially for people willing to think the worst."

Josh clasped his hands between his knees. "Let's clear the air right now—I love Anna and always will. No one could ever replace her and I don't want to even try, not in that way. What you have with my son is different. He needs a mother, and you love him like a mother should. When Anna dies, I'd like you to be his mother. Even if you leave one day, I'd still like that. Like with her accident, we never know how long we'll live. If something were to happen to me, he'll need you more than ever."

Eliza settled back into the chair, comforted at how Josh loved Anna to the point of wanting no one else. "David's easy to love, Josh. He's such a good boy. He never fusses or complains. Give him a toy or a book and he's happy."

Josh grinned. "Or a fishing pole. That boy loves to fish even more than I do."

"Well," Eliza said, trying not to laugh, "he almost loves playing in a mud puddle just as much."

Josh stood. "I need to get a Christmas tree soon. I've got something for him he'll love." He went down the hall and came back with a huge cardboard box, pushing it along the wooden floor to Eliza's feet. The flaps were already cut. "Open it and tell me if you think he'll like it."

Eliza folded the flaps back, removed several layers of bubble wrap and looked at Josh. "Don't you think he's too young for all these art supplies?" She rambled through the boxes of oil paints and different sizes of brushes. Beneath them she found a palette, several canvasses, and an easel. No wonder Josh had to slide the box across the floor; it must weight a lot. She took the palette out, slid it onto her thumb, and rested it across her forearm. "This is too big, Josh. David needs one for children."

"What about everything else? I searched the internet at the library in town to make sure I only bought quality supplies."

"You did a fine job. I could paint with these things myself."

"Good," Josh said with a gentle smile, "because I bought them for you."

Although Eliza appreciated his thoughtfulness, all these things cost quite a bit. "Thank you for thinking of me, but it's too much."

"Nothing's too much for you, Eliza. I haven't told you, but my mama left me a fair amount of money Papa had saved. If you look a little more in the box, I bought a palette for David too. Now you both can paint."

Eliza stood and went to Josh. "Stand up so I can hug you for being so thoughtful. I haven't felt like painting until ... well, until before my daughter died. This makes me want to try it again."

Josh stood and gave her a quick hug. "I'm happy when David's happy, Eliza. It's a good feeling to know I can count on you to be here for us."

He sat. Eliza went back to her chair to look through the box again.

"Eliza?"

She looked up from the box. "Yes?"

"You are happy here, right?"

"Very much."

"Do you miss your husband or your family?"

Eliza remembered what Ethan had told her about Denver dating someone. Since that was the case, no doubt Mama and Papa knew about it and approved. "Honestly, Josh, I hardly think of them. Knowing how I left Denver, and knowing how they would feel about it, it's best I don't see them anytime soon."

"What about Ethan? Have you talked to him lately?"

"I'll put it this way—if we all were still Amish, I would be shunned."

"I'm sorry to hear that. Like me, they should want you to be happy no matter what." Josh stood. "I'll clean up and go to bed. Looks like I'll have to shovel the driveway to see Anna tomorrow. Goodnight."

As Josh left the room, Eliza went to the door to open it and turn on the porch light. The huge flakes of snow had turned to tiny flakes, almost like sleet. Yes, Denver and her family had turned their backs on her. The thought stung her heart like sleet against her bare skin. No, no more pain. She was happy here, happy with David, happy with how Josh provided her a safe home, happy with his thoughtful ways, evidenced by his gift to her.

She closed the door and turned off the light. At the window, she wrapped her arms around herself.

Somewhere above the clouds in the dark of night, the stars twinkled. Would her icy heart ever thaw so she could return to Denver and her family again? Part of her wished it, but part of her was gradually giving up on the idea.

She left the window. Time for bed and a decision, including Josh's offer of adopting David.

visitor

In Absalom's workshop, Denver stopped sanding the guitar's back and drank a swallow of water from the crinkly plastic bottle. Beside him, Tess looked his way. "It was nice of Papa to make the form for shaping the sides of our guitar. It gave us time to work on the third top and back and neck when we got back from the mountains. That first guitar sounded terrible."

Denver gave her the bottle. "Good thing he did that, Miss Clumsy. You just had to go and break that spruce top on the second guitar after we got all the braces glued on."

Tess swallowed water. "Like you didn't press on the back of the first one too hard and split that gorgeous piece of rosewood while you were sanding it."

"True. I guess we're equally clumsy." He returned to sanding. "What's your mama making for Christmas supper? It's only two weeks away."

"A huge turkey. Instead of your southern cornbread stuffing, she's making apple, butternut squash, and sausage dressing."

"Is that a traditional Amish thing?"

"So is the apple pan pie she's making for dessert, except with vanilla ice cream."

Denver licked his lips. "Sounds great."

As the rosewood yielded a fine powder to his sanding block, he shook his head at his and Tess's mistakes with the first two guitar builds they had attempted after their mountain trip, which had kept them busy from August until now. This one was coming along great, and she had been practicing her inlay work, sawing intricate pieces of mother-of-pearl by hand and routing slightly oversized patterns in scrap pieces of wood for gluing them in.

He drank more water and went back to sanding.

Thoughts of Eliza lessened from every hour, to ten times a day, to ten times a week, accomplished by staying out of her room and taking the canoe out. Before the days grew shorter and colder, he and Absalom had spent time fishing. As if the man who Denver now considered a second dad could read his mind, he never mentioned Eliza's absence, and Denver appreciated it.

He checked the time on the clock over the work bench. "Think I'll head home and get a bite for supper, Tess."

She stopped sanding. "You know you're welcome to eat with us."

"I know. I'm just trying to get used to being on my own."

Tess brushed powdered wood from her hands. "Eliza pisses me off. If she keeps it up, I'll marry you for real to teach her a lesson."

Denver rubbed her arm. "No cursing, okay? You're much sweeter without it."

"I guess." She slipped her arms around his waist and lay her head on his shoulder. "You mean a lot to me."

Denver kissed her hair. "You mean a lot to me too. I might've gone crazy if you hadn't talked me into building guitars with you. It gets my mind off things."

Tess pulled away and kissed him quickly on the lips— something she had started after the mountain trip if they were alone and were saying goodbye. Denver couldn't fault her for it. Although they had never talked about the trip and how she had confessed to her mistake with that guy, including how it had affected her, it had created an intimacy between them that he couldn't deny. He kissed her back, lingering a bit longer than she did. If Eliza hadn't come back before Tess turned eighteen, his willpower to not sleep with her would be tested to the maximum of his ability.

Tess tapped his nose. "Nice smooch, Denny. Care for another one?"

"Dangerous territory, Tessy, and you know it." He eased her away. "Let me get on home."

Jacket on, Denver left for the road and his walk. He had missed his once common physical activity before he met Eliza, and the walks came in handy for building his cardio, along with the canoe outings.

At home, he opened the fridge and shoved things around until he settled on a salad and a bottle of water. At the coffee table in front of the TV, he thumbed the remote for the weather. In the middle of crunching lettuce, he stopped as the doorbell rang. Lettuce swallowed, he went to door and looked through the windows on its sides. On the porch, Akina waved. "You gonna let me in before I freeze out here?"

Denver let her in, grabbed her petite frame in a bear hug, and kissed her soundly. "Wow, you're the last person I expected to show up here."

Akina poked his stomach. "Does that kiss mean you approve?"

"Well, I guess old habits are hard to break. Want some supper? I'm having a salad." Denver closed the door and led her to the kitchen.

Taking a seat at the bar, Akina said, "I could use some coffee. I'm a little tired from the drive from D.C."

Denver powered up the coffee maker. "How are you and Dan? The last time I talked—"

The doorbell rang. "Huh, wonder who that is?" Denver left to open the door. Carrying a guitar case, Tess came in. "Feel like practicing?"

Denver closed the door. "You ate already?"

"I'll eat when I get—" She waved to Akina. "Well, look who's here. Hi, Akina, long time no see."

Denver and Tess went to the kitchen. "I was just asking Akina about Dan. You remember him from the wedding."

"That's right," Tess said. "What a hotty. He had muscles on his muscles."

Akina got up and looked Tess up and down. "Is this the same girl I saw at the wedding? My gosh, *you're* the hotty."

"Aw, I just clean up good."

Denver got coffee from a cabinet. "Want some, Tess? I'm making some for Akina."

"Why not? I can always use coffee." She set the guitar case in the hall and came back.

"You two learning to play?" Akina asked.

"Making the attempt," Denver said, measuring coffee.

"I'm surprised you haven't asked why I'm here and why I haven't asked about Eliza."

"You just got here."

"Jan called me the other day and told me what happened. I've been busy with my new job and thought I'd drive down and lend a sympathetic ear. Are you doing okay? You've been through a lot."

Denver knew Akina meant with losing Lily too. She hadn't been able to attend the funeral, but she had called and sent a card. "I'm hanging in there. It's not like I have choice."

"I'm keeping him occupied," Tess said. "We're building guitars too."

"More like breaking," Denver said.

"They seem complicated to make," Akina said.

Leaning against the counter by the coffee maker, Denver turned as the aroma and the ending drips told him he could get cups. He enjoyed seeing Akina. With her straight black hair and dark eyes, she looked exactly as he remembered from when they had carried on their short affair. "What about Dan? You two getting serious yet?"

"He wanted to settle down and have kids. I'm not ready to do that at twenty-five, if ever." She faced Tess. "You know what I mean. Men are good for a lot of things, but they don't exist so we can build our lives around them."

"Denver's not like that. He's a genuine sweetheart. My sister, on the other hand ..."

Akina shook her head. "I can see how losing a child could affect her, but to the point of leaving the one guy who was perfect her?"

Tess went to the fridge for vanilla creamer and took it to the counter. "My thoughts exactly. If it's the last thing I do, I'll make sure they're back together and happy again."

Denver filled two cups and offered sugar. Tess and Akina doctored their coffee. He suggested they go to the living room, where he was about to eat his supper. Tess sat beside him while Akina took a chair at Denver's end of the sofa. After a bite of salad and a swallow of water, he faced Akina. "You said something about a new job?"

"I'm a sign language interpreter for visitor tours at the Smithsonian."

"Wow, what a sweet job."

"It is, except for the high rent in D.C. I'm thinking about getting a roommate to share the costs, but I don't trust just anyone."

"Me neither," Tess said. "You never know what a person is capable of."

Denver swallowed salad. "You're not living with your folks, Akina?"

"And deal with that D.C. traffic every morning? No thanks. I scored an apartment within a thirty-minute walk or a ten-minute bike ride. Other than that I take the bus. I still drive for groceries and shopping."

"Shopping," Tess said. "One of my favorite words." She stood. "We'll practice another time, Denver. "I'll let you two catch up."

Denver walked her to door, where she lowered the guitar case to the floor and poked his stomach. "How do you feel about your old lover coming to visit?"

"Old friends now. Jealous?"

"Not since she said she isn't interested in marriage right now. As far as sex, I was willing in the mountains, but you wouldn't have me."

"Doesn't mean I wasn't tempted." Denver hugged and kissed her. "You know you mean more to me than your looks, right?"

Smirking, Tess returned the kiss. "I know, I'm the girl who keeps you from seriously hooking up with Leah and anyone else who might come along." She picked up the guitar case. "And don't forget keeping your mind off of Eliza with our guitar work." She opened the door. "Here's to a great Christmas for us. We'll probably gain ten pounds each from eating all of Mama's food."

Denver closed the door. At the window, he watched Tess put the guitar case in Oneita's car and drive away. She was right about keeping his mind off of Eliza. Unfortunately, about this time of night, when he was home alone, his mind usually wondered to that morning when Tess had hugged him naked at the cabin, including their conversation about the guy who had taken advantage of her.

Denver watched the red tail lights fade into the night. Could he really love her, or was it mostly sexual attraction? He would figure it out one day.

In the living room, Akina had moved to the sofa. Her shoes were off and her feet were curled beneath her. "I assume you know I need a place to sleep tonight. I'm not about to drive all the way back to D.C."

"No problem. I'll make the guestroom bed for you."

Akina left and came back with an overnight bag from her car. "I knew I could count on you."

Denver took the salad bowl and water bottle to the kitchen sink. "Need more coffee?"

"I'm good."

On the sofa again, he turned sideways to face Akina. "You can count on me like I could count on you when I was upset about losing my parents."

"Right, with sex."

Denver shrugged. "Stuff happens, just not with a gorgeous ex-Marine who happens to be Japanese."

"What about this thing with you and Eliza? Do you know any more than when she left you?"

"Not a thing. She doesn't call me or her family. She's teaching sign language at the school Jon made from her old home. Tess called Ethan to talk to her because she keeps her phone off. Eliza refused to take the call."

Akina twisted a length of hair around her finger, a habit Denver had noticed not long after they had met in Ohio. She lowered her hand. "You don't think ..."

"What?"

"No, she wouldn't do that. If any two people were made for each other, it's her and you."

Denver blinked several times. The thought of Eliza seeing someone else was as foreign as the idea of seriously considering marriage to Tess. "You mean her seeing another guy, right?"

"You've been apart six months. Were you sleeping together before then?"

"Not since before the funeral."

Akina's eyes widened. "Two years is a long time to go without physical intimacy when you're used to it. Have you failed in that category yet?"

Denver paused. Tell the truth or not? Not only had he wanted to sleep with Leah, he had wanted to make love to Tess—two separate things, really. Still, mentally failing in that category was pretty much the same as physically failing it. "I saw an old friend from high school a few times. We didn't sleep together because—"

Akina sat up straight. "All right, time to spill your guts."

"It's funny. We were right here on the sofa kissing, and Tess showed up. The girl and I went out on the pontoon boat to watch the Lakefest fireworks, and Tess and her family showed up there too."

"Curious," Akina said. "Did you know she was coming over to practice guitar tonight?"

"We hadn't talked about it."

"You realize she's in love you, don't you?"

"Not at all. Any time we talk about Eliza, all she says is we belong together."

"I thought so too. What if you married the wrong sister?"

"That's crazy."

Akina slid closer. "Are you still in love with Eliza? We could test it by doing what we used to do best. Speaking for myself, it was always a rousing success."

Akina's dark eyes drew Denver in, including her full lips shaded with pink lipstick and her low-cut blouse that hinted at her modest cleavage. Yes, she was the same old Akina, sensual to the max. Two years was a long time without physical intimacy. If they did sleep together, did it mean he didn't love Eliza? What a confusing question, one he hadn't asked himself when things were getting heated between him and Leah or Tess.

"Well, I always enjoyed our times together, but I wasn't married then."

Akina ran her fingertips along Denver's hand on the sofa. "You were dating Jan."

"Not the same."

"Do you think bad of me for trying?"

"We have a history together. Maybe you want to help me get over Eliza."

Sliding back to her end of the sofa, Akina positioned herself against the armrest and then raised her hands to clap three times. "Congratulations, you passed the test. You're still in love with Eliza." She stood. "Let's make my bed, I'm sleepy."

As Denver helped Akina put sheets on the bed, he couldn't help watching her. He may have passed the test this time, but what about another time? And that meant for Tess as well. Sure, he still loved Eliza, but he could only take so much before he failed, especially if he were to find out she was seeing someone else.

Christmas delivery

Denver finished his last bite of Oneita's apple pan pie, with its cinnamon hint and flaky crust. He drank tea and wiped his mouth with a napkin. "Wow, Tess, you were right about this pie." He faced Oneita. "You realize I can blame you if I gain weight from this meal."

Oneita pointed a fork at him. "You needed to gain some weight. You were almost skin and bones back in June."

"Papa," Ivy said, "when can we open presents?"

"When I say, young lady."

"But you wouldn't let us open them this morning."

Beside Ivy, Tess patted her reddish curls, similar in color to her own. "We told you we wanted to wait for Denver, okay?"

Denver pushed his lips out into a pout. "C'mon, doodlebug. You couldn't wait for me?"

"Put your lips back. That's fake."

Oneita stood. "If everyone's finished, we can open presents. Tess and I will do the dishes later."

Ivy ran from the dining room. "Yaaaaaaayyy!"

Denver laughed. "Oh, to be that age again." He kissed Oneita's cheek. "I hope you and Absalom know how much I appreciate you."

"We do," Absalom said. "I just wish Eliza were here."

Rising from her chair, Tess cut her eyes at him. "Papa, he needs to concentrate on anything but Eliza, at least until she comes back home."

"She's abandoned us, Tess. We might as well get used to that."

"I don't know," Oneita said. "As much as she loved Denver before what happened, I can't see her letting go so easily. A love like you two have is hard to find."

Absalom's crow's feet deepened. "Weren't you the one who was ashamed of her?"

"I still am, but I remember how devastated I was when we lost Lily." Oneita lowered her head. "How I miss her."

Ivy came to the doorway. "Are y'all coming or not?"

"I hear you, doodlebug," Denver said. "You're learning how to speak southern Virginia slang pretty good."

Tess left for the living room, where a tree glistened with tinsel, glass balls, and twinkling lights. She sat on the sofa and Denver sat beside her. "Too bad we couldn't have finished a guitar by now," he said. "One of us could've given it to the other for a present."

Tess kissed his cheek. "You're all the present I need."

Absalom came in. Ivy ran to him and whispered in his ear. He pulled her into his lap. "There's nothing wrong with Tess kissing Denver. We're family, we care about each other. He just kissed your mama in the kitchen."

Tess looked from Absalom to Denver and back. "They look at each other funny, Papa."

Denver bared his teeth and growled. "Now I'm looking at *you* funny, doodlebug."

"*Stop* it, Denver."

Oneita came in and sat in a chair across from Absalom. "What's going on in here?"

Ivy went to her and pointed at Denver. "Mama, he kissed Tess and made a mean face at me."

"He kissed me a minute ago, what of it?"

"Well ..."

"Well, what?"

"I saw them kiss on the mouth one day in Papa's workshop. They did it like you kiss Papa sometimes."

"Really?" Absalom said.

"Nothing wrong with that," Tess said. "Families kiss on the mouth sometimes."

"I agree," Oneita said. "Go hand out presents, you've fussed about it enough."

Ivy went toward the tree and stopped to point out the window. "Why's a policeman here?"

Denver and Tess went to the window. "It's a county deputy," she said. "He's got a big envelope."

Absalom opened the front door as the deputy climbed the porch steps. "Sorry to bother you folks on Christmas. I'm looking for a Denver Andrews."

Oneita went to the door. "What's this about?"

"Not allowed to say, ma'am. Is he here? I have this address listed as a secondary one."

Denver went to the door. "I'm Denver Andrews. What's going on?"

The deputy gave Denver the envelope. "Everything should be in here. I'd wish you a Merry Christmas, but envelopes like this from an attorney are rarely good news."

The deputy left. Absalom closed the door. "Denver, do you want to open that alone? We don't want to intrude on your privacy."

Denver's hands shook. He had heard stories like this from his friends when their parents— His knees buckled. Absalom caught him. "Whoa now, let's sit you down." Absalom helped him to the sofa. Oneita left and came back with water.

"Drink this before you faint. You're white as a ghost."

Denver pushed the water away. Yes, as white as Lily's ghost running her fingers through the water at the dock. Eliza … could she really—

Tess sat beside him. "Hey, whatever it is, you're with people who love you."

Ivy climbed onto the sofa. "Denver, what's wrong?"

Oneita placed her on the floor and give her a present. "Take this to your room."

"But I want—"

"Ivy," Absalom said, his voice firm, "do like your mama says."

"But, Papa, I love Denver too."

Absalom knelt in front of her. "Please go to your room. The adults need to talk about adult things."

Wiping tears, Ivy left without the present.

"Denver," Oneita said. "What do you think that envelope is?"

He gave it to Tess. "Open it."

Tess did so, took several papers out, and read them. "I … I don't believe it. Why would she do this? She loves you too much to—"

"What is it?" Absalom said.

"Eliza has filed to divorce Denver."

Absalom glanced at Oneita. "We were afraid this might happen."

"What do you mean, Papa?"

Absalom and Oneita returned to their seats. "Remember when we came home from our trip to Kansas early?"

"What about it?"

"Ethan called to tell us about Eliza leaving Denver. Your mama and I were so furious, we drove to Ohio to see why. When we got there …"

"Tell him," Oneita said. "He needs to know so he can move on with his life."

Absalom faced Denver again. "We were almost at the school. We passed a house just down the road. We saw Eliza on the porch, and a man ..."

"We couldn't believe it," Oneita said. "We kept making excuses for what we saw. I hate to say it, but that envelope proves we were wrong."

"What did you see?" Tess said. "Were they kissing?"

"The man was standing behind Eliza," Absalom said. "His arms were around her waist and his cheek was next to hers."

"That's right," Oneita said. "We drove straight home without talking to her or Ethan. If we had, I might've slapped her, it made me so mad."

"Maybe they're friends?" Denver said. "That's all it could be."

"What about those papers?" Oneita asked.

"She could be confused or— I don't know, I never thought she would divorce me. This just—it makes no sense."

"Call Ethan," Tess said. "Maybe he knows about that man."

Absalom made the call on a phone on the table beside him. "Ethan? Yes, Merry Christmas to you. Look, Denver just got some papers from a lawyer. They say Eliza wants a divorce. Yes ... yes ..." Absalom's cheeks reddened. "Really? She did that? Well, I suppose I have to believe it when you send them. Goodbye." Absalom faced Oneita. "Get my smart phone and bring it here."

Oneita did so. "What did Ethan say?"

Absalom swiped the screen several times. "I never would have thought she'd stoop so low."

Denver moved to the edge of the sofa. "What did she do?"

As Absalom watched his phone's screen, his cheeks paled. "Ethan said he heard some people gossiping about Eliza and that man—his name is Joshua Allen. His wife was hit by a truck around the first of July and has been in a coma ever since. They have a little boy who's three. Mr. Allen doesn't have any relatives, so he asked Eliza to watch the boy while he stayed with his wife at the hospital."

"That doesn't sound so bad," Tess said. "Maybe all this is a mistake."

A glimmer of hope took away Denver's sinking feeling—the same as when he had almost drowned himself in the lake over losing Eliza the first time—but decided against it because he loved her so much. "What else did Ethan say? Did he talk to Eliza? Did she explain anything?"

"She tried," Absalom said. "It seems she's been living with the man for several months and she's very fond of the boy." Absalom rubbed his eyes. "The thing is, while Ethan was talking to her, the boy called her mama."

Denver fell back to the sofa. Eliza had not only found another man, she had found another child to replace Lily with. Still, he believed in her, believed in their love. There had to be an explanation.

"Papa," Tess said, "what did Ethan send to your phone?"

Absalom held the phone toward Oneita, whose face contorted into the worst anger that Denver had ever seen from her. "That … that … how dare she—"

"Hush," Absalom said. "This is hard enough as it is." As he turned the phone toward Denver, Denver stood to take it. The picture showed four red streaks across Ethan's cheek. "She slapped him for asking about the gossip?"

"And told him what she did was none of his business."

Papers rattled behind Denver. He faced Tess, who was reading. "I wish it was a mistake but it isn't. She wants the money she earned from her paintings and nothing else. Her lawyer has already made the transfer."

"Can she do that?" Oneita said.

"She has her own account," Denver said.

As he stood there within the circle of people he loved most in the world, except for Willow who was visiting the family of a guy she was dating, his vision blurred and his hearing faded.

"Sit down before you faint," Absalom said. "You're turning pale."

Arms encircled Denver's neck. Tears wet his cheek. Soft sobs touched his heart. He eased away from … "Willow? Where's Mom and Dad? I need … Can you get them so I can talk to them?" Willow covered her face and sobbed harder. "What's wrong, Will—" A firm hand fell on his shoulder. "Son?"

Denver hugged Dad. "I don't know what to do, Dad. I tried to be a good person. I tried to find someone to love like you and Mom love each other."

Mom came over. "We're here for you, Denver. We'll get through this as a family."

Denver opened his arms, and Mom joined his and Dad's hug.

Still sobbing behind him, Willow slipped into the group hug. "We love you, Denver. It's going to be all right."

Time passed in tears and weeping. Somewhere in the night, stars glittered in the sky. The lake washed ashore with its familiar whisper. A bobwhite quail called for its mate.

Dad pulled away, took Denver by the shoulders, and gently shook him. "Denver, who am I?"

"You're …" From somewhere in the recesses of Denver's memories—the bobwhite's call, the lake's whisper, the stars glittering over the lake as he and Eliza had swum on the night he had fallen in love with her—from all those sights and sounds and visions in his mind, three words brought him back to the present.

I love you. And now our colors are in our baby.

He fell to his knees. "I don't … I don't know what to do."

He looked up into the tear-filled eyes of Absalom, Oneita, and Tess. "I don't know what to do. Why can't I just die and get it over with?"

"Can you stand?" Absalom said.

"Get him on the sofa," Oneita said. "Tess, make coffee. We need to talk this out until we know what to do."

* * *

Tess followed Mama into the kitchen. As she started to measure coffee, Tess went to her side. "I'm worried about Denver. You heard what he said about wanting to die."

"Eliza has broken his heart. We should shun her despite leaving the Amish. I never thought she would do such a dishonorable thing."

Tess got cups from a cabinet. Since Mama and Papa didn't mind her going to the mountains with Denver, they shouldn't mind this. She put the cups on the counter. "Mama, I think I should stay with Denver until he's through the worst of this mess. We don't have an extra bedroom, and I'd hate to ask him to sleep on the sofa."

The anger in Mama's eyes toward Eliza faded. "Well, your papa and I didn't mind you going to the mountains with Denver, so it should be fine."

In the living room again, Oneita gave Absalom coffee while Tess gave Denver his. Instead of sipping like everyone else, he put his on the end table. "What a way to spend Christmas, by getting a divorce notice and almost losing my mind."

"You just went away for a little while," Absalom said. "Considering the shock, it's understandable."

"Don't you worry about it," Oneita said. "We're your family and we're here for you no matter what."

Ivy's footsteps pattered in the hall. She peeked around the corner. "Can I come in?"

Tess slid over to make room for Ivy between her and Denver. "Get over here and hug Denver's neck and give him a smooch."

Ivy did so. "Are you okay, Denver?"

"Your hugs help, doodlebug."

"Why isn't Eliza here? I haven't seen her in a long time. When I ask, no one says anything."

"She's teaching sign language at your old house in Ohio. That's important, you know?"

"Will she ever come back?"

Denver blinked once, twice, and fingered a tear from his eye.

Tess pulled Ivy into her lap. "She'll be back. Her and Ethan are busy right now."

Tess waited while Papa sipped coffee. "Mama says I can stay with Denver for a while. He shouldn't be alone now."

Denver faced her. "You don't have to do that."

"That's a good idea," Absalom said. "Let's hear nothing else about it."

Tess stood. "I'll pack some things and be ready in a minute." In her room, she packed all her personal items plus clothes for a week. If she stayed longer, she could come back for everything else.

On the way to the living room with the suitcase, Tess stopped. She knew a way out of this mess for Denver, one to get his mind off of Eliza and to make sure he stayed single until she came back to her senses.

* * *

Waiting for Tess, Denver went to the Christmas tree and touched one of the glass balls. He and Eliza had their own tree the first year they were married, two months after their honeymoon at the cabin in Occoneechee State Park. They made love on the living room sofa, afterward talking about all their plans for a wonderful life. The following year they did the same thing, putting the tree up right after Thanksgiving, bathed in the glow of a love so deep from being pregnant, he thought he would drown.

And it had all fallen apart with Lily's death. Tears seared his eyes. No, no crying now. Wait until he was in bed—in bed where Tess couldn't hear.

"Denver? I'm ready."

Denver turned. Tess stood in the hall entrance with her suitcase. What a weakling he was, reduced to a sniffling mess who needed his sister-in-law to babysit him.

But he *did* need her, or he might paddle his canoe out to the middle of the lake and drown himself like he almost had before Eliza's family had decided to move here to be near her and any future grandchildren.

Family.

Some people didn't believe in it, or the tie between a married couple that could bind them together with love stronger than any chain ever made. He would like to have that again one day, and one day in the not-so-distant future. He held out his hand toward Tess. "Let's go."

Oneita came to him for a hug. "Let Tess get your mind off of things like she has since Eliza left. You know she can do it."

Absalom stood from the chair and took Denver into his arms in a huge bear hug. Pulling away, tears shone in his eyes. "I love you, boy. We'll get through this, all right?"

A slight smile upon Denver's lips surprised him. "Dad used to call me 'boy' during serious talks."

"Well, I'm your dad now, and don't you forget it." Absalom faced Tess. "I know how much you care about Denver. Help him any way you can."

"I will, Papa."

Ivy ran over from the sofa and raised her hands to Denver. "I want a hug too."

Denver did so, picking her up and nuzzling her soft curls, rich with the aroma of baby shampoo. He gave her a quick kiss on the lips. "See there, doodlebug, I love you exactly like I love Tess."

"It's not the same." Ivy wiped her mouth. "I'm too little for man kisses on my lips."

Denver laughed out loud. He kissed her cheek and set her down. "That better?"

Ivy nodded. "Merry Christmas, Denver." She went to the tree. "You want your present?"

"How about saving it for another time?"

She brought him the present anyway, about the size of a shoebox. "Here, take it with you."

Denver took the box and lay the large envelope with the divorce papers on top of it. "Thank you. Merry Christmas to you too."

"I don't know what it is. Tess didn't tell me when she wrapped it."

"It's a secret for grownups," Oneita said. "Papa and I know too."

"Why can't I know?"

Absalom scooped her up into his arms. "Maybe one day. Let Denver and Tess get home."

In Denver's pickup, he faced Tess. "They're something else."

"They are, aren't they?" Tess buckled her seatbelt. "Let's go, I'm as emotionally worn out as I've ever been."

At home again, Denver turned the heat up and took the envelope and present to the coffee table. Tess took her suitcase to the guest room and came back. "You might not want to open that."

"I'm curious about it now." He sat and tore the paper off, which did reveal a shoe box with a picture of the high-heels Tess had worn to the restaurant during their trip to the mountains. She sat beside him and he laughed. "Not sure how I'll look in a pair of these, Tessy."

"At least I can make you laugh. I thought you'd be okay with this when I wrapped it. After you got those stupid divorce papers from my stupid sister, I'm not sure."

Denver took the top off the box, found an envelope, opened it and read the Christmas card.

"Dear Denver, like the Gray family knows from losing our Lily, time eases the pain as the days and months and years go by. May they pain pass sooner for you than it did for us, and may Eliza come home to you one day. Love, Absalom, Oneita, Ethan, Tess, and Ivy."

Denver looked at Tess. "You guys are so great." He took a package wrapped in tissue paper and opened it. In his lap lay a plaster impression of a baby's tiny hand and footprints. Despite his intention to cry in bed, hot tears trailed down his cheeks. He ran his fingertips along the letters, written into the plaster below the prints: "To Mommy and Daddy, love always, Lily."

Tess grabbed his hand. "Are you okay?"

"When was this—" Denver swallowed the emotion filling his throat. "When was this made?"

"You know we were all in the hospital waiting room when Eliza was in labor. When the nurse came out and told us what happened, you can imagine our reactions. After I got to where I could talk, I asked her about making a plaster impression of the baby's hand and footprints. I read about it on the internet and thought it would make a nice present for you and Eliza. Even though Lily didn't make it, I still wanted to do it."

Denver touched the impressions, running his fingers along the tiny fingers and the tiny toes. He went the kitchen for a paper towel for his eyes and face and came back to the sofa. No, he wouldn't cry now, but he would probably float his bed away later.

Tess rubbed his shoulders. "I hope it didn't upset you too much."

"I don't know what to say. Between this and the headstone, I'm speechless." He took her hand from his shoulder and held it. "You are so amazing. I would be lost without you and your family." He kissed her hand and let it go. "I better see if I can get some sleep."

Tess stood with him and hugged him. Warm and firm at the same time, auburn hair pressed into his face, the floral aroma of shampoo filling his senses—she was everything he wanted at this moment.

No. Regardless of everything Eliza had done, he was still in love with her. Still, was it time to give up that dream and find someone else to fill his heart?

Tess pressed against him harder, arms tight against his back, breath hot against his neck.

As much as he needed her, would it be wrong to make love to her while he was married? Yes, it would. Not only would it be adultery, Tess was only seventeen, and he couldn't take advantage of her like that jerk had when she was fifteen.

* * *

Tess pulled away and fingered his hair away from his forehead. "I think we should get some sleep, okay?"

Denver didn't answer. Tell him about her idea now or not? The morning might be better. Let them sleep and have breakfast to return to some small bit of normalcy and tell him then. She let him go and yawned. "See you in the morning."

His footsteps plodded behind her. His door closed. Her door closed. She got ready for bed and pulled the chilly sheet to her chin, followed by a quilt.

As her eyes grew heavy, soft sobs pulled her from the edge of sleep. She couldn't just ignore Denver's pain. But what if she went to him and they— She didn't want that, not really. He and Eliza belonged together.

The sobs grew louder. She covered her head with the pillow but imagined them anyway. He needed her—needed her as much as she needed him.

She padded to Denver's door and opened it. In the moonlight pouring through his window, he lay on his stomach, face in his pillow, back heaving with heavy sobs.

Tess went to him. He must've felt the bed settle as she sat. He turned over, face wet, eyes red in the moonlight. "Tess— what—?"

She stood to slip the straps of the nightgown from her shoulders. It fell to her feet.

"Tess, you can't—we can't—"

"Shh," she whispered, getting in bed. "It's all right. It's all right."

"But—"

Tess kissed him. All hesitation gone, he pulled her over on top of him and buried his face into her neck.

She had never known it could be like this—could be like living inside another person. Denver alternated between holding her so tight she could hardly breath and running his fingertips along her back, until he rolled her over.

Their joining held an urgency she hadn't expected. Then again, it may have been because of the pain they both shared, of a family torn apart by the death of Lily.

Denver gasped in her ear. Tess rolled him back over, loving such an intimate thing as sharing herself with the man she loved.

But the man she couldn't have.

goodbye

Denver woke to Tess lying beside him. Her hair fell across the pillow, partially blocking her face. Several strands barely moved with her breath. What a wonder she was, knowing exactly what he needed when he needed it, which wasn't the act of making love but the closeness of someone who cared about him as much as she did, without expectations, without demands, just the sharing of two people who had been in tremendous pain from losing Lily.

He brushed her hair from her eyes, softly kissed her. She didn't wake, so he kissed her again. "Hey, you hungry?"

A huge grin appeared on her beautiful face. "Um-hmm," she said stretching. "And I know exactly what I want." She rolled on top of him for a long, luscious kiss.

They shared each other slowly, kissing, touching, lingering. Denver wanted to pull her down and whisper in her ear to say how much he loved her, but he couldn't do that, couldn't take a chance on breaking her heart when he was still in love with Eliza.

When they were done, Tess kissed his neck. "I think I'm pretty good at this. Want to try again after breakfast?"

Denver couldn't help but laugh. "Just pretty good? Try outstanding." He kissed her again, a quick one before he was tempted to love her again now instead of later. "What are you hungry for? And I mean for food instead of me."

Tess rolled to her pillow. "Oh, wow, I could eat the proverbial horse."

"Grilled, of course."

"You bet. How about french toast?"

"Well ..."

"What, you want something else?"

"I was afraid of this."

"Afraid of french toast?"

"While you were packing last night, I was looking at the glass balls on your Christmas tree. It brought back memories of mine and Eliza's first Christmas together. To say it hurt like hell is an understatement."

"Are you saying she liked french toast?"

"It was the first thing I made for her when she came here for her first art show with Jan."

Tess paused to look away, then back. "So this house is full of memories."

"More than I can name." Denver raised his palm to her cheek. "Don't take this the wrong way, but I feel bad about this."

"You mean sleeping together."

He tapped her nose. "You know that's not what I mean. I know I didn't take advantage of you, but I feel like I did. You're so young and sweet, and I'm—"

Tess covered his mouth. "Hush. What happened happened, and I'm glad it did. The worst thing for me is how no guy will ever measure up to you."

Covering his eyes, Denver laughed.

Tess slapped his chest. "Shut up. I didn't mean what you're thinking."

Denver uncovered his eyes. "I could get used to this."

"But you need to leave for a while to get away from the memories of Eliza ..."

"I think so. If we were to ever get serious, I'd like it to be when you're older, so I can take you out and people won't think I robbed the cradle."

"Or risk someone turning you in for dating a minor."

"Exactly."

"I can live with that." Tess rolled back to the pillow. "Huh."

"You decide on breakfast?" Denver asked

She rolled over to face him again. "What if you got a job at the Smithsonian like Akina? She needs a roommate to share the rent too. That would get your mind off of she who shall not be named, along with your memories."

Denver rubbed her nose with his. "You're pretty smart, you know that?"

"Smart enough to not get pregnant at seventeen."

"I didn't even think about that."

"After you told me about our cabin trip, I got a prescription for birth control. Just being safe, you know."

"Tell me about it. We came pretty close to doing exactly what we just did back then."

Tess raised her hand to gently rub his cheek. "Are you going to call Akina today?"

"Might as well."

"Will you miss me?"

"You can drive up when you get your license and we can see the D.C. sights. I've always wanted to do that."

"Sounds like a plan. Now, about breakfast, how about we practice dating and scarf down some grub at the buffet at that restaurant near the motel on the lake?"

"What if I called in an order and brought it back. Eliza and I used to eat there a lot and ... well."

"I get it." Tess got up and put her nightgown on. "I'm going to shower and get dressed. Order whatever you get for me." She leaned over to kiss Denver. "You know how well we get along."

Tees closed the door, and Denver got up to dress. Wearing jeans and a sweatshirt, he sat on his bed to call in the order and to call Akina.

"Hey there, Denver. I recognized your number in my phone. Has Eliza come home yet?"

"Would you believe she's divorcing me?"

"I'm sorry to hear that. I won't ask the particulars. I'm sure you're having a hard time dealing with it. It's like that day when she and Oneita had that talk, when we found out how she and Absalom had lost a child. You don't get over something like that overnight."

Denver couldn't argue that, which was one of the reasons he needed to get away. "What's that chance the Smithsonian needs another sign language interpreter and you need a roommate? I need to get away for a while and get my mind on something besides Eliza."

"The chances are great for both. I'll text you my address and you can come up any time. I'll put in a good word about you at work too."

"You've always been a great friend, Akina. I hope you know that."

"Is there any chance Eliza will change her mind?"

"I won't get into it over the phone, but it doesn't look like it."

"I'm sorry to hear that, Denver. I always thought you two were perfect for each other."

"Me too. Odds are I'll drive up today, if that's all right."

"Anytime you're ready. Bye for now."

Denver dropped the phone on the bed and turned. In his door, Tess, wrapped in a towel, her damp hair shining, blinked several times. "You're leaving today?"

"I think I better. The sooner I get away from here, the sooner I can come back."

She came in and sat on the bed. "I just lost my appetite for breakfast."

Denver sat beside her. "C'mon, don't be like that. Who knows when I'll be back."

Tess shoved him down and sat on top of him. "Gotcha." She kissed him once and got up. "If you've made that order, go get it and get your behind back here while I get dressed."

Denver put on a coat for the cold morning and drove to the restaurant. At the counter, a young woman was looking at the menus on a table. "Be right with you." She—Leah—looked up. "Denver!"

"Hey, Leah. I didn't know you were working here."

"Gotta make that down payment for a house, remember? Are you having breakfast?"

"I called in an order."

She left through a door and came back with a bag. "It's a good morning to stay in."

Denver paid the bill. "Mind if I ask you something?"

"You're wondering why I didn't call you after the fireworks, when Jan interrupted us."

"Well, yeah, but I didn't call you either."

"I'm pretty sure we both knew you needed to work things out with your wife. I wanted you, but we didn't know each other that well. After I thought about it for a while, I realized if we had slept together, it would because you missed her, not because you wanted me. Has she come back yet?"

Denver didn't know whether to tell Leah about the divorce or not. What the heck, he would be in D.C. soon, so what did it matter. "She gave me one hell of a Christmas present—a notice that she's divorcing me."

Leah touched his arm. "I'm so sorry. Were you expecting it?"

"It floored me, to say the least. I'm going to D.C. for a sign language job for a while. I need to get away and get my mind off things."

"I can imagine."

A couple came in, bringing cold air with them. "Let me seat these folks, be right back." She gave them menus, seated them in a booth, and returned to get a pot of coffee and two cups. "Look, you're a great guy. When you come back from D.C., I'd like to have another chance at us getting to know each other again without trying to rip each other's clothes off."

"I'll keep that in mind," Denver said. "See you."

Driving through town, he took in the shops, a new bakery about to open, the real estate places specializing in lake property, the barber shop where Steve liked to joke, and the bed and breakfast where he and Leah had enjoyed crab dip and that great crusty bread. He was glad she had said that about wanting to get to know each other without ripping each other's clothes off, as well as saying she was sorry about Eliza divorcing him. Both meant she was a good person at heart.

He found Tess in the kitchen making coffee. "Breakfast has arrived." He put the bags on the counter. "Coffee smells great."

As he took the food from the bag, Tess slipped her hands around his waist until they joined at his stomach. "Do you like this better with or without clothes?"

Denver covered her small hands with his. Was he really going to leave her? Last night had been perfect, without a single thought of Eliza to interfere in his and Tess's lovemaking.

"You're mighty quiet, Denny."

He turned within her arms. "Do you know how great you are?"

"Sure, you only tell me every five minutes or so." She took the food to the table. He brought coffee, creamer, and sugar. Better keep the upbeat attitude like Tess and pack and get out of here.

They ate quietly, remarking on the sunlight glistening on the lake, visible through the sliding glass doors. Tess asked him if he would tell Willow what was happening. He said he would after he got settled in D.C., that if Willow called either her or Oneita or Absalom, to have her call him, including how it was a good thing Eliza was keeping her phone off, because if Willow had called her and got no answer, she would've called him and she hadn't.

Tess took their silverware and cups to the sink to wash. He dried and put them away, went to his room to pack two suitcases with personal items and winter clothes—he'd buy spring and summer stuff later—and came back to the kitchen to give Tess a key from his ring. "This opens the front door. Do you mind keeping an eye on things while I'm gone?"

Tess put the key in her pocket. "You know I don't mind."

Denver started toward the door and stopped. "Stay as long as you want. Turn the heat down to about fifty to keep the plumbing from freezing. Swim at the dock if you want when it gets warm. Tell Absalom y'all can take the pontoon boat out to fish or whatever."

"I will."

* * *

Looking up into Denver's blue eyes, Tess expected her heart to break anytime now. She sniffled. "Ugh, wouldn't you know I'm getting a cold?"

Denver fingered the corner of one eye. "Me too." He picked up the suitcases. "Guess I better go."

Tess followed him to the door and opened it for him. As he got into his pickup, she wrapped her arms around herself, both from the cold and from missing his arms around her already.

He waved through the windshield. She waved back. His brown hair faded down the driveway.

Inside his and Eliza's home, Tess wandered around, looking at photos of Denver's family before he had met Eliza. He resembled his dad, about six feet tall with medium-brown hair that curled if he let it go too long between trips to the barber. His mom resembled Willow, with curly red hair and cute as could be.

Tess went to the fireplace mantle, where a wedding photo of Denver and Eliza sat. The perfect couple, so everyone at the wedding had said, and Tess still believed that.

She watched the lake for at least an hour. No boats hummed with their owner's search for fish. No jet skis roared with their speedy ride for their drivers. A flock of gulls, winter visitors to the area, were winging their way across the sky, white dots against a blanket of blue.

Tess touched the cold glass of the sliding glass doors.

What was love anyway? As a girl of thirteen, she had thought it was two people holding hands and looking at each other like she wanted a boy to look at her when she saw Eliza and Denver looking at each other that day. Now, she wasn't sure.

The tissue paper and box for the plaster impression of Lily's hands and feet were still on the coffee table. Denver must've packed his present while she had washed their breakfast dishes.

Tess went to his bed and covered up to snuggle his pillow, which still smelled faintly of his aftershave. Last night he had strummed her soul as if it were a guitar. No, sex wasn't love, but what she had felt—the completion of two people joined by loss and true caring for each other—that was love.

Where life would take them from here, she had no idea. He would be safe with Akina—safe from marriage in case Eliza came to her senses. Even if they slept together, it didn't mean what it had meant last night.

Tess tried not to cry but the tears came, wetting Denver's pillow, making her weep until she hiccupped, making her cough until her throat ached.

Yes, she loved him.

But like she had told herself last night, she couldn't have him.

Eliza had that hold on his heart.

And she always would.

1. In the first two chapters, we learn how Denver and Eliza lost their daughter at birth and how it affected their marriage. Is it understandable how this could happen?

2. When Eliza attempts to kiss Denver, why do you think it made her sick?

3. When Tess comes over and finds Denver drinking on the dock, do you think she's teasing when she almost kisses him?

4. Did you expect Eliza to leave Denver like she did?

5. Do you think Tess lied about locking herself out of the house so she could stay with Denver?

6. In Ohio, when Eliza stayed with Josh to take care of David after Anna was hit by the truck, do you think her decision had anything to do with losing her daughter?

7. As Tess and Denver grew close, she helped get his mind off of Eliza, which helped him stop drinking so much. Some readers might have a negative opinion of her for being attracted to Denver, but she always believed he and Eliza belonged together. Do you think she was sincere in that belief?

8. What did you think of Denver when he went out with Leah, and when he planned to sleep with her? Given everything he was going through, was it understandable?

9. How surprised were you to learn about Tess's past with the boy who slept with her and told people at school about it? Did it make sense how that made her not care about certain things, like how she changed so much from when she was Amish, even to the point of being nude around Denver?

10. Did you enjoy the scene when Denver and Tess went dancing?

11. As Eliza gets used to taking care of David, do you think her love for him is influenced by losing her daughter, or does she love him for the unique child he is?

12. Nearing the end of the book, did it feel like something bad was going to happen?

13. How shocked were you when Denver received the divorce notice from Eliza?

14. Tess fought to not sleep with Denver when he was crying. Did it make sense for her to finally give in?

15. In the last chapter, we learn how Tess sincerely loves Denver. What do you think will happen between them in the third book in the series?

About the Author

J. Willis Sanders lives in southern Virginia, with his wife and several stringed musical instruments.

With ten novels completed and more on the way, he enjoys crafting intriguing characters with equally intriguing conflicts to overcome. He also loves the natural world and, more often than not, his stories include those settings. Most also utilize intense love relationships and layered themes.

His first novel (not this one, but he plans to publish it) is a ghostly World War II era historical that takes place mostly in the midwestern United States, which utilizes some little-known facts about German POW camps there at that time. It's the first of a three-book series, in which characters from the first book continue their lives.

Although he loves history, he has written several contemporary novels as well, and some include interesting paranormal twists, both with and without religious themes.

He also loves the Outer Banks of North Carolina, and has published three novels within different time frames based on the area, what he calls his Outer Banks of North Carolina Series.

Another genre he enjoys is thriller novels, so he is launching a series with a main female character named Reid Stone.

Other hobbies include reading (of course), vegetable gardening, playing music with friends, and songwriting, some of which are in a few of his novels.

You can follow his author page at Facebook by searching for J. Willis Sanders, or at his Amazon Author page, or at his website at https://jwillissanders.wixsite.com/writer

Readers: to help those considering a purchase, please consider leaving a review on Amazon.com, Goodreads.com, or wherever you buy this book. It helps more than you know.